I0550409

PERDITION'S

GATE

Don Tynan

The cover art is an adaptation of original
photographs taken by, and owned by, the author.

By: Don Tynan
dtnapa@hotmail.com
DonTynan.com
Facebook =Don Tynan

Copyright © 2013 Don Tynan

All rights reserved.
(ISBN 978-0-615-85538-7)

All rights reserved. No part of this work may be
reproduced in any form without the permission, in
writing, from the copyright owner.

This is a work of fiction. Characters, names,
institutions, organizations, and incidents mentioned
in this novel are the product of the author's
imagination, or if real, are used fictionally, without
any intent to describe their actual conduct. Any
resemblance to actual persons, living or dead, events,
or locales is entirely coincidental.

U'buntu,

is a philosophy shared across the African continent. Its origin remains uncertain. To some it is a testament of brotherly love. To others, it is a system of laws.

One tenet of U'buntism is that punishment should extend beyond the criminal, that everyone in the greater community must suffer as well, evocating a law of retaliation; an eye for an eye, a tooth for a tooth, a death for a death.

Many people die of unknown causes in Africa every year. Some suspect hidden forces are responsible. Legends speak to an ultimate judger, one who possesses power beyond time and place.

This philosophy is enunciated differently in different countries, and among dissimilar ethnicities. In the south, it might be pronounced uMuthu, or Botho. In the north, indigenous peoples voice it as U'buntu, or obuntu. In one tongue it is spoken as, Motho.

Curiously, in America, a spectral-being thought to avenge long-standing societal injustices is known as the

Mothman

1:

Changes

It is late fall, autumn will soon be over. The trees here in Chicago have lost most of their leaves; they lay scattered and rotting on the ground. As I walk alone, the morning air hangs cold, gray, heavy, enshrouding all in a damp mist. Scanning ahead my gaze peers around, though, and beyond this wooded path now dressed in pre-winter death, sorrow drags my eyes downward. My friends have died, could I have saved them? Whether waking or sleeping, that question torments my every moment. Torn from me, so young, so soon, they do not exist, yet their thoughts still reach up from hell's depths to claw away at my sanity.

Friends now, have I none. Future? Have I a future? These barren woods are my friends now. Like them, I am changing with the seasons, growing older, and collecting the scars of aging upon my body, and upon my soul.

I raise a toast to you my departed friends—I cannot help but recall your deaths. Thoughts of you have burned a sadness into my face; it now drapes dark and sullen. The grief and tears have worn tracks into my skin. Ashamed of my sickly appearance I avoid eye contact with people. Few walk here this early, only the lonely. If someone does approach, I switch trails to avoid their hurtful glances. No happiness waits here to greet them.

No, I do not deserve happiness, only sorrow. For you my friends, I revel in sorrow's bleak and forbidding loneliness. It is what I deserve.

To you my friends, my mourning sings to you—your silent and sad requiescat—may you rest in peace.

*   *   *

Six months ago in Africa, the monster U'buntu touched me. That brief contact left me scarred mentally and emotionally—perhaps irreparably. For months I suffered from debilitating headaches and memory loss. Occasionally I still waken at night screaming from some horrific nightmare, but after the terrors I experienced who wouldn't? Should I consider myself fortunate? That demon was responsible for the deaths of thousands in Kenya. Yet, I survived. Why?

With the help of my psychiatrist, Dr. Henderson, most of my memory has returned, and bright lights no longer cause me immediate and blinding headaches. I deem myself healed enough to leave his charge, but I fear that emotional scars still remain, and might at inopportune times emerge again, and send me into that painful darkened place I so dread.

Contact with U'buntu has had additional effect on me. It is as though a doorway has opened up in my psyche. I now foresee things yet to happen, but who can deal with the insanity of such an ability, and what of my responsibility to my fellow man? Whom do I burden with this knowledge? Tortured by self-doubt, many times I have asked myself, "Do I really want this gift? Can I accept the things I see, and leave them be; or shall I walk in guilt, knowing I could have saved a life or diverted a disaster?" These are many age-old questions that now trouble my heart. Will experience gain me the wisdom to accept what is, or was, or what might have been? For that only time will tell.

Until today, I had not heard from my friend Dr. Bloome for a couple months. I still remember the first time we met. He sent me this ornate card of introduction in the mail; it was very unique and totally Bloome. My first impression of him was that of a scholar turned educated kook. He billed himself as 'Dr. Alan Bloome, Professor of Noetics,' which is a branch of science that delves into the paranormal. I mean, come on, wasn't that field of study just a lot of hooey? Nonetheless, with his tutelage, I learned that he almost single handedly took the world of the unbelievable and put a new and more scientific shine on it. Though I still view his beliefs with question, much of what he had imparted to me has a ring of truth to it. Our escapade together down in Africa sealed our friendship.

Sadly, he vacated his home in Chicago in July very shortly after our return to the US. Then he relocated to Amsterdam, and that is where he has been ever since. He said he liked the often overcast and cooler weather there, and I think their political atmosphere is a better fit with his libertarian lifestyle. Although I saw his move away from here and across an ocean as more of an attempt to hole up and disappear. Was he truly going to retire from the game?

Our encounter with U'buntu marked him emotionally as well. When I first met Alan, he mentioned he was on a quest to find answers to his wife's death. He said that some creature he called a Mothman had been involved with her plane crash ten years prior. Yet actually witnessing firsthand the death and destruction caused by these astral-creatures, as he calls them, may have been more than he could take. My thoughts go with him.

I no longer work as an epidemiologist for the World Health Organization. That job is on hold. Officially, none of my superiors believed in my claim that the deaths in Africa were the result of a monstrous demon. Still, they felt the trauma of dealing with my best friend Sam's death deserved a long sabbatical. About that, they are probably correct.

My conservative ideals hate not working. The agency paying me for doing nothing grates a little. Nonetheless, if this is a form of progressivism, and it is being forced on me, all I can say is, thanks for the free money.

My wife Amy is my best advocate, she has steadfastly remained at my side through these hard times. I doubt she has an unconditional belief in my story either. How could she? How could any sane person fully believe in such a fantastic assertion? Yet her aid and comfort during my disconsolate hours should not be understated, and her desire to help me make a complete recovery exemplify a wife's love for her husband.

Though I am much better than months ago, at times I still feel lost, as though a hazy blue-grey fog has enveloped me. Perhaps it is just that I have been lazy. I need to snap out of it. Alan's call yesterday has re-energized me. He said he is coming out of hibernation and mentioned something about a new expedition, and he wants me to join him. With my ailments healing, I am eager to get back into the hunt. He is on his way, and will be here in Chicago tomorrow. He said there was a recent news account of an unexplained happening here in North America that he wants to investigate. But first, before I agree to go along with him, I need to know exactly what it is he will be looking into. Moreover, I have to ask myself the question, "Am I really ready for this? … What if I have a relapse, what if I wind up back in the hospital, and have to face many more months of enervating rehab?"

2:

Amsterdam

Just arriving in Amsterdam is Dr. Wm. Henderson, Dr. John Carter's psychiatrist. He has just flown in from Chicago in an effort to locate Dr. Alan Bloome. For months, he has waged a fanatical one-man search to locate Bloome and confirm his existence. Dr. Bloome has been reclusive of late, but it is by way of a twist of circumstances that have kept these two from connecting sooner. Dr. Henderson does not believe in his patient's outlandish story of a monster from hell killing thousands in Africa. However, John's unwavering conviction left enough doubt in him to send him on a mission to find his friend and accomplice. His intent is to talk with Bloome and to compare their stories. Who else in the world would know the truth about what happened in Africa better than Bloome?

Bloome, though not eremite, is a man popular in only certain circles. The only people who know of him are those who have read his many books, and by way of the occasional speeches he gives to small crowds on the subject of Noetics.

Alan moved from his home in Chicago shortly after he and John returned to the US from their escapade in Kenya earlier this year. As is common these days, he had canceled his landline phone service years ago. His name, number, and address listing disappeared from the phonebook and related search programs, thus adding one level of difficulty in locating him.

As a consequence of his relocation, he changed his cell phone number. To complicate matters further, when renting his new residence, the property owner mistakenly listed his name as the resident. A small mistake, but it made Bloome's existence appear illusory.

Fortunately, an internet search showed a short article from a European newspaper about a talk Bloome gave two weeks ago in Belgium. With a little snooping, Dr. Henderson was able to get an address for him in Amsterdam. Without use of the internet, these two might have never met.

*   *   *

I have tried for nearly three months to locate Dr. Bloome, my patient's friend and supposed accomplice. Though I have found hints that there was once someone living in Chicago who went by that name, that was over ten years ago. I suspect that Carter's use of this name is just as fictitious as his belief in monsters. My inability to locate Bloome easily only adds to the mystery of his preposterous claims. I have decided to make one last attempt to find Bloome. John did say that he had recently immigrated to Amsterdam, which is just as crazy; who would do that? But that is where I am headed today.

After touching down at Schiphol International Airport, I rented a car, and with the aid of a map, took off for the supposed location of this supposed person.

My first impression of Amsterdam was very positive. The city, its streets, and its people appeared exceptionally neat and clean, and well-mannered, characteristics rare to find in my hometown of Chicago.

I had not travelled here before, or to any part of Europe, for that matter, and I immediately noticed that this was an ancient town. Its occupation must stretch back many centuries. They demonstrated this antiquity by placing ornately accented artistic sculptures and figurines along their thoroughfares, commemorating the grand achievements and the struggles of these people, no doubt.

This is such an interesting looking city—no urban sprawl here. People live one on top of the other. Every street, canal, or waterway, every turn or twist of road, by-way, or boulevard, is lined with tall, aged, multi-storied, multi-generation, multi-family, homes and apartments. The entire city is a deep maze of these four and five story buildings. Though it did not make me feel claustrophobic, I did wonder how these people manage to live so compactly, yet so neatly.

Perhaps it has something to do with the homogeneity of their society. In fact, everything here has an appearance of homogeneity. The monotony of the streets, all paved with dark brick laid in herringbone or thatch pattern, are homogeneous. The way the street brick blends into the walkway brick is homogeneous. The buildings, built of red brick, and little else, are homogeneous. The vehicles, all tiny and economy sized, are homogeneous. The people, all similar of appearance and of clothing, are homogeneous.

The ever-present haze above has me worried though. When does the sun shine here?

As the buildings loomed above, and driving on dark one-way roads below, I sensed one could get lost. However, one only had to proceed another block to find a crossway on which to turn back around.

This city is laid out so keenly that it is easy and fun to navigate, if only I had more time.

On the way to Bloome's residence, I drove by beautiful tree-lined canals. Small boats, neatly moored along the canal edges, add beauty and interest to this picturesque burg. Canals weave throughout the majority of the city, and offer an added means of transportation and housing. Each of these narrow waterways is framed on each side by even narrower side streets and walkways.

According to my map, Bloome's residence lies on a cross street on the next block. It should be located on the prow of a corner just before the curve.

Turning left, I rounded the corner onto a most narrow of streets. Autumn leaves were falling. They added a lovely color to the pavestone by-ways. Richly colored antique lampposts stood proudly at each street corner. The flow of auto traffic was separated from pedestrians by long lines of short sturdy iron posts that were connected together by lengths of heavy chain or rope. Over time they had become thickly coated with many layers of black paint.

All of this architecture tied together, and each street was singularly beautiful, but if taken as a whole, the city's sights blended into another rude homogeneity.

With only a short half-block to go, I thought it best to park and walk. I needed to stretch my legs anyway, and this would give me a chance to experience firsthand the beauty of this city.

The weather today was cool and cloudy, but not overly so. Zipping up my jacket, I set to walking, and actually enjoyed doing so. I didn't feel the need for wariness here that one has when walking the streets of my hometown.

As I walked, I counted down the building numbers. My destination was close by.

A large man was piling luggage and some boxes curbside a few doors up where the street begins to bend. He turned, and went back to his residence where I saw him fiddle with the front door lock. The building numbers hung prominently above each door, and with only a few doors to go, I followed the line of addresses with my eyes.

Where the man was standing, that was it. That was the residence. Was he the man I had searched for, for so long? Was this actually Dr. Alan Bloome? What serendipity if it was. Slowly, deliberately, I approached him.

* * * * *

Dr. Bloome was nearly ready to leave. His plane departs for Chicago in two hours. His many bags were packed and sitting out at the curbside. As he backs out of his home, being a tall man, he has to stoop down to lock the front door. With his back turned, he does not see the person approaching him from behind. After securing his door, and testing that it is locked, Bloome slips his house keys into his pants pockets, straightens, and turns around. There was someone standing only three feet behind him.

"Oh, Christ! You gave me a quite a scare, sir. You should know better than to sneak up on someone."

"Sorry. You were so absorbed with what you

were doing I guess you didn't see me walk up. I didn't mean to frighten you."

"Just an overreaction on my part. I used to live in a not so savory neighborhood. You'd think that by now I would've learned to watch my back."

"Are you Dr. Alan Bloome?"

"Why yes. Have we met?"

"No. Let me explain. My name is Dr. Henderson. I just arrived in Amsterdam today. My sole purpose in coming here was to find you Dr. Bloome. I must say that you are quite a difficult person to get a hold of."

"Oh, well, I am afraid you have come at a bad time Dr. Henderson. You see, my airporter will be arriving in a minute. I'm headed to the United States for a few weeks."

"It is imperative we talk sir. I have been trying to get in touch with you for months now. I must say I wasn't even sure that you existed." I can't let him slip away. After all the trouble I have gone to, I must find a way to slow him down and force him to talk with me.

"Yes, I have been in a self-enforced seclusion for the past few months. I have been so engrossed in finishing my latest book that I haven't stuck my head outside much."

"Was this book about the events down in Africa?" That's it Bill. That's it. Get him to talk about himself. Few people can resist that urge.

"Why yes. You have heard of them?"

"Dr. Bloome, I am John Carter's psychiatrist. I am the one he has been seeing for the past five months, and he is the reason I need to talk with you."

"If John is a patient of yours, are you sure we should be talking at all?"

"You see, there comes a time when you, as a

doctor, must seek out details in order to help your patient. You see, I am at a crossroad in treating him. It all revolves around his belief in a murderous monster on the loose in Africa." This was a lie, but a necessary one.

"So you have your doubts about the existence of U'buntu?"

"That is the reason I have sought you out Dr. Bloome. Dr. Carter weaves quite a believable story, and therein lays the problem."

"Not sure I understand you Dr. Henderson?"

"Yes, well, you see, certain people become so convinced in their delusions they become a reality to them. So much so, that no amount of psychotherapy can break them out of this cycle of denial. As part of his therapy, I had him recount his experiences in Kenya each time we met. I was looking for some little inconsistency in his storyline that I could use as a wedge to pry open some doorway into his self-doubt. But his story never wavered."

"Here is my airporter now," said Bloome. "I tell you what Dr. Henderson? If you help me load these bags, you can ride along with me to the airport, and we can talk further."

"Deal."

* * * * *

After helping Bloome stow his numerous boxes and travel bags in the back of the taxi, they got in the back seat and were off to Schiphol Airport.

"You do take an awful lot with you when you travel."

"Yes, it's mostly research materials, and of course several of these boxes are full of my new book. I plan to sell copies of it at a talk I'm giving next week titled 'Noetics and Alternative Scientific

Theory.'"

"I recall John saying that you had recently finished a new book. He was going to get me a signed copy of it, but I guess it slipped his mind."

"Dr. Henderson," started Bloome.

"Please, if you don't mind, call me Bill," interrupted Dr. Henderson.

"Thank you, I will. Then, Bill, your theory is that John made up the story of U'buntu. Why would he do that?"

"It is obvious that he is suffering from a trauma. Something injured him, and on a very deep and personal level. That troubles me. Whatever it was, it happened down in Africa, and you were there with him. So any information you can give me about your time in Kenya would help me to treat him."

"I sense that your concern for John's mental health is genuine. He should appreciate it that you are willing to go to such lengths to help him. ... You know, I was with John the evening he passed out and spent two days in the hospital. I remember that we were just sitting there going over some photos of one of the death sites when he yelled out in pain, grabbed for his temples, and then fainted. Previously he said he had been having these episodes of pain in his head. It seems it all caught up to him that night. Poor fellow. I know what it is like to be troubled by a demon."

"Yes, John had mentioned that your wife died years ago in a plane crash. Sorry for your loss. ... I believe that John's demon is also a woman. What I deduced from my talks with him is that many of his troubles revolved around that young woman, M Apurna. And her death, given John's previous run-in with her, appears suspicious to me. He was angered by the newspaper article that got him censured."

"What?" shot Bloome. "John told you that M

Apurna is dead? I only knew she had disappeared.
Now that is an interesting turn of events, isn't it? ...
Bill," staring down at the floor of the cab, Alan took a
long moment to gather a thought, "I can tell by our
discussion so far that you don't know who I am, and
what it is I do. I wish you had read my latest book
The Devil at 12:01. It is a tale about a true monster,
the one that caused the injury to John's mind. It also
recounts our entire time in Africa."

"True monster?" asked Henderson with a
perplexed yet unbelieving little smile on his face.

"Yes. A monster, or demon, whichever you
choose to call it, so frightening and deadly, that its
touch alone can kill. Bill, so far, you have been
ignoring the possibility that what John told you
actually happened. Believe me when I say that the
creature, U'buntu, is real. The thousands of deaths it
caused are real, and that it was solely responsible for
the total destruction of the city of Kenbe."

"Then you actually saw this monster for
yourself?"

Bloome pondered that question for a moment,
and then answered, "No. No one alive has seen it;
with the exception of John Carter."

After a brief pause, "Alan, listen to what you are
asking me to believe."

"Yes, I know. No pictures of U'buntu exist, and
you cannot believe in something unless you have
incontrovertible evidence. ... Let me tell you that this
is a spectral being. With its ability to slip into and
out of time, it probably cannot be photographed
anyway. However, I have witnessed the destruction
caused by its wrath. Many people John and I knew
well are dead now because of it." ... After taking
another long moment to think, Bloome continued,
"Actually, it might be best if you don't believe in it,
Doctor Henderson. Just go back to your comfortable

job, and your comfortable life, and forget about anything I have said. Death surrounds that monster. Searching after it will not bring you the answers you seek, and will cause you nothing but anguish and suffering. No good could come of it."

Just as Bloome finished his admonition of me, his cab pulled up to the airport's departure zone. He immediately got out of the cab, and walked to the rear of the vehicle where he motioned to a porter to help him retrieve his bags. I could tell he was in a hurry, but there was something else. His face had now turned sullen, as though a dark veil had pulled over his essence. Perhaps something had awakened in him a memory of his late wife? I didn't know. He then mentioned to me that his plane was scheduled to leave within the hour, and he still had to check in.

Before he parted my company he said, "Dr. Henderson, your insistence that U'buntu is nothing more than an invention John and I cooked up bothers me. However, I know from years of experience in dealing with a doubting public that no amount of chitchat will convert a non-believer. So, it is best for the two of us to part now. When two mentalities are that far apart, no common ground exists. Then it is better we go our separate ways than continue to sling more jabs at each other and let animosity get out of control, wouldn't you agree?"

I did not reply to him. I just looked at him in some disbelief. Then he said, "Let me pay for your cab ride back to your car. I apologize for your inconvenience in having to meet like this. If you need to talk with me in the future, please do so via my web site. You can get my web address inside any one of my books. I wish you well sir." Then he disappeared into the crowd.

* * * * *

Bloome's rebuke initially shocked me until I realized he seemed in more of a hurry to get away than he was upset with my questioning of his honesty. That alone made me more certain than ever that he and Carter were conspiring. I watched as he disappeared inside of the sliding glass doors of the airport along with a porter and a luggage caddy employed to handle his menagerie of bags and boxes. I was perplexed at his insistence that the U'buntu monster was real. At any rate, I found him to be quite kind, and he projected an almost chivalrous air about him. It was refreshing to find someone practicing social niceties these days.

Well, here I was, back at the airport in Amsterdam, which is where I started the day only hours ago, and now I have nothing to do. My encounter with Bloome only opened up more questions. I was hoping to gain some insight into Carter's scheme. Instead, now I have two individuals locked into some kind of silly belief. A shared delusion—is that possible? More likely, they were both trying to cover up something. However, Alan was right, I hadn't done my homework. I had no idea who he was, and I owed him a modicum of respect until I could prove him a criminal.

I jumped back into the cab we arrived in, the one he just paid for, and thought while the cabby pulled away from the departures zone. We left the airport grounds and got on the highway, and then the driver turned and asked me if I wanted to go directly back to Bloome's house?

"What, back to my car?" I asked. "Yes that would be fine. No, wait, actually, if you would, take me downtown. I want to go to the largest bookstore you have."

I started this day on a mission; it wasn't over yet. My driver dropped me off in front of one of the giants in the brick-and-mortar book industry. I thanked him, and sent him on his way. Inside the store, I hurried straight to the checkout counter.

"Can I help you, sir?" asked a young lady.

"I'm looking to see if you have any books in stock that were written by a Dr. Alan Bloome?" The young person behind the counter keyed in the author's name on her computer.

"Yes sir, we have two of his titles in stock." The clerk brought up the two books on her computer screen and showed them to me. I noticed that they were both dated pre-2008.

"No, it's neither of those. He has a new book out. I believe he called it *The Devil at 12:01*." She did another search for that specific title and found Bloome's latest book listed for sale on an internet web site, but it was not in the store's stock. Then she mentioned,

"We have a new service you might be interested in. It's called POD, or print on demand. If you find a book we don't have, and if it's formatted for computers, we can have it printed right here and now."

"What? That's remarkable," I said. We went to the vendor site offering Bloome's latest book, *The Devil at 12:01*. Then I paid her to pay them for the books download. She had only had to touch a few keys on her screen, and my new book was being printed while I waited. Five minutes later a young man emerged from the rear storeroom with my book in his hands, colorful cover and all. "WOW! That's amazing," I yelled. "Where will modern technology take us?"

I left the store with my purchase under arm, and

hailed a new cab for a ride back to my rental car. Later I took a room in a local hotel, and with no other ready plans, I spent the night delving into the psyche of Dr. Alan Bloome.

3:

Chicago

Alan's plane landed some twenty minutes ago. My head is spinning. This reunion has brought up feelings of doubt. Memories I have tried hard to forget have resurfaced. Why did I agree to this? Being around masses of people still causes me some discomfort. My mug hasn't appeared in any tabloid in six months, yet people still eye at me.

He asked me to pick him up here at O'Hare International. When he called yesterday, he said he was on a new mission to investigate something here in the states. It must be something important to get him to return to America. For security reasons I am not able to go straight to the plane's gate.

All this busied activity of people has me spinning. Dizzy, I need to sit. Spying a short cement bench located between to support columns, and hidden at the end of the room, I take a sit. I decided to hide away there until Bloome arrived to claim his baggage.

Many people were beginning to filter down the

escalator and cram into the carrousel area. Finally, I notice a tall and rather heavyset fellow with a big head and full scratchy looking beard. Yep, that's him.

Keeping a low profile, I wandered over to him. On seeing me, his eyes lit up, "Hello John, it's great to see you once again."

"Nice to see you also, Alan. How was your flight from Amsterdam?"

"Too long. I really need to stretch my legs," I found out in Africa that we both love to walk.

"Well, it is only a twenty minute ride to our house, and there is a beautiful park nearby. In fact, if you don't mind, I would like to join you on your leg stretcher."

"Great, then we can talk about how you've been doing." I accompanied Bloome over to the baggage claim where I was surprised to see that aside from his carry-on he had only one large bag to pick up. I was expecting a menagerie of boxes and suitcases.

"Where is all of your stuff, Alan?"

"What, I can't travel light like you?"

"Come on. I think I know you better than that."

"Yes, people don't really change, do they? I had most of my stuff, as you call it, sent on to a storage locker in New Mexico. That's where I'm headed next."

"New Mexico, the land of mystery and enchantment. Sounds like you're going to have a great vacation. Wish I could go along with you."

"You are!"

"Excuse me? When did I agree to fly off with you in search of monsters? I don't think that I am ready to do battle with another Mothman just yet."

"No, there will be no monsters this trip. That's not what we'll be looking into.

"Well, we can talk about that later," I said, "for now, let's get the hell out of here."

* * * * *

Alan and I spoke about nothing important on our drive to my house. Once home, I set him up in our spare bedroom, he will be spending the night. Then we headed out for our short stroll. Autumn arrived here several weeks ago, and the trees have already turned color in earnest and piles of leaves now carpet the ground. I was taking my friend to the famous Des Plaines River Trail. It is a collection of parks just a short drive from my new home north of the city. These heavily wooded parks meander on for miles. In my opinion, one of the few civilized things our politicians have done is to designate large tracts of land as parks, and set them aside from development. I have a need to be surrounded by nature, not wall-to-wall buildings, and the Algonquin Woods Park is just the respite to quiet my troubled nerves.

As ephemeral as they are, the changing seasons now displayed the fiery glow of maple and oak leaves. Viewing this explosion of color, the oranges, the reds, and the yellows, all interspersed with a touch of remaining green comforted my heart, and helped to soothe my tortured soul. As I walked these woods, I would kick through masses of multi-colored leaves that gather to cover the path. My thoughts would turn carefree as I recalled my childhood years. How I yearned to go back to a time when my biggest concern was getting home for dinner, or fighting with my brother over which cartoons to watch on Saturday morning. I rued the unnatural stresses I have had to bear, and deplored what I perceived to be the unfairness of it all. Why me?

"This place is beautiful, John." As we walked, Alan felt the need to break the pleasing silence.

"Yes it is. These past few months I have come here often. These trails go on for many miles. I've spent hours on them, just walking and sorting things out."

"Wish I could have enjoyed these woods with my wife while she was still living," said Alan, as he let out a sigh. "There are many things I regret not doing with her. Mostly I miss the simple little things the most. Like a stroll in the woods, or a walk along the lakeshore. Don't let too many regrets pile up in your life, John."

As he said that, a shiver ran though me from head to toe. "It's regrets that I am battling now, Alan. Dr. Henderson helped me to put my mind back together, and to understand and face the death and destruction wrought by that demon, U'buntu. However, now that I am fully cognizant of what happened those five months ago, I am forced to deal with another demon; the one called regret."

"You aren't responsible for the deaths in Kenya, John. Don't bother yourself with them."

"No, you are wrong about that, Alan." I paused for a moment to marshal my thoughts before I continued with the admission, "You know, Alan, I killed that young woman, M Apurna."

Alan's eyes winced in confusion, then he said, "John, stop. Don't tell me this. Think about what you're saying."

"No, I killed her and Sam too. ... It was my arrogance that killed them. I thought that if Apurna were in my presence on that day on our trek to the missioner's site that U'buntu wouldn't harm her. I was dead wrong about that. And my best friend Sam; I knew that murderous demon was responsible for the deaths we were investigating, yet I said nothing to him about it. I didn't even try to warn him about the danger. For that, I am guilty of their deaths as surely as if I had loaded a gun, and shot them dead myself. Those regrets I will have to carry with me for the rest of my life. I killed my best friend, Bloome. You can't imagine the sadness which constantly gnaws away at my soul."

"I don't know what is sadder," said Alan, "the tragedies themselves, or carrying them forward with us in our minds, and having to relive them each day of our lives? ... John, if there were words I could speak to exorcize you of your demons—I would not use them. I do not think you would want me to either. We learn from our missteps. They are what make us, and our species stronger. They are what help us to evolve."

"You have become some philosopher, Alan, you know that?" I have gained a stronger truth-sense as a result of my exposure to U'buntu. When I mentioned that I had killed Apurna, for a moment, I sensed that Alan actually took what I said literally. I found this a very curious reaction on his part. That this question still looms over me, troubles me on a personal level, though I will keep it secret for now. I knew the Minister of Health in Kenya thought Apurna's death suspicious, but I didn't know that Bloome also harbored some doubts about it—and that hurts.

"Let's talk about something positive, like our upcoming trip," he said.

"I don't feel that I am ready to tackle another Mothman right now."

"Not to worry," assured Alan. "This time we are chasing after space-aliens and UFO's, not some other-worldly monster."

"UFO's. What makes you think that there are UFO's to be found in New Mexico?" I said half laughing.

"I'm tied into a network of sorts. They notify me whenever there are unusual happenings anywhere in the world. My network is how I found out about your run-in with U'buntu," Alan retorted as we continued our stroll down the paths.

"If you chase after every mention of a UFO sighting, you are going to be running around like a chicken with its head chopped off."

"Give me a little credit, John. I screen these sightings closely. There are certain criterions they must meet before I run off after them. I'm too old and lazy to be chasing after wild fowl."

"Oh, and what are these criteria?" I was wearing a slight smile.

"I call it my three point method. Just because someone says they had a sighting isn't enough. As you know, there are reports of sightings showing up all of the time. So, when I get news of a sighting, or of an abduction, I look to see if there were other people involved who could lend it credibility. In addition, there might be multiple sightings of the same incident. That would also raise the credibility level. Then I look into the actual people who are involved. How they fit into their community is just as important. Do they have social ties, or are they itinerant? Further, could they possibly be media whores, and have they made claims like this before?"

"You check out all of that?"

"Generally, Yes." I sensed he was fibbing a little, but I let it slide.

"You know, I trust you Alan. I don't know why, but I do trust you. ... Let's finish with our walk, then head back home. You may want to freshen up a bit, and then Amy and I are taking you out to dinner."

We strolled along the Algonquin trails enjoying the fall splendor for about another twenty minutes before we arrived back at the car. Later that night, over dinner, he made his plea to my wife Amy.

"Alan," mentioned Amy, "I understand that you want to take my husband away from me."

With a smile, and hopeful eyes, Alan said, "Let's just say I want to borrow him for a week or two."

"I should be angry. After all, we don't live that far from New Mexico, yet John has never invited me there."

"Yes, I sense he has been remiss in certain inter-spousal areas," mused Alan. "Short trips and time spent together is very important to help couples bond. I promise I won't let him forget that." Amy thought that quip amusing and had a little laugh.

"Alright, I think this trip would be beneficial for you dear. You've been stuck at home long enough. It's time for you start getting out there again. … You take care of him, Alan."

So, I guess that my assent wasn't necessary. Is this what it's going to be like when I get old? Other people will be making all of my decisions for me. I didn't find it emasculating. Actually, I found their adlib word play games amusing. There is no way that I'm ready to start sucking pap through a straw, yet sitting back and letting others do my bidding could have hidden pleasures.

Later that night, back at home, we made plans for the two of us to fly to New Mexico the following morning.

4:

Jambo Africa

Nairobi, Kenya

Upon his arrival in Amsterdam, Dr. Wm. Henderson found himself alone and in an unfamiliar city. He had spent months searching for Alan Bloome. No sooner had he found him, than Bloome escaped his company, and headed back to America. Dismayed, but not deterred by Bloome's rebuke, he decided to dig deeper into this anomalous man's background.

Dr. Henderson is an imperfect man, one riddled with self-doubts, and a loathing of the common person. He also harbors an intense suspicion of others. This is jealousy bordering on paranoia.

His adult life so far has been spent living in a protected bubble of his own creation. Each day listening to his patients complain about their problems angers him. It is his anger that has stunted his ability to advance in his own career.

He thinks he has found a springboard that will catapult him to world acclaim. If he can find the clues that will disprove Carter and Bloome's absurd claims, then he can grab the spotlight for himself.

However, what awaits him in Africa will only test the limits of his personality, and bring him to the brink of irrationality.

*   *   *

Once I made it back to my hotel room in Amsterdam, I sprawled out on the bed, and spent most of the night reading Dr. Bloome's new book *The Devil at 12:01*. I found him to be an evocative and entertaining writer, and his tale did spark a curiosity in me. I was looking for any inconsistencies in his story line that would suggest it were concocted; sadly, I did not find any.

However, this could just be a polished piece of work on his part, and the sign of a devious mind. I didn't sense cunning in Bloome when I met him. My first impression of him was of a man of unusual intellect and education. He billed himself as a doctor, and as a Professor of Noetics. He did include a synopsis of his life as a forward in his book, which stated he got his doctorate from Harvard. Those facts are all readily verifiable, but Professor of Noetics; I actually had to look that term up. So he is also a person interested in the occult, or the paranormal. That fits well with his beliefs in spectral monsters, but ghosts and hobgoblins; I have my doubts?

His book conjured up enough inquisitiveness in me that I actually booked a trip to Kenya. I am still convinced that he and Carter's story, although well thought out, is a fraud, and I am going to prove it. Doesn't matter how smart you are, cons always slip up. Perhaps a forgotten detail here, or a misspoken fact there; these little fraying ends will appear. When they do, I will be there to unravel their scheme, and then I will be the one getting the notoriety.

My long trip from Amsterdam put me in Nairobi in the afternoon. I had not been to Africa before, and was eager to experience the new sights. With my carry-on bag thrown over my shoulder, I exited the airport, hailed a cabbie, and told him to take me into town.

That I was not prepared for the culture shock awaiting me here is an understatement. And I thought Chicago had some impoverished neighborhoods. True, before this week, I have never traveled outside of the United States. My only exposure to third world countries has been on the travel channels. However, seeing social strife and accepted poverty levels on TV is quite different from having it thrown right in your face. It was very easy to discount and ignore third world problems while sitting in my armchair at home. Witnessing firsthand how these people are forced to live was initially disgusting. After my revulsion tempered, I began to feel some sympathy for them, but I reminded myself that many of their problems are self-created. The dystopian morass that is present all around me, caused me to second-guess my decision to come here, and had me thinking to quickly run home. Why the fucking hell did I want to come here anyway?

Putting fucking monsters aside, I am the farthest thing from an *Indiana Jones* type. Nor am I a big nature bug, and this was not going to be a guided pleasure tour. Getting my hands dirty would be a first for me, and I began to think of it as a challenge to my bookish ego.

I have heard several of my patients mention how zip lining changed and empowered their lives. Now it was my turn to experience something new and out-of-bounds.

As best I can, I am going to retrace the steps taken by (Dr.) John Carter, and (Dr.) Alan Bloome. I question if those titles apply. Neither do I see how they are any better, or smarter than I am. Soon I will have an opportunity to disprove their preposterous claims, and perhaps to write a book of my own.

My plan is to use Bloome's book as a guide. First, I will rent a jeep, and then drive off to the city of Kisumu—that was where they based their excursions. Where they said this impressive old-world hotel lay, and that is where Carter's infamous bar was located. I just wanted to see how accurate their stories matched up with reality. Spectral monsters! Nonsense!

* * * * *

Office of the Kenyan Ministry, Nairobi

Ever since the occurrence of mysterious mass deaths earlier this year, the Kenyan Ministry has had an eye out to censure any possible media exposure to what they now call the *Incident*. They were intent on keeping a lid on the situation, even if this cover-up required them to tell lies. Their people had suffered enough recently, and telling them that a murderous Mothman monster was on the loose would only cause panic, more suffering, and death. Thousands of lives had already been taken. But they knew that people's memories were short, and that in a few weeks or months, they would start to forget the tragedy, and move on with their lives. All they needed was time.

So far, the zone of death patrolled by U'buntu hadn't grown. If it were something they could contain, that was to their advantage. They put forward some believable accounts that the ordinary person could relate to.

Initially, the deaths that occurred in the small border town with Uganda were attributed to a virus.

Viral outbreaks had happened before in Africa, and they seem to linger on the backs of peoples minds. It was a good story, and enough of a reason to set up a quarantined zone. So they came up with the idea of a Preserve, a vast restricted area to keep people out.

There were also a several reports of mass deaths in the area surrounding the virus outbreak. The authorities labeled them as revenge killings in response to the murder of a farmer and his family.

The crash of the small plane, and death of all aboard, including that of Sam Walters, was credited to pilot error, and nothing more.

The burning of the City of Kenbe was a much larger problem. However, local media were quick to grab ahold of a conflagration theory. In their papers, they said that the intense fire was the result of the crash of the helicopters, and that high winds that night produced an inferno no person could survive.

It was all very plausible, even though the government knew different. Out of respect for the deceased, they suggested that the Kenbe region be included inside of the Preserve they were forming. In addition, that it should be listed as a national memorial, and as such, declared off limits to visitation. The survivors accepted that. It made them feel good, and superstition wouldn't let them walk on another's grave.

One additional part of their strategy to obscure the truth from the world was to surreptitiously watch the people involved with the earlier investigations. Those who knew the truth had to be prevented from divulging it. They devised a watch list. That list included the names of Dr. Carter, and Dr. Alan Bloome; and their confidants. One of whom had just arrived in Africa.

* * *

Just entering the office of the Kenyan Minister of Defense is Mr. Um'fume, the Minister's aide. Moments ago, he received notification of the sudden appearance of Dr. Henderson in Nairobi. The intent behind his current atypical and peculiar movements is raising questions.

"Yes Mr. Um'fume. Please come right in," said the Minister.

Walking straight in, Um'fume's tall lissome frame, so common among many native blooded Kenyans, stood imposing in front of his shorter adipose boss, who remained seated behind his desk.

Um'fume was the man charged with overseeing the *Incident,* and has been involved with its investigation since the initial deaths appeared in the small border town with Uganda six months ago. He is also the person who gave Dr. Carter all of the aerial photos of the settler's death site north of the missionary school. Those were the very photos whose shocking revelation put Carter in the hospital.

"Minister," said Um'fume, "we have had a hit on Dr. John Carter's watch list."

"What?" he barked, in a cavernous and loud voice. "Don't tell me he is coming back here? You told him to stay away, did you not?"

"Yes, I made that quite clear to Carter, but it is not him. By your request, we have been having him and his friend Dr. Bloome under surveillance these past few months."

"So where are Carter and Bloome?"

"They are both in the US, sir. What is interesting is that Bloome boarded a plane to return to America a day ago. He had moved to Amsterdam. My sources tell me that Carter met him at the airport in Chicago. Apparently they have re-united, but for what purpose we cannot say."

"Let's continue to keep an eye on them. So far

our plan to keep the truth regarding the deaths under wraps has for the most part worked. People are relating the deaths in Kenbe to a tragic fire caused by the helicopter crashes, and as it fades from their memory, they are moving on. We do not need Carter and Bloome coming back here to stir things up again. ... Is there anything else?"

"Yes sir. The reason I came to you. It seems that Dr. Carter's psychiatrist is in our country. He flew in yesterday afternoon."

The Minister, looking straight down and over the rim of his glasses asked, "You had his psychiatrist put on the watch list? Why would you do that?"

"Just trying to be thorough, sir."

"Well, good job, Um'fume. But why would Carter's doctor want to come here, and why should that be of interest to us?"

"Can't say, but here is where it gets curious. His doctor, a Mr. Henderson, first flew to Amsterdam where he had a brief meeting with Bloome. The next morning he bought a plane ticket to come here. What do you think it means, sir?"

"Yes, this is looking suspicious. I am thinking that he is just a curiosity seeker. He knew about Carter's story and wanted to check it out for himself."

"How do you want to handle it, sir?"

"It is best if we do nothing. Just let him snoop around. If we act overly aggressive and question him, it would just raise his suspicions. I doubt he will find anything. The only eyewitness left alive is Carter, and aside from the Marks found on the fence line, there is nothing else left. No evidence exists that would countervail our story. In addition, if Henderson decides to enter the restricted zone? Well, then our problem will be solved for us, won't it?"

"Yes sir. ... I understand sir." Um'fume then left the Minister's office and went about sending out an alert. He advised his operatives of Dr. Henderson's presence, and he told them not to interfere with his actions in any way.

5:

New Mexico

On the way to Albuquerque

I should have been alarmed at how easily Alan
maneuvered me into joining him on this lark. I do
enjoy his camaraderie, and find his chivalrous
manner amusing, but should I succumb so easily to
his commanding way? It is easier to be a follower
than a leader. Is that it? Am I in danger of becoming
nothing more than a groupie? And what were we
investigating anyway, some strange claim of alien
abduction? A visitation by aliens? When did I begin
to believe in spacemen from Mars, or from any other
point in the cosmos for that matter? To me these
machinations are nothing more than zany stories
found only in the tabloids. Something to be laughed
at, and then ignored; unless you are ill advised.
However, here I am, flying at thirty thousand feet
and headed west in search of the para-whacky. To
pass the time I engaged him in some small talk.

"So Alan, you never told me what your theory is
about these alien abductions. You can't be serious in
believing that there are actually swarms of aliens

regularly visiting our planet?"

"Right you are John. Ten years ago, when I first set out on my quest to investigate the unknown I took it upon myself to rethink these weird claims. What impressed me about them was that these reports are for the most part, made by ordinary people. People like your next-door neighbor, or the waitress in your favorite restaurant. Just ordinary people who you would never expect to make lurid, or sensational claims, unless they thought that something had actually happened to them. Further, the similarity of their stories caught my curiosity. Although these reports were from people living in diverse places, and of different beliefs and educational backgrounds, they all contained common elements. It was just all too curious not to give some serious thought to. What was required was a more logical approach. I decided to develop a new scientific theory for them, and also a framework in which to classify and investigate them."

"And your new scientific theory is?"

"Well, let me tell you that first off I discounted the idea that the abductions were the work of aliens visiting Earth. Although I still believe that UFO's are possible, and that a visitation by aliens will happen someday, I don't think they have arrived here on Earth just yet. The galaxy is just too vast. Even if you traveled at the speed of light, you would still need hundreds if not thousands of years to get anywhere.

So, I thought on it, and came up with the idea that these abductions may not be physical attacks at all, but are more of a mental incident. Suppose for instance, that beings on another planet, when they arrived at their space age, they found the distance problem impossible to overcome. Instead of wasting precious resources on dubious multi-generational space flight, they switched their attention to the development of their mental and psychic abilities."

"I see where you're going with this, but aren't thoughts energy, and doesn't energy still travel at the speed of light making immediate and controllable psychic contact between planets impossible?"

"My, you are clever, John, but your assumption may not be correct. There are many different types of energy. Moreover, it is my belief that our brain is, at some level, a quantum machine, and operates according to the rules of quantum mechanics. Scientists have shown us that in a quantum world things behave quite differently, and it may be that instant telepathic communications are possible."

"You mean sub-space telecommunications. I just knew Star Trek would enter our conversation at some point. Jesus, Bloome."

"Well, whether you call it sub-space, inter-space, or inter-dimensional, I think the premise is all pretty much the same, John. Moreover, the penner's of Star Trek, and of all sci-fi may have been less imaginative than clairvoyant. Isn't it possible that they were in sub-space subconscious contact with more advanced minds from other worlds, and that these alien minds imparted their thoughts to them? Thoughts about scientific principles far advanced from ours at that time?"

"Now wait just a second, Bloome. You are getting ahead of me. What do you mean that there are many types of energy?"

"Sorry, John, guess I misspoke. I don't think that our science has any idea yet as to what energy really is. Glad you caught me on that one."

"Oh, come on Alan. Everyone, including me, knows that light and heat is a form of energy."

"Actually, no, light consists of photons, and heat, or what was once called black body radiation, is nothing more than photons in the infrared spectrum.

They carry and can impart energy to other particles, but exactly what that energy is has not been defined yet.

We are just now getting a handle on the many different types of particles, and to do so, science has of itself, postulated the existence of other types of energy. You hear it called dark energy. What I suggest is that just as there are dozens of different kinds of particles, so to, there are many types of energy. Learning about these other types of energy may be our ticket to the stars, or to inner-space and to the use of extra dimensions, just as your U'buntu monster does, or have you forgotten about him?"

"Alan, I can see that you have given all of this a lot of thought."

"Yes I have."

"So, your working premise is that these stories of abduction are actually misunderstood psychic attacks. I will have to think about that one."

"I hope I answered your questions with clarity?"

"Hah! God you make me laugh. By the way, you haven't mentioned any sort of itinerary yet. Where are we off to first?"

"First, I have to give my speech at the University of New Mexico, in the small town of Las Vegas."

"There is a Las Vegas in New Mexico?"

"Yes, it's a lovely little town set on the edge of the Great Plains. I just know you're going to like it."

Alan may have suspected it, but I was laughing inside at his kooky ideas. He never fails to amuse me. Thanks to our conversation, our flight seemed to pass quickly. We landed at Albuquerque International around noon. I say around noon as the one thing you can't predict is time spent getting into or out of airports. I arranged for the rental of a four-wheeler jeep, while Alan collected his bags. As usual,

I have only my carry-on. Traveling light is a habit I strictly enforce.

As I was the invitee on this trip, and still felt more like a tag along than an important member of a fully functioning team, I let Alan drive. He said he had some local knowledge as he had been to New Mexico before.

No sooner had we left the car rental property than things began to go wrong. He missed the turn that would have taken us to the freeway, and directly to LV. Instead, we wound up lost in the back streets of Albuquerque. I do not believe that I am an edgy and ill-mannered passenger, and I don't mind letting someone else drive for a change, but riding with Alan was like sitting in the backseat with a killer toothache while you grandparents slowly and meticulously lost their way to the dentist's office. It was torturous!

After about twenty minutes of frantically driving down one dead-end, and then another, Alan said, "John, see if you can get the map computer turned on?"

"Lost are we?" All the while, I am fiddling with the computerized trip guide, Alan is zipping around corners, and blasting through dips in the road, and searching one neighborhood to the next looking for a freeway exit.

"Alan, please, just pull over to the side of the street while I play with this thing."

"They're supposed to be very easy to use," he said. "You just input your destination, and it will tell you where to go."

"Yes, Alan, I know that. I can't get the damn thing to work, but if you really want someone to tell you where to go?" I offered.

"No need to get testy."

"You've been driving around this neighborhood

for twenty minutes. You're lost!"

"If you could only get the map guide to work we won't be. The rental agent said that they were very easy to use."

"Well they aren't," I shouted. "Damn it, I'm not some nerdy tech whiz. I swear my fraying nerves are turning the hairs on my head white. Just go back to the rental agency, and let them show us how to use the damn thing."

"Agreed, any ideas on which way it is from here?"

"Geezzas! ... Why don't you just follow one of those landing planes?"

Another twenty minutes passed before we located the car agency. After a short in-service we were wired up, and now Bloome had a computer telling him when and where to turn. Leaning back, I got some much-needed rest. Our destination, the small college town of Las Vegas, was located about one hundred and twenty miles to the northeast.

The rest I so desired was not to happen. Had this man never driven before? When we were lost back in the city of Albuquerque he couldn't speed through the neighborhoods fast enough, but now that he is on the interstate he's creeping along at fifty. People wanting to get somewhere kept honking at us; several of them gave us the one finger salute. I tried playing the coward by keeping a low profile, but it was no use.

When we finally arrived in Las Vegas, it was just past four in the afternoon. Alan's speech wasn't until seven, so we had plenty of time to stop and grab a cup. We were both tired and thirsty from the long drive, but not feeling hungry. We spied a coffee shop just off the I-89 and pulled in.

"None too soon for me, John," said Alan. "I hate

driving. Here, I surrender the keys to you. You can be my chauffeur for the rest of the week if you like."

"Thank you, Alan. I accept. Besides, your driving was getting to me. If I wanted to be kind, I would say that you drive like an old woman."

"Why bother being kind. Just say it like it is."

"Alright. Here it goes—your driving sucks. You need to learn to drive as if you have somewhere to go. The speed limit is 65. You never got over 51. God, I hate being flipped off, especially by teenage girls with those long slender little fingers sticking it at you."

"OK, John. OK. Boy you sure get surly when you are tired. Come on, let's go and get some coffee in you."

We entered the coffee shop. It was one of those modern 24hour chain restaurants; neat and clean, and the first smell to hit you was one of vanilla flavored pancakes. A great place to sit and work on your diabetes, and get hooked up to a coffee IV.

Taking a booth along an outside wall, a line of windows offered us an unobstructed view of the plains to the east. Just miles and miles of barren nothingness. Bit looked quite boring, unless you are a fan of grasslands.

Our waitress wasted no time in filling our cups. For several minutes, we both sat silent and stared blankly out across the landscape. After our trip, we needed time to decompress and enjoy our coffee. Alan was right, I do get a bit surly when tired; I am not a fan of long tedious rides.

Our section of the restaurant was empty except for a solitary person sitting four tables away. To me he looked like just one of the locals. That southwestern dress, the denims, cowboy shirt, and bolo tie, but no boots. I guess modern cowboy's all wear sneakers and ball caps.

We sat and relaxed for about twenty minutes, the man never once turned away from his eastward looking stare. It was as though he was locked in a trance state. His was a good place to sit and ponder.

After our third coffee refill, and with life returning to our bodies, we decided to order some dinner. After our server took our order, I noticed the man's spell break. He turned and briefly made notice of Bloome and me, and then turned away again. Over the next few minutes, he repeated his glance at us two more times.

"Aw Christ," moaned Bloome.

"Jesus, Alan. I have never heard you use cuss words before. What's up?

"Oh, that guy over there. He's a lookie loo. I should have warned you that there would be competition showing up. Quite a number of people follow these UFO sightings, and most of them are uninformed wannabes."

I turned to assess the man again. "I don't see that, Alan. To me, he appears to be a native to these parts. Look at how he's dressed."

"No, he keeps giving me that knowing look. He must be someone on the fringe of the network. He would have to be connected to know who I am."

"Isn't this just paranoia, big boy?"

"Well, we'll see."

I felt embarrassed. The man must have heard Alan's ranting, and sat quietly. He didn't leer at us again as we finished our meals.

Finally sated, I reached to my coffee cup for one last gulp when I noticed him get up and walk toward us. He came up to our table, and in a soft and polite voice he said, "Hello, Alan."

"Do I know you sir?" replied Bloome.

"I'm Don," he said, as though his name should

carry some great significance to us. He was definitely a local though. You could tell from his accent. There is a distinct dialect here in northeastern New Mexico. It is a combination of a soft Texas drawl infused with Mexican/American slang. It is quite distinct, yet subtle, and you have to listen closely to pick it out.

"I'm sorry. You have me at a loss," said Bloome. "If we have met before let me apologize, but I don't remember meeting you."

"No, we haven't met before." He paused for a moment in apparent thought, and then switched his gaze to me. His unfocused stare at my chest area pierced right through me. His stare bothered me. I also don't like pauses in conversation. Alan might have been right about this guy.

After an eternal second or two of stabbing me with his gaze, he turned to Bloome and said, "Alan, John Burningtree's father was my closest friend. We grew up together." After another long pause, "Would you mind if I sat and talked with you two for a moment?"

OK, my weirdness radar just went off. How did this person know who we were? How did he know that we would be here in the restaurant? And who the hell is John Burningtree?

Apparently, the information Don offered up was important, and really got Bloome's attention.

"W—W—Why yes. P—Please have a s—seat, Don. ... D—Do you have a last name?" Alan stutters; never had I heard him stutter? With perplexed curiosity, I bent my head, and keenly listened on. This was amusing.

"Yes ... but I prefer to be known only as Don."

OK, so this guy is not a sterling conversationalist, but this isn't a job interview, and I am dying to get answers to my questions. While I sat with rapt attention he added, "Alan, you can find John in Taos. He is in mediation on the reservation's holy ground. I am certain he will want to talk with you. Just go there and wait at the front gate. He will know when you arrive." That put a smile on Alan's face.

I just felt another turn in the universe's giant cog. A nexus was forming around us, and as would become clear to me later, pieces to Bloome's puzzle were falling into place.

"Thank you, Don. Thank you," said Bloome.

Well, Alan was elated, but I felt a growing unease in all the mystery that grew worse. Don again turned to me and used his blank stare to check me out. What the hell was he looking at? I didn't know this fellow, yet somehow, by his presence; I knew I had seen him before, but where? This was one of those deja vu moments.

"John," he erupted, and without an introduction. Startled, my chin jumped backward and my eyes flared open wide. Just as he called out my name, he raised his gaze and we made complete eye contact for the first time. "You have been having terrible headaches?" he said.

That sounded more like a statement than a question. Then he went on to say, "There is a problem with your aura." Excuse me? Aura? If not for the startling accuracy of his first statement, I would have gotten up and left to find saner company.

Alan, with his left arm stretched, and with his hand open, reached out and across the table in an attempt to grab a hold of me. I hear him say, "John, no, be patient, and listen to what he is telling you."

Following Bloome's directive, I decided to play along to see where this was leading, "Yes," I answered, "for several months I did suffer from blinding headaches, but they have subsided now."

"No, John," argued Don, "your problems are not over. I can see it in your aura. You were touched by a Skinwalker."

I had never been around an insane person that is until today. Wondering if there might be a mental hospital nearby, I interlocked my fingers over my now full stomach, which was growling uncomfortably.

The man in front of me then went on to say, "There is a Navajo cleansing ceremony to remove this demon if you no longer want it inside of you."

OK, in the real world you do not get bonus points for being succinct. A little more lengthy discussion might be advised here. I heeded Alan's plea for me to be patient, but what have I run into?

Don, the man of few words, then pushed his chair back, and stood, saying, "You two need to talk alone. It was nice to have met both of you. Alan, mention me to Burningtree if you will."

Then, before he turned to leave the restaurant, he added, "John, don't worry. We will meet again before you return to your home." Then he turned and headed for the front door, and soon disappeared into the waning daylight.

I gave Bloome this two wide-open eyeballs look, my chin sunken down and resting on my chest as I stared at him. While wondering to myself whether I'm cut out for this weirdo stuff, Alan chimes in, and needless to say, he is in his element.

His body movements grew animated, and his speech raced. "John, do you know who, and what that was?"

My brain can't process information like Alan's can. He seems able to handle any number of unrelated data points at one time. He is truly a gifted man. I, on the other hand, need to outline info into a hierarchy, and then proceed in logical fashion.

"Alan," I said, "let's just ignore Oddball Don, and his strange approach for the moment. Why don't we start with the term, Skinwalker?"

"OK, John, OK. I'll slow down. Let's take it one small step at a time. Besides, I really need to be getting ready for my talk tonight. So, why don't we get going, and I'll give you some homework to do while I'm busy teaching this class.

You see, it all has to do with Navajo lore and tradition. As you will find out as you read up on it, there is no precise definition of a Skinwalker. You could call it a witch or demon. That is where it gets interesting. One corollary to it would be your Mothman, or U'buntu, over in Africa. I'm sorry, but when these striking coincidences crop up across vastly different cultures, and lands separated by oceans, I get all excited. So, write this down. You can use the college library computers to do some research. I want you to read up on one: Skinwalkers, and two: the Navajo Creation Myth."

* * * * *

After Alan and I left the restaurant, we remembered one other thing, which had slipped both our minds—a room for the night. After securing lodging, we both set out for the college campus. This was a small town, and the campus was only five blocks away so we decided to walk, which gave me time to clear my mind of Oddball Don.

As towns go this one was compact, old, and had some interesting history. The homes in this central part of town must date from the forties or earlier. What struck me the most were these hugely wide parking strips that surrounded each block; they must be at least fifteen feet wide This placed the sidewalks we walked on far back, and deep into the grasp of the eerie and ever changing mature landscapes they encircled.

As we strolled, my gaze wandered under, around, and through overgrown shrubs and trees. Together they created a spooky disguise of shadow and form, and lent an eerie feel to the night air. I only wish the landscaping around my home in Chicago had such a mysterious feel to it.

We split up at the campus. Alan was off to give his speech, and I was off to the library. I had homework to do. Besides, I had suffered through enough kookiness earlier. Besides, I looked forward to some alone time.

Following Alan's orders, I read up on the Navajo. I wasn't exactly certain what he wanted me to learn, so I just read everything that came up on the computer. An hour and a half in I was confident I had covered the bases, and turned my attention to current events—events of the UFO kind that is.

I came across the newspaper story that had Bloome so interested he traveled halfway around the globe to investigate it.

It was a short article about a local citizen who claimed to have been abducted by aliens while hunting in the hills. It gave a date of the incident, and mentioned the name and age of the supposed victim, a John Burningtree, Jr., 54, son of the late John Burningtree, Sr., of Santa Anita Pueblo near Taos, New Mexico. There was no follow up article.

"So what is there to investigate?" I asked myself.

I made a print screen copy of it to show to Alan. Then I decided to dig a little deeper, and did a search for any information on John Jr.'s dad. Amazing how much of our lives are online.

I came across John Sr.'s obituary, and read it. The lead line read: Long time native son John Burningtree Sr. died on Saturday, March 11, 2001, at the age of 64.

It went on to mention his only living relative, his son, John Jr. ... Then it hit me.

Doing some mental math, if John Jr. is 54, then his dad today, if he had lived, would be about 75. Don, the oddball man from the restaurant, who said he was senior's best friend as a child, should now be about 75 also. I met Odd Don, and he appeared to be between my age and Alan's, or about mid-forties, well over a whole generation too young?

When Alan's speech was over, he poked his head into the library; it was just after ten o'clock. His appearance broke my concentration; it was time to stop anyway. It was late and I was tired. Alan said he was going out with a few of his lecture participants for a late night snack, and some more talk on ghosts, and what have you. I declined to join them, and went back to my room to sleep. My little nugget of information would have to wait for morning.

6:

Trip to Kisumu

Lake Victoria, Kenya, Africa
Along the northeastern shore of Lake Victoria lies
the old port town of Kisumu. Nestled up against a
bay at the top of the lake, years ago it became a locus
for trade. The name Kisumu literally means a place of
barter trade. At over 3,700 feet in altitude, even
though I sits atop the equator, the climate there is
generally temperate.

It is the largest city in this corner of Kenya. That
is the reason that John Carter's former boss, Sam
Walters, chose it as their base of operations. Much of
Africa's colorful colonial history can still be seen
there.

Dr. Henderson is about to arrive there.

*   *   *

Yesterday when I arrived in Nairobi, it was late in
the afternoon. Way too late to do anything but take a
quick look around, get an overnighter room, eat, and
sleep.

This morning, with a log of Dr. Bloome's journey confidently fixed in my head, I rented a jeep and drove to Kisumu.

It took the better part of a day just to get there. On arriving, the first thing I wanted to checkout was the hotel Carter raved about. He never gave me the name, just a lavish description. He did mention that it was only a block to two from one end of the airport compound.

On the outskirts of Kisumu, I pulled into a gas station to fill up. I also bought a map of the surrounding area. Conveniently, I found one in English. Tourism drives commerce everywhere, I guess.

A quick peruse of it showed a hotel icon only two blocks from the north end of the airport. That must be it. I walked over to the attendant, pointed a finger at the icon, and asked him if he knew anything about it?

His English was broken, but understandable, "Yes sir. That very fine hotel. Very old."

Had a dagger just been thrust into my conspiracy theory? I reassured myself that it was quite possible that much of John Carter's story was based on fact. That the places he stayed, and many of the sights he saw were quite real. Only that in his delusional state of mind he embellished his story with tales of nightmarish monsters, and that his friend, Alan Bloome, went along with it either willingly or naively wishing it so. So finding the hotel proved nothing, but I still had to lay my eyes on it.

Gas tank full, target located, I pushed in the clutch, slipped my jeep into gear, and touched the gas pedal. I was off directly for the hotel. The city of Kisumu has a curious and interesting simplicity as to how its roads are laid out. They were overly wide, and easy to navigate. I had no problem finding the hotel. It was right there, and just as Carter had described. Definitely old colonial, and very well maintained. Its white exterior almost glistened, and made a striking contrast to the other buildings surrounding it.

I parked my jeep on the street across from the hotel. There I sat for a moment to admire the building, and to pat myself on the back for the great detective job I was doing. I made note that the porters and the valet were in formal attire just as Carter said. It was now late afternoon, and there was a flurry of activity in front. People were coming in, presumably to register.

When through cajoling myself for my detective prowess, I remembered that I had no planned itinerary, and no room in which to spend the night. Certainly, a $300 an hour psychiatrist could afford a couple well deserved night's stay in this Grand Old Manor.

I wheeled the car around and pulled right up to the front steps. The valet came running over. "Will you be spending the night, sir?" he asked.

"If there is a room available," I said.

"Very well, sir. I will hold your car while you check with the front desk."

It felt good to be waited on, and if the other services here are as genial, I will be spoiled. As I climbed the front steps and entered the foyer, I noticed that although the architecture of this old building was uncomplicated, inside it was cool, clean, and lavishly adorned. Ferns and flower arrangements were set atop quarter columns. The wood parquet floor shined spotless. Huge paintings hung on the walls. They were larger than life depictions of the hunt, and fit well with the feel of an early twentieth century gentlemen's club.

A brass plaque on the middle bottom of each painting told a story to commemorate who it was, and when it was painted. One caption read 'Painted in 1914.'

Many animal heads hung up high on the overly tall walls. Some great white hunter no doubt killed each of these beasts. I imagined myself a big game hunter, or perhaps part of the peerage of old, sent to Africa to conquer and settle new land for the empire, and this fine hotel my home away from home.

I poked around a while longer, then strode to the front desk, a woman asked, "How long would you be staying, sir."

"Please register me in for a one-week stay." I could venture out from here during the day. No matter how tough it got out there, I knew that when I returned here, humble personnel would be waiting to cater to me—it felt very comforting.

After settling in, I went downstairs and ate a nice meal in their formal restaurant. Again, it was everything Carter mentioned.

Later that night I took out Bloome's book to do a re-read. I needed a plan of action, and used his book as my outline. My first step tomorrow would be their last. I would trek to the lost city of Kenbe. John always ended the recount of his tragic saga with his most outrageous claim. He blamed the burning deaths of thousands in the city of Kenbe on his monster U'buntu. He said that his monster caused a conflagration that engulfed an entire city, reducing everyone and everything there to ashes. How preposterous. That should be easy to disprove.

Then his whole story will immediately fall apart. "*Tomorrow*, Dr. Carter, *tomorrow*."

7:

The Taos Mystery

Back in New Mexico

Alan and I met the following morning and ate breakfast at a greasy spoon next to our motor lodge. Before we drove to Taos, I thought it appropriate to discuss the inconsistencies regarding Oddball Don. I wanted to keep an open mind. I knew all too well that in my new endeavor of investigating the paranormal I would be in contact with a fair amount of kooks. However, I was experiencing unease from the meeting with Odd Don, a person who I deemed a nut. Perhaps I am making too much of it, but I have never done well around wacky people.

"Good morning, John. How did you reading go last night?"

Alan looked unusually well rested for someone who was out quite late. He got in sometime between one and two. A couple times after that, loud knocking against the wall that separates our two rooms disturbed my sleep. I reminded myself that he is an adult, and that this was a college town; so I didn't pursue it any further. We got right into my research.

"I completed your homework assignment, but I'm not exactly sure as to what you wanted me to learn from it?"

"You may be looking at this way too deeply, John. My intent was only to help acquaint you with the beliefs and culture of the Navajo. I hoped that in gaining some knowledge of them, you would realize that they aren't the simple band of roaming savages as portrayed by Hollywood, and, I am afraid, by most grade school history teachers. They have had a presence in the southwest for over three thousand years, and have a language and belief system rich in lore about the world we live in. There is much we can learn from them."

Alan can get a bit full of himself at times, so this was the perfect opportunity to put him in his place.

"Your point is well taken, Alan, I will have to buy some of their art. I love its colorful simplicity, and I know that Amy would enjoy having some pottery and paintings of fanciful horses and wolves strewn all around the house." This was a purposeful missive aimed right at him. How I love to torture him.

Its effect was immediate. I watched as he put his hands to his face, and rubbed his palms around and around over his eyes. Then he pulled his fingers down scratching at his face through his beard. Then he let out an exasperated groan, and said, "No, no, no, you missed the point entirely..."

Sitting across from him, and in quite a relaxed pose, I had my hands clasped together and resting on the table. I made a wide smirk as I twiddled my thumbs.

He pulled his hands away from his face, and we made eye contact. That is when he got it. His look of scorn quickly faded, and then he mumbled, "Oh."

"That's right, big fella. I got you again."

"I suppose that I deserved that one. Sometimes I forget that I expect way too much of you."

"Ouch, don't forget who's driving you around today. Now, if we can stop sparring with one another for a moment, there is something I dug up last night that needs your attention? ... Here, I printed out a couple of things. This one here, I believe, is a copy of the article on the UFO abduction we are investigating."

I handed Alan the news item, and gave him time to read it. "Yes, that is it. Hopefully we will meet with Burningtree later today."

"Yes, well, I got a little curious and dug deeper into his life. I wanted to know something about his father. Here is a copy of his obituary. What I found of interest was his age at the time of his death."

"Yes, he was sixty-four," noted Bloome. "I'm not sure where are you taking this, John?"

"OK, here, let me explain it in simple terms so that even your Harvard trained mind can comprehend. If Burningtree senior had lived, today he would be 75 years old. Let me ask you, just how old do you think his childhood friend Oddball Don appears to be?" It didn't take Alan long to connect the dots.

"Now, that is interesting."

"Yeah, well, Oddball Don is either a loon, or a conniving liar."

"Or, extremely long-lived."

"Oh, you can't be suggesting?"

"I'm not suggesting anything, just recounting the possibilities. Keep an open mind, John. Besides, I had a glimpse of something about him burst upon my consciousness last night when he sat down."

"So, what, now you're a psychic?"

"All I know is that a strange image burst onto my consciousness. It is not something I can explain or quantify, but I did make note of it. Remember how we talked about journalizing our thoughts to improve awareness of what is going on up there? There is a lot that goes on in the mind that we ignore which could be useful. Perhaps what I saw was my mind picking up on a thought that was in his?"

"Thought transference, now I've had experience with that one," I said. "So, tell me about what you think you saw."

"Alright, now don't laugh. What I saw could be described as a scene from the old west. My vision was of the inside a building, probably a house. It was just one room; square, about twenty feet wide, and the walls appeared to be made of nothing but wood boards. It was dark inside; only a lamp was lit for lighting.

There was a lot of clutter lying about; mostly objects that were common a century ago, but which have disappeared from our use today. I couldn't even name them. I saw two people, a man and a woman. The man was tall, had a full thick beard, and was dressed in what looked to be work coveralls. The woman had on a drab one-piece dress. That was it."

"I see," I said, as I bobbed my head up and down. That got a little chuckle out of him.

"Trust me John; you don't want me in your psychiatrist's chair. Now can we get on with the day?"

"Huh, just now, when you mentioned the word psychiatrist, a mental image of Dr. Henderson shot across my mind. I wonder what he's doing today."

"Oh, if you have a need to call and chat with your doctor, I'll go and wait in the jeep."

"That's not funny, Alan. OK, enough banter, let's just go."

Tired of our friendly verbal repartee, we left the restaurant, and prepared to drive to Taos. I did not understand why I had a mental image of Henderson run through my head just then. A curiosity I supposed, and I thought nothing more of it.

This early morning in autumn here in NM was sunny and really quite comfortable considering the time of year, and being well over a mile high in elevation. The town of Las Vegas is nestled up against the eastern side of the bottom end of the majestic Rocky Mountain Chain. Before entering the jeep, I took a moment to survey the scenery surrounding us.

Immediately to the west, verdant hills lay covered in pine forests speckled with stands of aspen that were now showing their golden glow. Turning to the east, and shading my eyes from the still rising sun, my eyeshot enjoyed an unobstructed view of the beginning of the Great Plains. A thousand mile expanse of flat to rolling grasslands stretched in every direction from north and south.

The vista I was enjoying was quite a treat. I felt relaxed for a change. The edges of my mouth turned upwards in a slight smile. Bloome, spying across the top of the jeep, noticed my peaceful smile, and just before he jumped into the passenger side he said, "Your welcome, John."

Today we first drove west to the historic town of Santa Fe, and then turned north to the Taos Pueblo. Given the distance we had to drive, my estimates put us into Taos around one in the afternoon.

A few miles down the road I turned to Alan and asked, "Alan, what do you think Odd Don meant when he said that Burningtree would know when we showed up? How does he even know we are coming today?"

He said, "I assume it's because he's an Indian."

"Damn." I exclaimed, and took my eyes off the road long enough to give him a power stare. Then I forced him to endure an hour in the silence box for that one.

Intent on getting there we drove through the lunch hour. We were both eager to meet this person, and were willing to suffer some to do so.

Once in the town of Taos, we drove straight to the pueblo where Odd Don said Burningtree would be. The pueblo itself consisted of numerous buildings. One of which appeared to be a church or mission. The buildings were all made of adobe, a mud and straw mixture, giving them an old southwest appearance. It must also be an economical way to build.

There was a metal gate barring access to the native's compound, and we noticed no one roaming about to yell at for help. We decided it best not to trespass on sovereign Native American ground, so we stood and waited at the gate.

Minutes clicked off. After twenty, I tired, and suggested to Alan that we linger back in town where we could get lunch. He agreed, but just as we were turning to leave we noticed the figure of a man about three hundred yards away. He raised his arm and waved at us. He was walking our way, but not in a hurry. At his slow pace, it would take him five more minutes to reach us.

At about forty yards out he yelled, "Hello, I'm John Burningtree." Amazed by such a serendipitous event, I felt a strange rush through my temples, and wondered whether or not Native American's shake hands.

Alan spoke up first, "My name is Dr. Alan Bloome. It is very nice to meet you Mr. Burningtree." They shook. I followed suit.

"Nice to meet you, Mr. Burningtree, I'm Dr. John Carter."

"Wow, two doctors, gosh, gee, how much is this

going to cost me?" he quipped, and then he let out a robust belly laugh that got us joining in.

My curiosity got the better of me, and I had to ask the question, "Mr. Burningtree,"

"Please, call me John," he interjected, "or JB might be better to prevent any confusion with our two names."

"Then, JB, if you don't mind my asking, how did you know we were waiting here for you?"

Growing a smile on his face, he said, "Smoke signals, of course." Then he lets fly with another raucous laugh. I liked his ever present and easy jocularity. JB was not tall, and his robust girth gave him a stocky look. He had dark hair, which stuck out long and straight from beneath his ball cap. His naturally brown skin and thick round face were distinctive among the Navajo people. "OK, enough Indian jokes for a while," he said. "Actually it was Jenny who called me. I guess you two didn't see the museum and curio store just across the way and behind you? That is where Jenny works as a docent and clerk. Most tourists who come here to view the pueblo start there first."

Alan and I turned in unison. Yep, there it was, bigger than life. A sign on the front says it all, 'Pueblo Museum and Curio Store, pueblo entrance permits sold here.'

We turned to look at each other. "Well, that's embarrassing," I said.

"It was a long drive to get here," added Alan, "and we are starved."

Then JB blurted out, "If you two are hungry, come on and let's go in to town and get some lunch? It'll be my treat."

All of a sudden, I was really liking this guy. Plus, there was an actual interchange in his style of conversation. That was something that was missing from Oddball Don's personality.

The three of us jumped into our jeep. JB steered us to a restaurant that he said served excellent New Mexican food. This is not to be confused with Mexican food, or so I was told. However, the two were very similar, or is it that there is only so much you can do with rice, beans, and chilies?

We seated ourselves, and then conversation broke out. No disrespect to Jenny at the museum, but I still had some nagging questions surrounding JB's seemingly freaky pre-knowledge of our visit.

Alan went first, and began asking him some questions, but in a rather delicate tone. I found his methodical approach painful and slow, and what was with the rather mundane questions. If I were JB, I would have found his way of dancing around the issue insulting. Was his soft method of inquiry a reaction to JB being a Native American?

Tired of Alan's dull line of questioning, I broke-in and asked something more pointed, "JB, do you live here on the reservation?"

"Absolutely not. I just come here to hunt and think. The reservation is a safe haven for me. "

"If you don't mind my asking, what is it you do for a living?" Alan winced; he must have thought my question too forward.

"No, I don't mind talking about it, John. I am a software engineer. Got my degree in engineering at Stanford, but that was a lifetime ago. ... So, you two are doctors. Mind if I ask what your degrees are in?"

Alan looked dumbfounded. Seems he had a preconceived notion that our Native friend from the reservation would be backwards.

"My profession is in epidemiology. I have worked for the World Health Organization for the past fifteen years, and my silent friend here actually managed to get a P.H.D. from Harvard. He used to work in materials science, but nowadays he just chases ghosts for a living."

Bloome finally snapped out of his stupor and said, "I'm sorry JB. Let me apologize, I originally thought you were a pueblo dweller. I guess my information about you is sketchy."

"No, I haven't lived in these parts for perhaps thirty years. I only come here to hunt as I did with my dad when I was a child. This reservation contains a sacred hunting ground, so to speak. Only us Indians can hunt there. I think of it as a great perk, one I take advantage of each year."

"So, who the hell is Don?" I blurted out.

On hearing my question, his mouth opened slightly, and his face gained a ghostly look. "What?" he asked.

"Who is this Don guy? We met him last night in Las Vegas. He said he knew you, and that he was your father's childhood friend."

"Don!?" he said, still looking startled. "You met, Don?" His face went pale. Apparently, the knowledge of our meeting Don shocked him. "I didn't know he was back in these parts. Wow, now that is huge."

"So, you do know him?" He brushed my question off.

"So, you two met Don, and it was he who told you to come here? ... That's big. It's a power sign, or omen, or something. I was going to leave for home tomorrow. If you weren't led here today, we would never have met at all, and that would be that. Interesting how one mystery always leads to another?"

"Then you weren't expecting us?" I asked.

"Sorry, no. People have been showing up at that gate looking for me ever since the newspaper article slipped out. I am always happy to meet and talk with them, but, as yet, I hadn't found any of them worthy to share the true story with. So I would just make up something and blow them off. I really didn't feel comfortable discussing my wild experience with strangers anyway. I do have a life back in LA, and I don't want to be tagged with some kook moniker for the rest of my life."

"I am a little confused then JB. How would this Don fellow know who we are, and that we were interested in talking with you?" His face grew dark and long again. Something about that question, about that man, bothered him on a deep and personal level.

"That requires some explaining," he said. "You see, Don is a Nagual."

Ah, crap! Just when I thought Burningtree was a standup member of the twenty-first century he reverted to the weird side. Moreover, he said it with the straightest of faces. Last night, while I was doing some research on the Navaho for Bloome, I came across that term, and I remembered that I had heard it years before in my childhood.

"JB, you're suggesting that Don is some sort of witch?" I said. "I met the man, and he's not even an Indian."

"Doesn't matter," he said. "Let me give you some background on him, and the only reason I know so much about him is that he was my dad's best friend for many years. I'm not surprised that you met him in Las Vegas that is where he first met my dad. Supposedly he has some connection to that area of the state."

"So he is human after all?" I wanted to break-in at this point and ask some more questions, but quickly got shushed by Bloome who was all ears now.

"As I was saying, my father was sixteen at the time. For some reason my grandparents moved from

Taos to LV. Probably to take some low paying jobs. Reservation life has always been a financial negative for our people. Because my dad was the new kid, and an Indian, the school children would constantly taunt and bully him. Such was the sad life of a modern Native American.

Then one day, while out in the school's play yard, some boys began pushing my dad around. That is when they all sensed something and turned east to look down the sidewalk. They said this figure of a young man seemed to appear out of nowhere, that he walked right over to where they were, and stood before them. It was Don. He said that at that time Don looked to be about four years older than the other boys were. He was taller, stronger, and his appearance was threatening, so the bullies backed off.

He introduced himself to my dad. He told my dad that he knew that he possessed a peace loving spirit, and would not fight back to protect himself, so he stepped right in to protect him. They became friends on that day, and remained close through the years.

Don was prescient about things, and whenever my dad was about to get into trouble he would mysteriously appear. However, for all his troubles, my dad grew to hate this life. He was one of those people who have too gentle a soul to survive in this world. I think the Nagual knew that, and that is why he stayed close to him, and I have always had great respect for Don for caring after my dad like that.

Life in the modern and changing world hurt my dad. When he was old enough to emancipate himself from his parents, he ran back to this pueblo. Here, he fell into a reservation state of mind, and was never able to escape from it. There was no way he was going to be able to apply himself and take a white man's job, but he did have an innate talent for art, and his gentle spirit guided his hands to paint beautiful watercolors. He would often sell them at the town squares down in Santa Fe and Albuquerque.

His artworks became quite famous, but not him. He shied away from any kind of publicity. He spent the rest of his life living here in Taos in relative peace and happiness. If it hadn't been for the Nagual's help, I am sure he would have turned bitter, and his rage would have destroyed him.

The only information I have on Don comes from my father. I did meet the Nagual once when I was too young to remember, and once more many years later. It was here in Taos at the town square. I was on my annual vacation from work, and came to visit my dad. He was there setting up his vendor stand when I showed up. He told me I was in for a surprise that day. That a great spirit was coming to visit. I have never been big on the Indian Way so I blew his statement off as just mumbo jumbo. Anyway, I sat with him for about an hour while he showed his art and made some sales.

A wide overhang covers the north side of the sidewalks, and we had been standing in its dark shade. It was about eleven, and just passing that part of the day where cool shivers give way to the sun's warming bliss. Then, for a reason I can't explain, I felt this presence across the street in the central square.

When I looked up and turned south to see it, the sun's glare nearly blinded me. Squinting, I noticed the figure of a man standing across the street. Somehow, I knew it was my dad's friend Don.

He walked over to us and he and dad hugged. Then he introduced himself to me. I did not know whether I was still part blinded from the sun's glare, but his face contained a fierce glow, as if he had pulled this mask of radiance over his true being. It startled me, but his kind charm assuaged my fears.

He helped us pack up my dad's wares, and then the three of us went to have lunch. He and my dad talked some about how his life was going, but for the most part the Nagual sat quiet with this far-off look in his face. After lunch, he politely said goodbye and left. I never saw him again."

"Yep, that sounds like the man we met in LV last night. So, he is a mystery man," I said. "He must have a home somewhere around here?"

"No, I don't know where he lives, or how he managed to live. Dad once said he was from the plains of the old west just east of LV, and that he was much older that he looks. But where he was born, or where he can be found, I cannot say. Over the years as I corresponded with my father and on my summer hunting trips with him, he occasionally talked about Don. He said that he was a powerful Nagual. That he was possessed with the Eagle Spirit, and that he had a total knowledge of the Navajo way. That at times when members of our community got sick he would mysteriously show up and perform the healing ceremonies for them. To the Navajo, the sand and the sand paintings hold special power, but only shaman's know how to make and use these intricate of sand paintings.

Anyway, Don disappeared around the time my dad passed away, and he hasn't been seen in these parts since. That is until you met him yesterday in LV. I heard rumors that he went south down below the Mexico border and took up residence with a small obscure tribe there. I hadn't seen or heard of him again until today."

Our discussion in the restaurant with JB continued

for some hours. We sat, drank more coffee, and had some dessert. I felt his description of Oddball Don was a little afield. I mean calling the man a Nagual. In my youth, I remember reading about that term. It was described by an author who wrote stories about the Yaqui Indians in Northern Mexico, but that was nearly thirty years ago, and these books were considered fantasy anyway. So I decided to put away any further discussion of Don for now.

The immediate plan of attack was to interview Burningtree about his alien abduction. We changed the topic of conversation over to UFOs. Bloome was an adept interviewer, but he was taking notes by scribbling on napkins. His unpreparedness had me scratching my head. This was his gig. One he had crossed an ocean for, so why no notepad?

Anyway, JB was engaging and did not appear to have any hesitation about relating to us any of his personal experiences with the aliens. Apparently, our chance meeting with Don opened up a door, and he accepted us now as part of his inner circle.

"So the abduction took place while you were out hunting," asked Bloome, "and that was on the Northside Reservation?"

"Yes, I was way back in the Sangre de Christo Mountains, and all alone except for my horse. This was a place my dad I came to often. It is high up on top where the mountain opens up into a long flat rocky spine. We would camp there near an outcrop situated above a large pond a few hundred feet in a valley below. From this vantage point, we would lay in wait for bears and deer coming to drink. That is the way Indians hunt. We let the animals come to us.

Anyway, it was clear and very cold that night. To stay warm I cozied up inside my sleeping bag. Looking skyward and counting stars brought back memories of times spent up there with my dad as I listened to him tell me tales of Navajo lore. I don't remember falling asleep. It was one of those times when you're so tired that you just fade out, you know.

I was in deep sleep when a loud noise startled me awake. I tried to move, but found I couldn't. It's as if I was paralyzed, or in some sort of trance.

I struggled with it a little bit, and then I looked up to the sky, but the stars were gone. That's when I realized there was an object hovering above me. It is hard for a good Indian to admit, but I was really scared right then."

Alan mumbled, "H'mm," and then jotted something down on one of his paper napkins, and then asked, "Do you recall about how long this feeling of paralysis lasted?"

"It wasn't long. The object over me was making this buzzing noise. Still lying on my back and looking straight up at it, I made note that it had yellow and gold or amber colored lights in several places on its bottom. Its hull wasn't flat or smooth. There were shapes like different sized boxes protruding from it."

"Did it spin?"

"Spin? No, it didn't. After about thirty seconds, it floated off me. Once it was away from me, I could move again. I slowly rolled over on to my stomach and scootched on my elbows and toes the short way over to an embankment at the edge of the overlook. The object had descended down and was hovering over the front of the pond below."

"Was that an official Indian maneuver?" I asked.

JB broke out in a raucous laugh and said, "Jesus, John, you kill me."

Alan was not as amused, and gave me the evil eye. Well, I had to ask. Then I shut up and let JB continue, but it was nice to have him back in his jocular mien.

"From the edge of the overlook I watched it for a minute while it hovered. I thought it was going to land. I wanted to see if people came out of it."

"And did they?" asked Bloome.

"No, and that's where it got bizarre. My elbows were hurting so I tried to move forward a little to find a more comfortable spot when I guess it noticed my movement.

The flying machine sort of rose up, and I saw a row of lights come on around its periphery. I heard an odd clanging noise, and then I was bathed in some kind of light. It was hugely bright, and I had to close my eyes. I must have passed out then, and I do not recall waking up again until the morning.

The next day I kept getting these strange thoughts running through my head. They were like pieces of memories of something that happened to me the previous night while I was unconscious."

"How would you describe them?" asked Alan.

"Alan, I don't know. I only remember parts of it. It was like being inside a foggy dream. I was inside what looked to be an operating room. I remember feeling very cold, and I think I was lying naked on a metal table. I saw beings moving about around me, but I couldn't focus clearly enough to make out their details. Then there are the mental images of the personal things they did to me. But I don't want to talk about those right now."

"No, and I don't think that I would either," said Alan. "Huh, you know JB; it is interesting how these abductions always have very similar details. I have interviewed other abductees, and have read of incidents spread across the globe, and they all have striking similarities."

"What do you think it means, Alan?"

"I'm not sure, but I do have a theory. Let me think about what you've just said, and then tomorrow I can explain what I think is going on for you. ... By the way, do you think we could visit the site of your encounter?"

"Sure, I can take you there tomorrow if you like."

"Excellent!" cried Alan.

"We'll meet at the front gate at eight. You will have to prepare yourselves. There will be plenty of water to drink in the mountain streams, but there won't be anything to eat. So grab some jerky and trail mix. You should plan to be gone about ten hours. Oh, one other thing, this tribe is very sensitive about having their pictures taken. They do not allow cameras of any type. That includes cell phones."

We concluded our talks for the night, and took JB back to the Northside Pueblo. After making plans for a room for a couple of nights stay, we went shopping for our trip tomorrow. We were both excited about being able to go on a long hike back into these beautiful mountains.

8:

Return to Kenbe

City of Kisumu, Kenya, Africa

My first night's stay in this old Gentlemen's Club turned pricey hotel piqued my interest in the times of the great white hunter. What it must have been like to go off on a safari and shoot big game? Throughout the halls and meeting rooms of this old Maison hang paintings of scenes of the hunt. Khaki-clad gents standing with gun in hand and one leg raised with foot resting atop some poor dead beast. Was it really that romantic, or has our perception of colonial Africa been incorrectly molded by media and ignorance? I am going with the later, and now we have modern day adventurers taking advantage of the naïve with tall stories of avenging extra-dimensional demons hunting humans. I was not having anything of it. I am convinced that Bloome and Carter have conjured up this story for profit, and to cover-up a crime, and I am going to prove it.

Today, my explorations will take me north to the city of Kenbe, or where it used to be. I want to inspect the fence Carter mentioned. The one supposedly erected to keep people out of that area. There is little doubt that the city suffered grievous damage from a fire; that much was on the international cable news networks. However, building a fence to prevent survivors from returning there sounds odd to me, and perfidious governments and unsavory individuals, might be tempted to manipulate and misconstrue this drastic action, and allow it to become the basis for wild and unfounded accusations.

My destination lies eighty miles away. With clear intent and a single purpose in mind, I jumped into my jeep and hurried off to the north. The amount of activity on the streets in Kisumu this morning felt normal. The city was abuzz, and the pace did not seem out of the ordinary. Some six months had passed since the staggering loss of life up in Kenbe. Had these people been able to move on so fast? I find it amazing how quickly we can forget.

Outside of town was no exception. People were busying themselves everywhere. Many pedestrians were walking within an arm's reach of speeding autos. That is a sight not common in America. Trains of humans, colorfully clad, walking with wares, be it clothes, food, or sundries, balanced carefully atop their heads. Has economics here forced the masses to travel primarily by foot, or is it a custom? I did not know with certainty, yet the apparent dystopian plight seemed out of character with a modern society.

The first forty miles of my trek went as any trip would on a modern American highway. Then I began to notice a marked decrease in the amount of traffic, cars and people. About ten miles farther, they disappeared entirely.

The sudden cessation of peopled commotion was spooky; there was no one out here. I found myself completely alone, and driving on an unknown road, and in an unfamiliar country. Ignoring the dangers of being alone, unarmed, and unescorted, I pressed right on.

The line of telephone poles Dr. Bloome mentioned in his book was directly off to the left. I was on the right road. I became absorbed in the drama of following in his exact footsteps, and revved my jeep forward.

Speeding by, I read a road sign that said, Kenbe, 5KM. Almost there, my ego slapped me on the back once again—Dr. Henderson, detective extraordinaire—Ha-Ha!

About a mile farther, the road abruptly ended, and the corners of my smirk turned suddenly downward. Well, it didn't exactly end, the road went on, but it was sealed off by a ten foot tall chain link fence laced with barbed wire on top. My mouth gaped in amazement, and I hit the brakes.

The tall fence spread wide in both directions. To the west from where the road ends, an open savanna grassland extended slowly down to sweep across a broad plain. You could follow the line of the fence with your eyes as it ran for miles in a wide sweeping arc to the north. To the east of the road, the rocky landscape rose up slightly and turned into an acacia forest.

They had erected this fence in a hurry, that much was obvious. An army of bulldozers had ripped clear a strip of land that exposed the red African soil. Now a giant bloody streak scarred the earth, and faded off to the horizon.

Was this the end of the line? Was I alone here? I climbed up on my jeeps bumper to gander about. I spied no one. No people were mulling around or gathering into small groups, which was so common back in town. I saw nothing; heard nothing—not even a bird. The eerie silence of it was in stark contrast to my built-up prejudices of Africa. "What, no massive herds of animals; no lions roaring; no hyenas, with their hideous laugh, and ganging about? What, no myriad of flying birds with their colorful plumage and raucous cries?" How odd it all seemed.

There was another vehicle nearby. Somebody had parked a very dusty and beat-up jeep off to the east side of the road. It could have been there for days, or even weeks by the look of it. If Bloome's time line is accurate, this fence was no more than five months old. However, people have been here, and recently. A noticeable footpath straggled along the outward side of the fence.

Making sure I had locked my car, I threw a daypack over my shoulder, and began to hike the bush. I came here to see what I could see, and without thinking, headed off to walk east along its length. This is where my ignorance could have cost me my life. I had forgotten that I was not at home in Chicago where I often roamed our streets and parks freely. This was Africa, and for the most part still untamed and dangerous. Wild animals still roam here, and the predatory type prefers to eat defenseless humans.

It was not hot, I am standing right on the equator, and my long pants and heavy shirt do not feel uncomfortable—making a mental note—I will checkout the local weather patterns later.

I walked for the better part of an hour, and traveled what I guessed to be about two miles. The terrain turned monotonous. For the thicket of trees and man-tall grasses, you couldn't see far. If the rest of this trail was just as obscured, I was wasting my time. Even atop a horse, you still could not see farther than several hundred feet in any direction.

"I'll go another half-mile. That's it. If the terrain hasn't changed by then I'm going to walk back to the jeep and re-assess my options," I declared.

Only a few minutes farther down the path, the loud caw, caw, of a bird startled me. Its alarm rang out as though something had just flushed it from the grasses. My scrotal area twitched, and a pang of apprehension shot through my body.

The rashness of my choice to walk alone and unarmed in the bush has me shaking. Fearing a wild animal attack, I asked myself, "What should I do?"

Run, of course. But, I'm trapped against a razor-topped fence. Halting, I wait and listen for any movement. The air is still. The crackling of a dried blade of grass quickly drew my attention, and I jerked my head around. I knew if an animal were present, sneaking through the bush, and eyeing me for attack, that the insects and birds would draw quiet. All was quiet. Right now, I would have preferred a cacophony of insects to this deafening silence.

Suddenly a shape on the path in front of me draws my attention. It was still far off, but getting closer. Now I'm trapped along three cardinal points. My heart is pounding. My only clear choice of action is retreat back the way I came. I scanned the grasses to my side keenly looking for any telltale sign of a large predator. There is none, but I know that lions are stealthy.

Paralyzed with indecision, the creature in front of me nears. I turned to face it, to eye it down.

Slowly, ever so slowly, I walked backwards. I was not going to run and trigger its attack instinct.

Now focused on the threat in front of me, I see it raise a limb high up into the air—and it waved. For Christ's sake, it's a human animal—I mean a man. He moved slowly in my direction. My fears assuaged a little, but another person out for a walk in the bush. Someone I do not know. This could be even worse.

At about two hundred feet distant, he threw up his right arm again to wave, and then yelled, "Hello." What a relief. I returned his greeting.

"My god, you're an American," he laughed with a slight smile on his face.

"Why, yes I am. Why do you find that amusing?" I asked.

"Well, I mean, here we are, in the African bush, on one of the most populated continents, and the only two people for miles are both from the other side of the planet. Don't you find that funny, and a little odd?"

"Yes, I see what you mean." Oh great, I sensed that he was a conspiracy theorist. Just my luck.

"Gerald Hicks."

"Oh," stretching my hand to meet his, "nice to meet you, Gerald. I'm Dr. William Henderson." Gerald was a younger man than I was, probably in his mid to late thirties. He was also a little shorter than I was; I put him at about 5' 8". His bushy, ruddy-blond hair feathered out from under his faded ball cap. My experience as a psychologist pegged him as an unprofessional, and probably a fringe kook.

"I can't believe you're out here just to walk the fence," said Gerald. "You must be here for the same reason I am? Kenbe being wiped off the map. Very interesting isn't it?"

I supposed that was the most reasonable conclusion to reach considering. "Yes, you're right about that Gerald. I flew in yesterday. Today, I had planned to scope it out up here. Does the terrain keep on like this for many more miles?"

"Yes, this acacia plain extends for another fifteen miles, then the farther north and east you get it turns more arid, but the west side of that mountain chain there is quite tropical. What, you didn't do a Google search first? I always like to fly over an area I'm going to investigate first."

"Interesting!" I said. A feeling of inferiority just punched me in the stomach. This guy was more prepared than I was, so I had to change the subject immediately. "I didn't bring my computer. What do you believe happened here Gerald?"

"What? You mean the destruction of Kenbe? That's what I'm trying to make sense of. My group and I investigate strange and mysterious events all of the time. Anything from ghost sightings, to UFO abductions, but this one stretches my ability to fathom. This one is all too real, and all too scary."

"So, Gerald, do you believe that this is the handiwork of a monster?"

"Yes, no doubt about it. Talk about it is all over the internet. We even have a video of the night it happened. That was before any news of that night was scrubbed from the net. Our working theory is that some astral-monster killed all of those people."

"Astral-monster, that's what Bloome said," I mentioned.

"What? Bloome? Dr. Alan Bloome? You know Dr. Alan Bloome?" he seemed surprised.

"Why, yes. I talked with him just the other day in Amsterdam. We chatted a little about his experiences down here in Africa last June. That is what spurred my interest to come here and see it for myself. I brought his new book with me. In it he details what he believes happened here. So, are you also a friend of Dr. Bloome?" I asked cautiously.

"Me, no, I've never met him. To me, and many of my associates, he remains a mystery, and I am relieved to know someone who has actually met him. Up to now we thought his name was fictitious; just a pseudonym. That perhaps that name was a code name for a group of authors."

"No, Bloome is real alright. Gerald, where are the other members of your group?"

"I had to come here alone, the other members all have day jobs, and recent economics have hurt our funding for research. I'm a member of GUFON. That's an acronym for Global UFO Network. We have been in competition with your friend Bloome for years. Somehow he has always managed to beat us out in learning about and getting to these events, but we have never been able to figure out how he does it."

"Gerald, when you walked up, I was just turning around to head back to my jeep. I would be happy if you would accompany me."

As we walked back to our vehicles, Gerald gabbed on about the death of Kenbe, government cover-ups, other conspiracies, and spectral-monsters. I took him to be a bit of a kook, but even a kook is a welcome accomplice when you realize how lost and out of place you are.

"Gerald, are you staying in Kisumu?"

"Yes, it's about the only town in this part of Kenya with a modern motel. I have a room in a travel lodge."

"I'm staying at the Grand Colonial. Perhaps we can get together when we return to Kisumu. I would be very interested in seeing your internet files, that is, if you wouldn't mind sharing them with me."

"Why no, not at all. I would love to share what we have. Perhaps we could talk about working together on this project. I'm not comfortable operating alone in this country."

Gerald was quite obliging—the purview of the

uninitiated—yet, I had no "group" of my own.

I followed him back to his motel room where he agreed to let me have a look at his internet data. He was staying in a fleabag motel. His choice of lodging forced on him no doubt by lack of money, but it did offer free internet access, and I didn't even bring a computer.

"What I am going to show you first is a short video clip of the night Kenbe burned. It was taken by someone aboard one of the helicopters that crashed."

Gerald brought up and played the video file on his laptop screen. The movie clip was slightly less than three minutes long, and the quality was very poor. The images were grainy and lacked color. They were taken at night with the use of spotlights, and from hundreds of feet in elevation.

"Can you explain what I am looking at here?"

"This in the only footage that survives of the night Kenbe died. What you are looking at are people down on the streets below. You can see them mulling about until about half a minute past midnight. Then you will notice that they all appear to freeze in place. It's really eerie. I mean, they don't appear to be looking at anything. They don't move their heads. Their gaze appears frozen, as if locked on to some object right in front of them, but as you can see, there is nothing there.

Now, let me play it forward slowly, and watch. There, do you see it? Look at the time stamp. At one minute past midnight, everyone collapses. It's as if someone flipped a switch, then everybody simply shut off and fell to his or her feet dead. Then the video goes blank. Witnesses two miles away said that that was the exact time the helicopters crashed."

I couldn't believe what Gerald and his ilk take as proof for their claims. Are there that many gullible soles out there?

"And you think this video is proof of what?" I asked. "I mean, the quality of this film is terrible. Who knows what we are looking at? This video might have been dubbed over, and the part where everyone stops could be where some genius decided to copy the film while it was on pause. The graininess of it also makes it suspect. I don't know, Gerald, all we can say with certainty is that the helicopters crashed, and then there was a horrendous wind-whipped conflagration which destroyed that city and killed those thousands of people."

"Yes, I understand where you're coming from, Doctor Henderson. *Question Everything*. That is a good philosophy to follow. My friends and I think that same way. In fact, that is GLUFON's motto. Those two words standout in large bold type right at the top of our web page, and whether you or I, are right or wrong, it is the curious circumstances that surrounding these deaths that lead me to believe Dr. Bloome's conclusions are the right ones."

"And you think that the government is covering up the truth about Kenbe?"

"There is a lot to be suspicious of. First, this video circulated around the web for just a day, and then it was wiped clean. It just vanished and with no explanation. Only governments can do that. Then you have to ask yourself why they pulled it? What were they afraid of? Next, the fence, which when finished will encircle an area forty miles in diameter.

Further, Kenbe was not alone; there were several other small towns near to it. Can you explain to me why the Kenyan government unexpectedly evacuated everyone from those towns, and then decided to encircle them with a fenced Preserve?

Then there are the personal accounts from people who fled the city. Their stories of the visions of horror that led up to the destruction of Kenbe, they all match up. All in all, something very odd, something very out of this world, happened there."

"OK, but none of the stories are firsthand accounts, are they? None of them are from people who lived through it, and who can now tell us exactly what transpired that night?"

"No, but that's just one more of the weird circumstances. Surely, if this were, as you say, just an unfortunate accident and fire, then wouldn't some of the residents of that town survive to tell their story?"

Well, Gerald had me there. That was a tough question; one I could not readily explain away. This argument was pointless. I was not going to sway him, or he me, and I still needed an aide and guide. As not to burn a bridge that I desperately needed, I decided to make him a proposal.

"Alright, Gerald, I think we both have totally opposing views on what happened here in Kenya. However, those differences could make us stronger as a team. As long as we know that we have differences, and so long as we respect each other's point of view, I am willing to put aside any criticisms of your and Bloome's outrageous ideas for the time being. If you are willing to do the same, I propose we form an alliance, and work this mystery together. I'm willing to give it one week. In fact, I challenge you to convince me in that short amount of time that my take on the deaths is wrong."

As a psychiatrist, I have learned to recognize facial and body language. On hearing my proposal, Gerald's demeanor turned to one of cocky suspicion. He thought he was right. It was just as obvious that he was not used to working with someone he hadn't known and had trusted for years, but on that point we were both breaking new ground. What? Me, buddy up with some nutcase just to prove a point? Oh, the sacrifices I make in the name of research.

After a few moments of soul searching, he said to me, "OK, Dr. Henderson. I am giving your idea some serious consideration, but first I need to clear-up a couple things. First off, do you have a business card on you?"

"Yes?" I took out my wallet, slipped a business card out of its neat pocket, and handed it to him. "Might I ask why you need one of my cards?"

"Well, your claim to be who you say you are could be made up. I mean, I don't know you, but I figure if you have business cards all printed up, it is a good clue that you are."

The little twerp. This was becoming painful. "Is there anything else?" I added crossly.

"Credits. There might be books written on what we discover together. How do we handle the business end of it?"

He had a valid point. "How about this, I agree not to write anything regarding our exploits that crosses into the paranormal, but if this turns out to all be a hoax, then you agree to let me write that part of the story. Plus I will mention you in the credits, and allow you to insert your personal findings, if you so choose."

"Agreed. ... Finally, if you and I are going to work together as partners, and if you want access to all of my extensive files, then we should be on a first name basis."

"Jesus Christ!" I thought to myself. "He was kidding, wasn't he?" I had earned my title through years of education and work, but alas.

I let out a noticeable exhale to show my rancor at this last request, and begrudgingly bent to his demands. What other choice do I have? My time here is limited, and he has some necessary research. I was certain I could easily disprove Bloome's assertions, and peg Carter as a murderer. "Alright, I agree. Let's shake hands on it partner."

I spent a few more hours picking Gerald's brain. Of particular interest to me, was his knowledge regarding the fence. It was not finished yet. Up on the far northern side they were still in the process of completing the huge circle. I wanted to go there and see the construction for myself. Perhaps we could talk with the construction crews. If they had been here working for these many months surely they had heard of something. With the only road up north fenced off, no direct route led there from Kisumu. The only way to get there was to fly.

9:

The Blood of Christ

Taos, New Mexico

Alan and I were both eager to go on this hike. We woke early and made our way to the front gate of the Northside Indian Reservation promptly at 8am. JB was there and waiting for us. With our daypacks filled with jerky, trail mix, and sodas, we might get tired, but not hungry. Throwing our packs on our backs, Burningtree then ushered us onto the reservation property. And we were off, or so we thought.

A small creek runs through the middle of the reservation property, over the past century the locals have raised a berm on either side of it for flood control. A well-worn path follows the top of the embankment.

The rising sun was glinting on the waters of this tiny rivulet. My eyes followed its silver streak as it swept in a long lazy curve for over a mile to the east. Then it turned south and disappeared behind a mountain. As we approached the berm, JB stopped by a small wooden footbridge that crosses the creek.

There he raised a finger to point to the hills to the east.

"That's where we are heading boys. We'll just follow this path through the valley here. The trailhead begins right where this creek turns south."

I noticed JB had not brought a daypack. After we had crossed the creek, he said, "OK, follow me boys. Let's go and pick up our taxi."

"Taxi?" we asked.

"What? You two didn't think we were going to walk there, did you? It is over ten miles up there."

"Oh, no. Nooo," we responded, and proceeded to march on behind him to a large barn.

There, two young men were tending to three horses. JB walked around one of the horses and gave it a big slap on its flank. "This here is my old friend Randy."

He took the reins of the other two and walked them over to Alan and me. "Here you go. Alan, you had better ride on this bigger one. John, why don't you take this little Appaloosa?"

I had never ridden a horse, and to alleviate my fears I resorted to asking some dumb questions. "Do these horses have names?"

JB and the two stable boys rattled off something in Navajo. Then they shared a laugh.

"They said yours is called Horse A, and that Alan's is Horse B." Then the three of them busted out in laughter again. I found their joke mildly amusing, and laughed with them, but I began to find JB's Indian humor taxing.

JB mounted his horse and maneuvered it around to my side. Then he called out to one of the boys who immediately came over to me and said, and in plain English, "John, here, before you pull yourself up, wrap the reins equally and loosely around the saddle horn." Then he showed me how to do it. "Now, remember, even though these horses are big, they are still dumb animals. They only obey the rein. You can talk to them all day if you like, but they don't understand English, only Navajo." JB sitting atop his horse had another belly laugh.

"OK." I then muttered something under my breath. ... The boy continued giving me his in-service on how to ride a horse.

"Remember, always get up on the left side. Horses are creatures of habit, and are trained to follow simple commands. Now, grab the saddle horn with your left hand, put your left foot into the stirrup, and climb on up."

Doing as he said, I managed to mount the beast. "OK," he said, "it's best if you hold the reins in your hands at all times, and just like in the movies, to get him to move, gently kick him in the ribs with your feet. To turn, just touch the rein to one side of his neck, or the other. To stop easily pull back on both reins at the same time. See it's very simple, even a white man can do it."

"Very funny." Alan had been snooping in on my lesson. Copying my instructions, he was already walking his horse around the front of the barn; plying it right and left with the reins.

"One last word of warning," he said, "if you need to stop and get off the horse, be sure and wrap the reins around the horn, don't let them fall free. Also, whatever you do, do not pull back hard on the reins."

I thanked the young man, and then got in behind Alan to practice maneuvering the animal. After I had a few quick turns, JB yelled out, "Let's go, you two follow me."

Learning to maneuver the animal was quick and easy, but I found having to be taught how to ride a horse a little emasculating. "Alan, how did they know that I had never ridden a horse before?"

"I think it was rather obvious, don't you?"

"Yeah, right back at ya, city slicker." Yes, neither of us had ever ridden a horse before. That is something I guess horse people can easily pick up on. JB took the lead, and we fell in behind him. I enjoyed ridding atop the beast, but it was somewhat bumpy, and I wondered what was my butt going to feel like after hours in the saddle?

We were gently loping down the path that edged the creek. 'JB was right," I said, "this was going to be much faster and easier than walking."

We followed the creek east through the valley. After about fifteen minutes, we arrived at the base of the Sangre de Cristo mountain range. It seemed to just pop up from the sea of flatness that bordered it to the west. We followed on as the little stream turned and ran south to chase the mountain. Half a mile farther, we came to a noticeable trail that led up and into the hills.

Stopping his horse, JB pointed up to a trail worn into the side of the mountain. "Alright boys. Here is the trailhead. We will be going into the heart of some of the most remote and pristine forest left in America, much of it protected by the Indian Nations. I'll take the lead. It is a bit steep at the start, so grab on tight to your saddle horns."

JB went first. He jabbed his horse in the ribs, and together they shot up the slope. Alan was right behind him. I waited a moment to give my horse and myself room. Then I gently kicked him in the ribs three times.

The horse took off at a fast gallop. The ferocity of it tossed me out of the saddle and into the air. My behind came down hard and slammed against the now rising saddle. Holding on for dear life, this violent jerking action repeated several more times.

I had lost control of the beast, good thing he

knew where to go. Thankfully, the steep entry to the trail was only two hundred feet long, and then it leveled off into a wide fire trail.

When I had caught up with my friends, JB turned and gave me a quizzical look, and asked if we were all right. I turned to Alan. The look on his face told me that he had just had the same butt spanking that I had. We were both excited to have survived.

JB then smiled and said, "Riding horses is an easy art to learn, you two will pick up on it soon enough.

The three of us were now riding side by side, and entertained ourselves with conversation just to pass the time. "John," I asked, "did you say that you were born here on this reservation?"

"No, I was born on a pueblo south of here closer to Santa Fe."

"And yet they let you come here whenever you want?"

"It's OK, I have a multi-reservation pass."

"Oh, Jesus!" I exclaimed, and I did have a laugh at that one. "But you came here to be with your father and to hunt?"

"Yeah, I guess the family secret is out."

"I don't mean to pry," I said.

"No, it's OK. As you might have guessed, my dad and mom split-up when I was only four. My dad lived here on Northside, but I stayed with my mom down south, and only visited dad in the summer months. He would take me up into these hills and try to teach me about nature, but the Indian way didn't catch on with me. There just wasn't much for a twentieth century city dweller to do here. I think dad was upset with me, but he knew times were changing. Like I said, he himself grew up in the town of LV, and where he found modernity poison, I, on the other hand, ate it up.

Fortunately for me, when I was ten, mom and I moved to Albuquerque. There I got an education, and went on to study computer engineering. It saved my life."

JB continued to talk, that is one thing I have noticed he does well. I found his life's story and quirky sidesteps interesting, so much so, that neither Bloome nor I had noticed we were now hundreds of feet above the valley floor. The view to the west, occasionally poking through the tall pine trees, was just majestic. The day was sunny, and the late fall air was warm and clear, and laced with the scent of pine. For the first time in months, no thought of the deaths in Africa intruded upon my mind. I relaxed and was truly enjoying myself.

The fire road we were on wound around the contours of the mountain in a generally southern direction. The horses followed it with no effort on our part. It was almost as though they knew where to go. As we climbed ever upward the trees grew taller and thicker. We soon lost any sight of the valley below.

By midmorning, the sun had risen high above the treetops. Its rays pierced the scattered wisps of clouds bringing forth a skyfall of bright glare turning the azure skies creamy white. This glow highlighted nature's palette. The few remaining aspen leaves cast a fiery golden glow amid a sea of dark green pine. In reverence, I thanked our Native American friends for having the insight to set this beautiful land aside from development and destruction. "JB, this is truly beautiful scenery," I said. "Will this road take us all the way to your hunting ground?"

"Nah, wish it did. That would be too easy. We'll have to get off trail up ahead. To reach my happy hunting grounds we need to cross over to the top of the mountain and then take the ridge a little more south. I hope I don't get us lost."

I thought that was a joke, and was expecting another one of his riotous laughs, but this time he remained silent. Out of curiosity, I had to ask,

"What, no follow up belly laugh?"

Then as serious as he could be, he turned to stare at me and said, "No, we Indians would never joke about getting lost."

Together, Alan and I turned to look him in the eye, and then unable to hold it in any longer, he broke out in uncontrollable laughter. You really couldn't help but like JB.

We spent another hour on horseback plodding through and around aspen groves and stands of tall pine. The city of Taos has a base elevation of 7,100 feet. My map shows we were going to wind up three thousand feet above that.

When we reached the top, the terrain finally leveled off, but finding our way along this ancient hill was daunting. Water seeps collected in the low spots, and an overgrowth of brush created an impassable thicket. We couldn't see more than a hundred yards ahead, and trusted in our friend not to get us lost.

"We're almost there boys," yelled JB. A small rill raked the wide flat crest of this mountain that runs north and south. JB found a clear spot where the small stream was free of brush and undergrowth. There small pools of water were exposed. We stopped long enough to allow our horses to lower their heads to drink. Afterwards we crossed over the stream, and slowly trod along a deer trail to the eastern side.

Shortly the forest gave way to a more rocky terrain. From the crest of the mountain, we could see forever across this vast country. Tall mountaintops poked up to the sky in all directions.

Immediately before us, monolith outcrops framed high mountain meadows. The summer wildflowers had already lost their colorful blooms, and frost had taken the carpeting plants. Nature was preparing for another change soon to come. The air this high up was cool and thin. Within weeks, gentle snows will begin to fall and hide this beauty in deep white slumber.

We followed this rocky spine for about half a mile. After we passed another huge monolith, the mountaintop spread out flat, wide, and open. "Here it is," yelled JB. The three of us stopped our horses at the edge of a treacherous overhang.

The sun was warming our backs as we looked through a short valley that spread out south and east below us. At its far end two steep hillsides turned inward like giant fingers forming the hollow that was the valley. The floor of the valley was engroved with aspen, birch, and a few tall cottonwood trees. Protected from the high winds that blow across the ridges, they still retained their leaves that were ablaze in bright yellow to red-orange and green.

Just below us, at the front end of the valley, lay a small alpine lake that backed up against a steep rocky rise.

"This is the place, Alan," said JB. "This is where my dad and I would come each year to hunt and to talk. We would camp out right here on top. At night, I would try to count the stars, and watch them as they turned in a great wheel above us, and marveled in the mystery of it.

From our perch here on this ledge we could spy on the lake, and all the way down and through the valley for game. We shot deer and sage grouse. At night, after dinner, we would look up at the clear starry sky and my dad would weave stories for me from ancient Navajo lore."

"This is where you were camping the night you had your abduction experience?" asked Alan.

"Yep. Your horse just made road apples right where I threw out my bedding."

"Oh, sorry."

"Don't worry, I won't be coming up here again to sleep for at least a year. ... Come on. Let's go down to the lake. It's warmer down there. We can rest there and eat our lunch."

We followed a deer trail that led down to the lake. Once there I happily jumped off the beast I had been riding. My butt was quite sore. I walked a bit to stretch my legs. JB remained in the saddle; he sat tall and upright on his mount, eyeing the autumn solitude that was this place. We let him have a private moment to reminisce.

Alan found a fallen tree where the three of us could sit. Hungry, I didn't wait for the others, and dug in. I only wished I had thought to bring a sandwich. The others soon joined me. As we ate, JB mentioned that we were the only white men to share this sacred spot with him. He called it sacred. Part of the Indians' belief system is to talk about the intrinsic power of things. That inside of every object, every tree, or every place there resides a spirit. About that belief being true, I cannot say, but judging from its beauty, this place certainly deserved admiration.

After lunch Alan was the first to break the silence, "I can see how your mind can wander up here. At night, the aloneness must be overwhelming. Where might your dreams take you?"

"You know, Alan, you haven't yet told me your take on my encounter."

"So, this is where it happened. The scene is just as you described it for us the other night. ... JB, my belief regarding the many alien abduction cases may differ from other people's hysterical accounts. Let me ask you; is it possible that what you saw all took place in a dream? Moreover, I do not doubt the experience you claim to have had. Only the method by which it occurred."

"Don't worry Alan; I don't get angry over being questioned. I just want to get to the bottom of it. And you're right, for part of my experience I may well have been asleep. However, it was a strange waking sleep, and I swear that before they knocked me out with that light ray, I was quite aware. I even gave myself a stone bruise here on my forearm when I scootched over to the embankment. I can even point out to you the rock that caused it. So, how do you explain that?"

"I can't explain it, JB. That's what makes these abduction claims so interesting. What I attempt to do is gather information on as many visitation accounts as I can. There is already a pattern to them. Perhaps someday we will gain enough pieces so that we can actually put this puzzle together."

"Last night I did some research on you, Alan. I found out that you have written numerous books on this subject. I downloaded and read one of them. I know you feel they're psychic attacks rather than real visitations. I understand your reasoning for thinking that, but from my point of view, trust me, it seemed quite real."

"Yes, but these encounters all occur either inside of, or next to that twilight realm of consciousness, and lacking any physical proof, all we are left with is a mystery. And thank you for buying my book."

"I like to know who I'm dealing with, plus it helps if we're communicating with a common reference point."

"This is one smart Indian," I said.

JB, laughing, said, "John, I like you."

We were sitting down in a valley on the morning

side of a mountain. The sun was now well past one in the afternoon, and soon our little paradise would be left in the dark.

"Well, come on guys," said JB. "We better hit the trail for home unless you two want to spend the night up here?" Not geared for an overnighter, we declined the invite. "Let's untie our horses first, and let them have a quick drink."

We walked our rides over to the lakeshore so they could lap up some water. While they drank, the three of us stood quietly to have one last look around. In mystery, I felt my awareness expand.

In the sublime entirety of the picture before me all else fell silent. I noticed not the cool air against my skin, nor did I hear the gentle quake of the aspen leaves tingling through the air. I forgot about my friends presence close by. In that moment, the passing present collapsed into the now.

There were no sounds intruding upon my solace. Neither did the freshening aroma of the forest come to mind, nor did my eyes any longer bear witness to a singular beauty. I was no longer the embodiment of a man; my soul had dissolved and became one with nature, a part of the totality of life; my awareness blended into a perfect moment.

Then in realization of what was happening to me, a warm shiver coursed through my body. When I was young I read many books on the subject of spirituality and the sense of at-oneness many mystics talk about, however, until now, I had never experienced the spiritual nunc stans, or the eternal now. Even though it was brief, the stark change from what I considered normal consciousness will have me wondering over this experience for a lifetime.

Before we mounted up to leave, we both thanked JB for taking us here. What a wonderful experience he shared with us.

Alan and JB turned their horses away from the pond, put a foot into a stirrup, and pulled themselves up into their saddles. As I reached up to mount my horse, still mystified by my experience, I forgot to grab the reins and hang them over and around the saddle horn.

As I slipped my foot into the stirrup, it gently, yet unwittingly, nudged the horse in the ribs. He immediately responded by taking off at a gallop. This sudden action caught me unprepared. The bolt of the horse threw me free of the stirrup, and tossed me sideways out into the cold waters of the lake.

The near shore wasn't deep. Startled and drenched, I rose up on all fours. Muddied water dripped down the hairs of my head and face, and ran into my gaping mouth.

My eyes, looking down, saw my reflection on the surface of the water. Falling droplets fell to pierce my image, and then expanding rings of water grew ever wider to surround and encompass it. In a fleeting glance, I saw my reflection looking back at me. For a moment, I thought I had become my reflection, as though my mind had turned inside out, and now I was looking at me, only from an alternate perspective. Had I momentarily switched sides with reality?

However, I soon realized I wasn't experiencing a change in perspective. No, I was an experiencing for the first time the totality of reality. Had I stumbled upon an ancient Navajo mystery? Their mystic folklore talks of everything being one. That inside every blade of grass, every speck of sand, and every leaf of every tree, resides the Great Spirit. Now, in a sense, I understood the symbology behind the serpent eating his tail. It was the circle of life. As god, or man, looks out on the world, he sees himself staring back, and in that sense, he becomes locked into an eternal circle of creation.

When the shock of being tossed into frigid waters had passed, I heard my two buddies having one hell of a laugh. Cold, wet, embarrassed, I did not join them in their levity, but there was no way I could blame them for laughing at my flub up.

"Aw, shit!" I said, and stood up and walked to shore. JB shaking his head back and forth said, and in deep Indian gargle, "Hmm, white man can't ride horse." That put Alan in stitches. Luckily, Burningtree had a towel in one of his saddlebags.

Our ride back to Taos mirrored the ride up. What a long day. Never was I happier to get back to my room and take a hot soak. Chafed butt aside, I guess the experience was well worth the pain. After a chance to rest and freshen up, we later met JB at a restaurant for dinner, where he invited us to some sort of special Indian event tomorrow evening.

10:

Trivialisms

Kisumu, Africa

The sun was just rising on my third day in Africa. I am up early, and don't bother to stop to have breakfast in the hotel's restaurant. Spending my nights in Carter's much-touted Grand Colonial Hotel might make for a comfortable vacation, but I felt the cushy extravagances were distracting me from my one purpose—proving him a murderer. Likewise, the excessive services poured over every guest here made me question his priorities. After all, he was sent here to Africa to investigate a deadly virus outbreak. While people were dying in large numbers, I suspect that he and Bloome were sitting back sipping tea with their crumpets; that just angered me even more. I was going to teach those two charlatans a lesson the world will long remember.

I felt I was making progress in my investigations, and with the addition of Gerald to my team, I now had access to some powerful research tools. Dr. Bloome's book was also very helpful, and may ironically prove to be his undoing. He chronicled his and Carter's travels in great detail. His expert descriptions of scenes of death, and of the roads to the towns they visited laid out a path easy for me to follow. Of greatest help was the detailed map Bloome included in his book. He actually pinpointed each of his and John's brash adventures on a map. Thank you Dr. Bloome.

For reasons I cannot explain, I doubted Carter's protestation of having amnesia and blinding headaches, even from the start. During each of his sessions as my patient, I purposefully asked him to recount his exploits to me, expecting to catch him in a trap. Yet each week during his therapy, he never varied his story, not one aspect. He practiced his lies well. Together, he and Bloome must have rehearsed each sordid detail.

Bloome chronicled these details perfectly in his new book. However, there was one very ominous omission. There is no mention of John's trip to the missionary's settlement, or any mention of the death site just north of there, which is where M Apurna met her end. I suspect I know the answer to why he omitted those details. I further suspect that the clues I need to prove it will be found there.

I must now focus my quest. I will concentrate on the far north and the missionary's school. Even though it has been six months, some evidence of M's murder might still exist. Perhaps even now her bleached white bones might whisper her murderer's name.

I am hesitant to enter and view the dead city of Kenbe. The tall fence has it walled off. Although no security is visible on the ground, the Kenyan government could be policing the area from overhead with UAVs. I doubt anything relevant to my investigation remains there.

According to Gerald, the fence enclosing the

northern part of the preserve is not yet complete. If Dr. Carter's story has any ring of truth to it, then the missionary's compound should be only a couple of miles south of that northern perimeter. More importantly, the place where M Apurna was murdered would be even closer to that fence line. Certainty of purpose is now drawing me to the northern border of Kenya.

* * *

I arrived at Gerald's motel room at 8:30. I wanted to pour over the aerial photos he had of the north. He was already up and eagerly waiting to be engaged in our endeavor. His computer was already out and booted up. I spent quite a while going over the huge number of photos he had stored. Out of some curiosity, I had to ask, "Gerald, how did your group come into possession of all of these remarkable photos?"

"A member of our group, who shall remain nameless, frequently hacks internet satellites. He's always looking for something new. He monitors internet activity and noticed an unusual amount of it coming from this usually quiet part of the world.

By way of his hacking activities, he uncovered these aerial photos. You see, the Kenyan government was using UAV's to fly over trouble spots in their country. They originally transmitted the data collected via an internet service. That was a quick and easy way for them to do it, but it was not a secure method.

They have since encrypted the signals, and have switched to using a secure satellite, probably one that belongs to our CIA. Anyway, my friend came across these photos. With a little digging, he was able to determine that they were photos taken of a supposed virus outbreak here in northeast Kenya.

"I don't remember hearing about these deaths on the news?"

"No, multiple deaths here in Africa are not uncommon, and probably for that reason they weren't picked up on the news wires. Either that, or the government was trying to suppress them."

"Why do you call it a supposed viral outbreak?"

"That's where it starts getting interesting. Originally, we all thought that it was just that, a viral outbreak. That's why we didn't investigate sooner. All we had were some nice close-ups of the African countryside shot from above, and we knew of the report of a supposed Ebola outbreak; nothing unusual about that. But then, three weeks ago, we came into possession of a report made by the senior World Health Organization investigator here in Kenya. Here, go ahead and read it."

Gerald handed me some papers. It wasn't much, just two short pages of a mostly boilerplate report. It looked credible enough, and was signed by a Dr. Sam Walter. I took a minute to read it, and then asked,

"Where is Sam Walter today?"

"Sam Walter is dead. He died a day following the date on this report. Interesting, huh?"

"Oh, that's right, John did mention that his boss died, but he offered little as to how. What do you know about his death?"

"That, we can't say for certain. A source said his death was due to a plane crash, but the exact details either have been kept secret, or are not known. All we could dig up regarding his death was a very short obituary in a Nairobi newspaper. He lived there with his wife."

"This report makes no specific determination as to how the people he was investigating died. It just says, UNKNOWN, again and again."

"Doesn't that suggest anything to you, Bill?"

"Gerald, unknown is just that: unknown. And how did you come into possession of this report? How do I know that it is official?"

"The report came to us in the mail, and you're right, we do not know who sent it, why they sent it to us, or even if it is a copy of an original report. All we know for certain is that the man in charge of the investigating the many deaths here in Africa died under mysterious circumstances. ... You don't believe much in coincidences, do you Bill?"

"No, just hard facts."

"Well, when we received this report, we went back and looked at these photos in a new light. Notice they are all time and date stamped, and contain GPS coordinates. If you look at them chronologically, a story starts to emerge.

First, we have the photos of the twenty-three deaths in a small town on the border with Uganda. That is where the supposed viral outbreak occurred.

A couple days later, more photos of that town are taken, and of a farm twenty miles to the east. On the photos of the farm, notice the circles around where the bodies lie. The descriptions are written in Swahili. We had them translated. It says, *Umb'we'bwe farm. Family found murdered, as well as two area police.*

Then, a day later, there are photos taken of the site where twelve men died. The coordinates put that scene only a few miles from the small town.

A day after that, we have photos of a helicopter that crashed at that site where the twelve men died. The description says that it was a news chopper that went down.

The next day their UAV returned to the site of the helicopter crash. Apparently, a small plane crashed in the same spot. We have determined that

that was the accident that killed Dr. Walter. It was about a mile from the small town where the original supposed viral outbreak happened.

Some photos were taken the next day that traversed that entire area, but we spotted nothing in particular of interest in them. After that, the photo record stops. No more photos. Not even of the Kenbe area, which is where thousands of people died? Which made no sense? Why take all of these photos, and then nothing? It is almost as though someone expunged them in an effort to cover-up whatever they showed."

"Carter kept mentioning his trip to a missionary's settlement up north. Are there any photos of that area?"

"I'm sorry, who is this Carter person?"

"Oh, that's right, you've never met John Carter, and Bloome's book is careful not to mention him by name, except in a footnote."

"Well, Carter, or Dr. John Carter, to be precise, is the original investigator called in by the W.H.O. Sam Walter was his boss. John is the one who, in my opinion, cooked up this story about the monster he calls U'buntu. He did it to cover up his murder of a young woman, a reporter who cut him off at the balls with a newspaper article about him. I'm surprised you haven't heard of it?"

"Bill, you seem to be privy to an awful lot of detailed information that my team is unaware of? We really do need to start sharing notes. This is the first I have heard of Carter or of an article about him."

"Why don't you do an internet search right now? I think it might help open your eyes regarding who you are putting your trust in." Gerald opened up a web browser on his laptop, "I'll need a key word to use?"

"The article was written by a woman reporter. John only referred to her as M Apurna." We entered M Apurna's name as a search, and got no results, as though she never existed. "How is that possible?" I asked.

"I can't say," said Gerald. "Where is she from?"

"John never said."

"Let me try a search engine from another country."

"You can do that?"

"Sometimes you can. I'll try searching again from a European server site." Gerald tried again to find anything on an M Apurna, and came up empty.

I was beginning to get a feeling in my stomach that Carter had lied to me even about the woman's name. Had I been taken? Was his whole story, including the existence, and death, of the woman concocted? "No," I thought, "I can't accept that. We'll have to dig deeper."

"Gerald, let's approach this from another angle. Do you have the date of the deaths at that ranch up north?"

"Yes, it's stamped right onto the photos."

"Then, let's do a search of the local paper; say a day or two after that date. See if we can bring up past issues of that paper. Then we can read them searching for the article."

Gerald did a new search, and quickly brought up old copies of the local rag. We browsed through the front pages looking for the story, and sure enough, two days after his arrival in Kenya, Carter is excoriated in the tabloid press.

"Wow," I said to Gerald, "I hadn't read the entire article before. I just had John's portrayal of it to go on. However, she really let him have it. He was sent home the very next day. No wonder he flipped out. Publicly humiliated, his career in jeopardy; those are reasons enough to seek revenge."

* * * * *

The Article:

Scientist Claims Weird Creature

Responsible for Deaths! People are dying on the border of Kenya and Uganda. According to Dr. John Carter, a representative of the W.H.O. an Eeerie extra-dimensional creature resembling the Mothman is on the loose in Africa. I sat down with this formerly acclaimed doctor, and he revealed to me that that very day he had a run-in with this ghostly diamond-eyed apparition from Mars. He did seem quite serious about it. Certainly, if a demon were to appear in front of me I would be a bit scared too. However, I think this doctor was suffering more from a spaced-out imagination fueled by an alcoholic binge, and that the ghost he saw was his own shadow viewed through drunken delirium. As real people have died, as rumors of disease and wars intensify and threaten to take more lives, what we need is a sober scientist, not a boozed out has-been...

* * * * *

"Yes, I agree," said Gerald. "However, it's still possible that he actually saw something, and I am well versed in the Mothman legend."

"Gerald, are you serious?" I was dismayed that even after reading such an article on Carter, he was still willing to give him some leeway.

"Bill, all I ask is that you keep an open mind. This article doesn't prove that Carter didn't have an encounter. It appears that something scared him, we are only in disagreement as to what."

Gerald's remarks stung. I stood tall and rigid for a long moment while I considered them. With my hands behind me, and clenched in fists, I fretted over my young partner's response. How can I conduct a serious investigation with someone who believes in monsters? But I still need him.

"Very well," I said. "It's good that we approach this with opposing beliefs. ... I promise you Gerald, by the time this week is over, you will see things differently."

Gerald did not hear my words; he was sitting on his chair and staring blankly off into space.

"Gerald!"

Shaking his head as to get the cobwebs out, "Oh, sorry Bill, I just realized something. We have always wondered how Bloome managed to get the jump on us. This time it was this article. He must have built-up quite a powerful network to be able to dig this article up from such a remote paper. Did your friend Carter ever mention how and when he met up with Bloome?"

"Why, yes. He said it was the day after he was sent home to Chicago. He said there was a letter of introduction from Bloome waiting for him in the mail."

"But he didn't say anything more, anything about his network?"

"No, and I think that I mentioned previously that I spent about two months myself trying to locate Dr. Bloome. ... Not to worry, the air of mystery he manufactures around himself is an indication that he is hiding from something. We'll ... Gerald, are you listening to me?"

Gerald was still sitting with a pensive, blank, and

almost dejected look on his face. Obviously, I was not getting through to him. I could not have him in awe of someone I had tagged as a crook, and promptly changed the direction of our discussion.

"OK, let's get on with today. ... What I want to do is find a town close by this northern edge of the fence line. We'll fly there. We need to check that area out; somehow, I need to visit that missionary school? It must be located on one of these photos here?"

Gerald snapped out of his trance, and we poured over the photos from up north, "The only thing that looks like a small village, or group of buildings, is right here," he said.

"Yes, that must be it. Carter said it was about one mile from an area of devastation. Look how the vegetation along the whole northern area has been laid bare."

"Look here on the map; there is a town by the upper fence line. It's about twenty miles to the north of it though."

"That's OK. I'm sure we can hire a taxi, or rent a car there."

"Then let's get going," said Gerald, "and you can fill me in on the rest that you know about this Carter person on the way."

The Plane Ride North

We located a public airport in Kisumu, and then chartered a plane to take us up north. The remoteness of where we were headed had me excited, and at the same time worried. Our destination was only one-hundred and fifty miles away, but with no direct and modern roads leading there, and our only access by plane, we could get stuck. This country is alien to me. I don't know the languages, or the customs. The only reason the locals interact with me is the green cash in my pocket. Too little of it, and you can't get along. Too much, and you make yourself a target. That I don't trust the African people probably shows through to them. That's all right. Just five more days and I'll be done here. Then I can get out of this third world country.

The plane we hired was a small single engine high-wing. It offered great views, but was slow. The flight up took almost three hours. The airspace above what has now been dubbed the Kenbe Preserve is restricted. Our pilot had to fly around the preserve, which added more time. I enjoyed looking out across the African countryside, yet the view wasn't as entertaining as those portrayals of Africa on TV. I saw no massive herds of roaming animals. In fact, most of the terrain below us was either scrub plain, or worse, what was once dense forest had now been hewn bare.

From the sky, it was easy to notice that the inhabitants had scarified vast tracts of land. They had cut deep gashes into the skin of our planet that now oozed reddish blood. The wounds as they bled spread and widened. Nature, in her attempt to heal, had only eroded further, and worsened the wounds. The spoil that washed away from these gashes washed into the rivers and turned them muddy red. The sight of such devastation disheartened me.

As we neared our destination, the winds picked up, and severely buffeted our little plane. Our pilot pointed down, and said, "That's where were going to land." I moved my head closer to the window to peer down. The runway was nothing more than one more gash cut into this country's fragile hide.

Bang! Suddenly my head is slammed against the window. Strong crosswinds near the ground pitched the plane violently.

The pilot broke hard into a diving turn to lose

altitude quickly. Twice the severe winds rocked the plane sideways, and nearly inverted us.

Pilots of larger commercial jets are concerned for the comfort of their passengers; ours wasn't. He made several abrupt chinks before we came into position to land. Visions of dying in a burning crash swept across my mind. As with riding on any wild roller coaster, my stomach was exceedingly happy when we finally came to a stop.

The town we found ourselves in was just a hot, dry, dusty, windy place. Not really an established town as I was accustomed to seeing. Just a line of unconnected buildings, all with their backs to the dirt landing strip which is probably this town's only source of income.

Immediately after deplaning, I had to take a few steps. After sitting for three hours, I needed to stretch. As I walked away from the plane, several street urchins immediately set upon me. This was uncomfortable. They were all showing me their outstretched arms and waiting palms. This was a new experience for me, and I had no idea how to handle it. I didn't want to insult the local folk for fear of reprisal. Fortunately, for me, the pilot came running to my aid, and shooed them away.

We thanked the pilot and bid him farewell. Gerald and I then walked around to the front of the buildings, and scanned the sights before us. This town contained nothing that looked official. There were no banks. I saw no police station, no hardware store, and no hospital. Neither did I see any visible signs of robust commerce. This was as raw and primitive as a town can get—just old, beat-up looking buildings.

One of the buildings doubled as a gas station and everything-mart. It had two gas pumps, but they looked to be out of the 1940's, however they fit well with the stores exterior.

The early afternoon sun felt hot. Tiny bits of sand blown by the arid winds stung as they hit my skin. I noticed several people hanging out at the stores north side taking advantage of the patch of shade afforded by a small overhang. An out of place looking modern vending machine stood beside the front door. We walked over to it. At this point, I was feeling quite generous, and bought Gerald and me both cold cokes.

One of the men who had been standing there came over to us, and in broken but understandable English asked, "You two want taxi ride?"

I interpreted him to be offering us his taxi service. Surprised, I said, "Yes, we will need to hire a taxi." I questioned myself if I should inquire as to how much it might cost, but decided it better just to go with the flow.

He made motioned with his arms urging us to follow him. He led us to an older sedan parked in front of a house two doors down. Yeah, my expectations had to be lowered, but there was nothing better in sight.

This town, or gathering of shanties, sat at the intersection of three roads, each leading off to where I did not know.

OAs we stood beside his beat up car, our cabby asked, "Where you two want to go?" Gerald had a geodetic survey map folded up and stashed in his back pocket. He took it out to show the man. Following Bloome's actions six months earlier he had drawn a circle on it outlining the restricted area. Gerald pointed his index finger to its northern edge.

"Very good, you want to go to Preserve," said the driver. "Fifty bucks."

All of a sudden, his English seemed to improve. Fifty dollars for a twenty-mile cab ride, who could be unhappy with that? We nodded in agreement.

As we reached for the cab's doors, he stopped us and mentioned, "No, no, pay first." So, the rules were backwards here. I gave the man his bucks, and he allowed us entry to his filthy beat-up sedan.

Not much sooner than we had arrived in his town, we were leaving it again. Once we were all inside, he quickly wheeled around raising a cloud of dust. He took the one of the three roads that ran essentially south.

Our cab zoomed along at a high rate of speed for perhaps ten minutes. Then the driver hit the brakes hard, and made a sudden left-hand turn onto a dirt road, and leaving our stomachs behind.

All evidence showed that this road had been recently cut, and appeared to be heavily trafficked. Nothing more than a bumpy swath of barren dirt, a cloud of dust rooster-tailed high behind our cab as we sped along.

The countryside here consisted of flat tablelands separated by shallow swales. Most of the land had been clear-cut or showed sparse vegetation. Only an occasional acacia tree sprung up to meet our eyes. There was no scrub brush, no fallen snags, and no dead wood lying about; the ground was picked clean.

Seeing this scrubby vista, I wondered what strange forces were at work here. If people had cleared and burned what wood was available, where did they all go? I have heard of the poverty that exists in many parts of Africa. But what intelligent and thinking creature destroys the environment on which it must survive?

After a hair-raising thirty minutes ride we came to the top of the tableland. The terrain changed into a broad flat plain that gently sloped upward toward the base of a high mountain range that must have been ten miles farther off. Immediately the

Preserve's fence came into view.

It was a massive undertaking. We were still a mile away from it, yet it stretched tall and wide to fill the horizon in both directions. Off in the near distance construction equipment: bulldozers and trucks were clearly visible. All of this hectic activity, just to build a fence? In amazement, Gerald and I looked at each other and scratched our heads.

For that last mile, our driver slowed down. As the dust cloud dispersed, we could see that the fence was nearing completion. Such an enormous undertaking it was, but why? It stretched in a wide arc to the east right up to the base of the mountain. To the west, it ran for as far as my eyes could focus. The road we were driving on led directly to the fence, and ended there at a large steel gateway.

Crews had not yet erected the gate, which left a large opening cut into it. At the opening were three armed guards, all dressed in military garb. As we approached, two of them took their weapons down from their shoulders, and aimed them right at our vehicle. Smartly, the cabby stopped.

I didn't wait for an invitation to exit the cab. Just as I got out, two of the guards came at me, and started talking loudly in some African language. Waving their weapons around, they appeared to want me to get back into the cab and go.

"Gerald," I shouted, "why don't you get out of the cab, and join me over here?" I expected safety in numbers.

As Gerald got out and rounded the car's rear, the two guards called out to the third man one who was now sitting in a military jeep they used to block the gates opening.

Though their posture was threatening, and they had their guns pointed at us, in my arrogance, I wasn't thinking on fear right then. "No one would shoot an American just for wanting to look at a fence," I thought.

The third man, who was shorter and lighter in complexion that the other two, somewhat slowly and deliberately, got out of his jeep. He walked over to where we were all standing, and in clear spoken English demanded to know who I was.

"I am Doctor William Henderson, and this is Mr. Gerald Hicks."

"There is nothing here for you, Doctor Henderson. You two should leave."

"We just want to see the Preserve," I said defiantly.

"There it is," he said in a stern voice. "You are looking at it, now go." Obviously, I was not going to sway this man. They were serious about keeping anyone from entering the preserve, but we had come far, and had just gotten here, I wasn't ready to give up. Not yet.

We got back in the cab, and I asked the driver to pull back a little and stop. There were construction vehicles coming and going. I noticed from the company name painted on the doors that the contractor was from Holland, of all places. Whoever ordered this fence built was serious about getting it done. There was an army of workers strewn along the fence line.

Where could all of these workers be staying? Not here, there is nothing here but barren dirt, and certainly not back in that shantytown we had just come from. Just then, a line of trucks came barreling down the dirt road, and entered the construction site passing by us. Curious, I got out of the cab and hailed one of them hoping he understood some English.

"Hello," I yelled, "mind if I ask you some questions?"

"You're American, nice?" he muttered.

"Why you speak perfect English," I said.

"Of course, all northern Europeans speak the Kings English, we're all neighbors, you know?" Then he said, "It appears you have gotten the guards attention. They don't have much of a personality, do they?"

"No," I said.

"If Khan there comes over here, let me take care of it," he said.

"Khan," I asked.

"Yes, the short one there is Lieutenant Khalid Khan; he is in charge of keeping the peace up here. He is a serious man, and you don't want to anger him. ... So, are you a reporter or something?"

"No, have there been many reporters snooping about?"

"Every day it seems. This place has got quite a few people asking questions, you know?"

"I'm not a reporter, but I am interested in the Preserve. My name is Dr. Bill Henderson."

"Nice to meet you Bill, my name is Günter. Oops, here comes Khan. Let's not talk here. Meet me later tonight back at our motel, and I will tell you all of the stories."

"Where are you guys staying?"

"When you get back to the highway, have your cabby turn left. Ten miles further on is a small town with a motor lodge and a restaurant. That is where we are all staying while we work on this project. Why don't you wait for me at the restaurant later tonight?"

What luck, I almost began to believe like Gerald in coincidences. I thanked the young man for the information, and let him get on with his job. Before Khan got to me, I put my hands halfway up into the air as if to surrender, turned, and got back into our cab, and we left.

* * * * *

Sitting on the front seat of Khan's jeep was a clipboard full of information sheets. They were all mug shots of persons deemed of interest to the Kenyan Ministry—reporters and the like. The front page held a photo and personal data of one Dr. William Henderson, Psychiatrist.

Using his two-way radio, Khan contacted a Mr. Um'fume, in the Kenyan Minister's office.

"Yes, Um'fume, this is Khan. The psychiatrist fellow on our watch list just showed up here."

"What? He is up there in the north. What would he be wanting up there?"

"I have no idea sir, but I saw him talking to one of the contractors. I sent him away, but if he returns, how do you want me to handle it?"

"We don't want to raise anyone's suspicions. The story is the same as if he were a reporter. Tell him that we have set aside this land as a preserve to reforest it, and that the fence is to keep the animals in, and people out."

"Yes sir, I can handle it."

"And Khan, if Henderson shows up again, I want to know about it right away."

"Yes, sir."

* * * * *

Fifteen miles to the west, in the town Henderson is heading to now, a news team has been listening in on Khan's unencrypted transmissions. A reporter and three broadcast technicians have been here in northern Kenya for several weeks attempting to gather up what information they can on this fishy preserve story. The reporter, Michael Mills, was a onetime friend and co-worker of M Apurna.

"We should thank the Kenyan government for using open communication channels," said Mr. Mills. "We already have the names of the officials involved in this clandestine act, hopefully soon we will figure out the truth behind it. I tell you, I know there is a bigger story here, and I won't rest until I find out what happened to M."

"I'm beginning to smell a rat too, Mike," said his companion, Terry Gelow, in stern agreement. "And now we learn that they had an American psychiatrist on their watch list. What the hell could some head shrink from America possibly have to do with a tract of land here in Africa?"

"That is something we need to find out," said Mike. "We have his name, let's get on the net and figure out just who this person is, and what it is that ties him to the preserve. What could possibly inspire anyone to travel half a world to this remote hell hole?"

* * * * *

On the drive out, I turned to my companion and said, "Gerald, this is all very exciting. And now we have an English speaking comrade on our side; one willing to spill the beans." I was patting myself on the back again for my investigatory prowess; probably underserved, but nonetheless.

"Bill, don't you think that you are overlooking some important facts?"

"Huh?" Gerald's question snapped me out of my well-deserved, yet delusional euphoria.

"Think on it for a moment," he said, "What reason on Earth could possibly prompt the Kenyan government to fence off such a huge area, and force them to concoct some phony story. Something is being covered up here."

"It could be just what they are calling it, a preserve. You can see the ecological devastation in this area. I believe they are trying to protect the land. The best way to do that is to keep people out."

"Do you need such a tall fence and guards to do that?" he asked.

"Well, apparently here, you do."

"And what about the city of Kenbe; why fence it off. In addition, what about the original deaths in that small town Carter was investigating. What caused all of those deaths?"

Gerald had asked some biting questions for which I had no ready answer. And although I was certain they could all have quite natural explanations, some doubt remained, and in the pit of my stomach I began to feel a twinge of unease.

As Gerald suspected, certain things, little things, were not adding up. Why hire a high priced contractor from abroad when you can hire locally for so much less. The only answer I could come up for that was immediacy. They wanted it done, and done now. But why the urgency?

Further, I keep going back to the report filed by Sam Walter. I am also a medical doctor, and I didn't spend those many years in medical school for nothing. I know full well, that with the state of medical technology being where it is today, that the term *UNKNOWN* doesn't really apply. That the deaths he was investigating would have to be due to either a chemical, viral, or bacteriological agent; or an attack by man—all of which were readily discernible.

Before I had a chance to think further on Gerald's doubts we arrived at the highway intersection. I had to motion quickly for the driver to stop or he would have turned right, and at a blistering speed returned us to the cesspool we landed in.

"No, stop! We want to go left to the next town," I said as I made hand gestures in that direction.

"You want to go to Kilali?"

"Kilali, yes, we want to go to Kilali." Then I see this hand reach up and hang over the front seat, palm up.

"Kilali, fifty bucks."

"Oh, dear god. ... Gerald, I'm tapped out for the moment. Do you have any cash?"

We paid our cabby his confiscatory fee, which was nothing more than blackmail. After suffering through another one of his high-speed zips, he dropped us off at the edge of this new town. Then in a cloud of dust, he sped back to the rundown dump we found him in.

Kilali was a step back into civilization. It appeared to have a vibrant economy with signs of progress toward the twenty-first century. We easily found the motel described by Günter.

We had no idea when he would get off work, and I didn't want to waste another day. So, after securing a room for the night we decided to walk to the town's main street. I thought that perhaps we could find some locals and ferret out information from them regarding this so-called Preserve. This was seat of your pants investigating. I was formulating my plans on the run. Who knew where the next turn of a corner would take us? I was pumped, and felt more alive than I had in years. Here, there were no sniveling, whiney patients to coddle, just raw, wild, and untamed territory to explore, and explore we did.

We spent the afternoon snooping about in downtown Kilali, but we failed learn much. Sure people knew of the Preserve, however, they were just as confused over it as we. Later that night, as suggested by Günter, we found ourselves in the restaurant next to the motel.

Gerald and I were both eager to talk to him. If he had worked up here for months, he must have some heard some interesting stories. That opportunity conveniently arose just as we were ordering our meals. In walked Günter and he appeared to be alone.

"Günter, hello again. Remember me from earlier today?" I muttered.

"Yes, you are the American Doctor."

"You are welcome to join us for diner if you like?" Günter was an interesting young fellow. With his blonde hair cropped short and gelled to stand straight up he looked more like a stocky, six foot two Bart Simpson.

"Why, thank you, it would be a pleasure to have someone from the US to talk with," he said politely, and then took a seat next to me. "I'm sorry; I have forgotten your name."

"I'm Bill, and this is my partner, Gerald."

"Nice to meet you Gerald, are you a doctor also?"

"No, I'm a founding member of GLUFON."

"Oh, I have heard of this organization." A sly little smile of recognition appeared on his Günter's face. "Back at my home in Antwerp, I visit your website often. I think it is very cool what you guys do. Why, that must be why you are here, isn't it? You're investigating the monster sightings."

"Yes, we are," said Gerald, "but I think that the Doctor here, and I, are approaching this story from opposite ends?"

"What? Bill, you're not a believer?" exclaimed

Günter.

"No, and I'm not afraid of little green monsters, or things that go bump in the night either."

"Well, you will be, you will!" emphasized Günter with a rasping sound—aping Yoda. I got it, and we all shared a little laugh, then I steered the conversation toward something more concrete.

"So, Günter, how long have you been on this job?"

"Since the beginning, about five months now. We started down south where we put in forty miles of fencing, and then we were instructed to complete this northern section. There is going to be around one hundred miles of fencing in total, you know. If it weren't for the mountain and the long lake along the eastern edge making up the other side of the Preserve, it would've been much longer."

"So, why the large gate," I asked, "I didn't see any gates along the southern side?"

"What?" he asked with a look of dismay on his face. After he had a chance to figure out what I was asking, "Why, it's for the people living in there to get supplies in, of course."

"Wait? ... You just said there are still people living inside of the Preserve? I thought everyone died at Kenbe?"

Günter moved his head back and forth a few times, and then stared down at the table. I sensed he was showing some disbelief in my question. "Boy, you two are uninformed as to what has been going on here." ... He continued, "Yes, Kenbe was a total kill, but there are still a few of the native farmers scattered across the high plain that were unharmed and remain so, and also everyone at the missionary school. In fact, one of the school's missionaries walks out with his donkey almost daily to pick up supplies."

"You don't say."

That was startling information, and I would need time to process it. Clearly though, this bolstered my opinion that what killed all of those people was no monster, just a tragic accident. My two friends here surely don't think that I am supposed to believe that an astral-monster killed thousands, yet left a handful of humans alive?

"Günter, what I want to do is to get inside of the compound. Is there any time of day, or week, when the guards are not present?"

My question grabbed his attention. He turned away. A pained look grew on his face. Clearly, he was having mixed emotions, as though torn between amusement and disbelief.

Then he stared at me, motionless, his mouth agape, his wide smirk of a smile tempered by a slight downturn of the corners of his open mouth. With his short blond hair standing straight up, his countenance looked almost comical. "Yes, that is right," I reiterated, "we are going in there."

He sat mute. After a moment, he closed his mouth, and then looking down at the table, said, "Bill," then raising his head to make eye contact, "I don't know of anyone who has contemplated that." His facial expression then turned to one of deep concern, "Guy's, I can't be a part of this. Bill, I know my beliefs may sound simple-minded to you, but take my advice. Don't go in there, neither of you."

Then, turning to Gerald, he said, "If you two want to hear about what is going on inside of the preserve what you should do is talk with the missionary. He can be seen crossing the barren area walking towards the gate most mornings around eleven."

I didn't push him for any more information. Why bother. I just sat quietly while I finished my meal. His concern for us was touching, yet in my opinion, his fear was irrational, and a plan was hatching in the back of my mind to prove it.

Günter and Gerald were on the same wavelength, so to speak, and got into a lively conversation about ghost sightings and UFO's. Nothing I cared to be entertained with. While the two of them yakked it up, I noticed that a group of men at the other end of the room kept leering over at me.

Suddenly, griped with self-doubt, a creepy unease grew in my stomach. For the first time since I arrived in Africa, I felt unsure. People must have noticed my unease and they were staring at me. The conversation of two weirdoes sitting next to me and chatting about supernatural nonsense didn't help. I pulled my arms in close, tucked my shoulders in a bit, gave myself a cowering hug, and thought, "For god's sake, you're a psychiatrist Bill, snap out of it."

Just then, one of the men who had been eyeballing me from across the room stood and started to walk my way. Even though he was in casual dress now, I could tell that he had a polished almost movie star mien, and must have worn a suit and tie often. He was no unsophisticated cretin like the two next to me.

With a prominent air, he walked right over to me and said, "Excuse me, Doctor Henderson. My name is Mike Mills. I'm a freelance reporter working for a world news syndicate."

Gulp. What an unexpected shock. Had I heard him correctly? In my private moment of paranoia, I couldn't be sure. A freelance reporter. In the middle of the African bush, and he is familiar with who I am? I braced myself for the unknown.

"I'm sorry, could you repeat that?" I asked.

"Yes, I said my name is Mike Mills. I'm a

freelance reporter working for a world news syndicate."

"Oh, hello, Mike, how may I help you?"

"First, do you mind if I sit down."

"Please do, it would be nice to have someone levelheaded to talk with for a change." I was throwing a snipe at Gerald and Günter, but they were lost in their own conversation, and ignored us.

"Let me not keep you in the dark, Dr. Henderson. I know who you are because we reporters are a snoopy lot. The other members of my team over there, and I have been working here in Kenya for weeks now. As investigative reporters, we monitor the airwaves. Believe it or not, your name became the center of a conversation today between the Khan, who you met at the preserve gate, and a senior staff member at the Kenyan Ministry in Nairobi. Apparently, they already knew who you were, and were waiting for you to show up."

My paranoia had been justified after all, but now an odd sinking feeling deep in my bowels had me shivering. Was I in danger of being arrested, or prevented from finishing my quest? Or worse, sent home before I had a chance to discredit Carter and Bloome? In some disbelief, I replied, "What? How could they possibly know who I am, let alone be expecting me?"

"Apparently, you are on some sort of watch list they put together."

"I was put on a government watch list? My god, but why?"

"That was the question we have been asking ourselves, Dr. Henderson. Somehow, you fit into all of this craziness here in Africa, and we, like you, want to know why. Perhaps if we put our heads together we can figure this one out. We are still trying to get our heads around this whole phony preserve story, and it seems you are just as curious."

At last, I had found a sane person who thinks as I do. My shivers of fear eased, and my body warmed again. I opened up, put my arms away from my sides, and out on the restaurant table. "Yes, Mike," I said. "I find the idea of a fenced in preserve ludicrous, and I'm eager to find an answer to some other inconsistencies that have been nagging at me."

"Dr. Henderson, or could I call you Bill?"

"Certainly."

"Bill, let's try and figure this out. If you don't mind my asking, how is it that you found yourself here in Africa?"

"Six months ago, a man came to me complaining of severe blinding headaches and memory loss, and asked me to help him. During his treatment, he related to me how he and a friend were here in Kenya when they encountered a monster. He said that the monster was responsible for the deaths of thousands. That man's name was Dr. John Carter."

"Yes, we know about Dr. Carter," said Mike. "He was one of the W.H.O. doctors sent here to investigate a virus outbreak. However, our research shows he left Africa almost immediately after the burning of Kenbe. With the destruction of a major city to deal with, news of the virus outbreak faded away overnight. I don't see how he ties into all of this?"

"What? ... Then you don't know the whole story? ... Somehow, that does not surprise me. Well, Mike, as I was treating him, I came to think of Carter as a fraud. I never believed his story; it was just too incredible to be true. That is why I am here. I intend to expose him and his accomplice for the cons that they are."

"We have all heard stories about the Monster of Kenbe, but like all things on the internet, we thought them for the most part just the work of over active imaginations. Is Carter one of those spreading wild tales of a Mothman in Africa?"

"Yes, he claims to be the first person to have encountered the creature he calls U'buntu. I won't bother you with the minutia, but my take on it is that he concocted this story of a monster to cover-up the murder of the young woman, M Apurna."

As I mentioned Apurna's name Mike's face went pale, and his lower jaw nearly fell to the floor. His hands began shaking as he pushed his coffee cup aside. Then I noticed tears form in the corners of his eyes. He tried hard to hold it back, but my trained eye knew he was in utter shock—obviously, he knew her—and well. "Mike, tell me how you knew Miss Apurna." Now I had a chance to play psychologist again.

"Yes, you guessed it. We were lovers," he said blowing his nose. "We had just broken up right before her disappearance. I will admit she was a difficult and headstrong woman, but I loved her just the same. ... I suspected all along that she might have died in the fires at Kenbe. Still, I held out hope. She would often mysteriously disappear for days on end, probably off following some story, so I thought little of it when she did not check in at the office.

Then, as the days turned into weeks, I began to suspect she had returned to Kenbe. She had friends there, and they began to talk about rumors of weird occurrences. ... It is just so sad. She was so young and beautiful."

As Mike took a moment to compose, I remembered something, something that conflicted with John Carter's saga of terror. He said that he and Bloome saw M Apurna in Kenbe the very day before it burned. Was that just one more strange twisted wrinkle in his convoluted fairy tale? Was Carter that intelligent? Was he even then building up some reasonable doubt surrounding Apurna's death? That must be it, for there is no way to connect this detail with anything sane.

"Mike, let me tell you what I know about M Apurna. John told me, now this was during his therapy sessions, that he saw M Apurna in Kenbe. That was the day before the city burned. He went there that day following the directions of the Minister of Health. His friend, Alan Bloome, accompanied him. The story goes they both saw a woman whom they took to be M go into this small clothing store. John went on to say that when he saw her enter the store that he ran into it to talk with her, but she wasn't there. She had disappeared."

Before I could finish with my thought, Mike burst in saying, "Yes, I know that store. That is where I bought her a white crop top just two weeks prior to our breaking up. Talk about looking sexy."

"Mike, wait. Don't you see what is going on? She wasn't there. It is my belief that Carter and Bloome never saw her in Kenbe. That story is all made-up. In fact, they couldn't have seen her there. During my last session with Dr. Carter he as much as admitted to me that she died up north days earlier in a place not far from the missionary's camp."

"What are you trying to tell me?"

"That she didn't die in the conflagration at Kenbe. That it was no monster that killed her. Listen, Carter's story never wavered. He said that she had accompanied him to this death site he was investigating north of a missionary school, but that was days before the conflagration at Kenbe. Moreover, regardless of what Bloome and Carter want everyone to believe, and unless you believe in monsters, he is the one who murdered her, and it was there at the settler's camp. What better place to do it. There were already more than a dozen bodies lying about, who would question one more? Further, the Kenyan authorities did not intend to collect the bodies for burial. I am led to believe that all of them were left to rot in the open."

"You are suggesting that John Carter murdered M. Do you have any proof of that, and why would he want to kill her anyway?"

"Mike, he killed her as revenge for her slamming him with that newspaper article, and he is using this tall tale of a monster on the lose as a cover-up for her murder. There is something else that you will find very interesting. I suspect the Kenyan government knows that he did it, but for some reason they have decided to go along with his cover up. And this is where Carter's story starts to fall apart. You see, he didn't know that the Kenyan Ministry was using UAV's to fly over every death site and take photos of them. He only found that out during his last night's stay in Kisumu.

When he found out that there were aerial photos of the settler's site, and that there was an unaccounted for body there, he freaked out. That is when he faked having a blinding headache, and passed out. He spent a couple days in the hospital where he claimed to be having some permutated form of amnesia, but these are all just pieces of a huge lie. The only piece to the puzzle that doesn't fit yet is why the Kenyan government gave him the damning pictures."

"If Carter had government help, then it sounds as though he had all of his loose ends already tied up. So why would he come and tell you he murdered her, and wouldn't that put him in jeopardy if he were arrested?"

"No, not at all, and that is why we psychiatrists have to be on the lookout for patients like him. If he were ever charged, his story would be used in court as a backup plan. He would call me in to testify, and I would have to tell the court that in my opinion it was quite possible that he was suffering from delusions and was quite possibly temporarily insane when he killed her.

This has happened before. Many psychiatrists have been duped that way. Just last year a close friend of mine lost his business and livelihood when one of his clients sued him over a similar incident. That is why I take it very seriously."

On hearing the truth, Mike looked angry. I could see the rage and anger written on his face. I can use that. He will want revenge on the person who killed his lover. He will not give up. He will struggle even unto his own death to learn the truth about how and where Apurna died. All I need to do is point him in the right direction. His ardor for vengeance will drive him to uncover Carter's lies. All I need to do is follow his lead. Then I will have my proof.

"Bill, if what you say is true then M's body lay close to the north side fence, and clues to her murder might lie there also. Then that is where I need to go. I won't rest until I solve the mystery surrounding her disappearance, and if that leads me to her killer, all the better."

"Then let's work together, Mike. The only place we are going to find answers is inside of that Preserve. I intend to get in there. I am going to start with the missionaries, and they were the last people to see Apurna alive."

"Very well, Dr. Henderson, we will work together on this. Let's go ahead and plan something for tomorrow."

11:

The Blue Moon Flute

Taos, New Mexico

Our journey into the Sangre de Christo Mountains yesterday left Alan and me with a memorable experience, one that will no doubt stay with us for the rest of our lives. It also left us with extremely sore rumps. Neither of us had ever ridden a horse before. My upper leg muscles were stiff, and they hurt to move. Riding was more work than we expected, and had us quite run down. Needless to say, we missed the morning bugle call.

Hunger roused us around noon. I suggested we straighten our bowlegs by walking to the town plaza and have some lunch. It was only a few short blocks.

After freshening up, we headed out to eat. My first steps were very difficult and painful, and I had to yell out, "Arrgghhhh!"

"I think that you have confused your phrases again, John," quipped Alan.

"No, that one feels right." My saddle sore pains lessened by the time we reached the town square. There are several eateries located close-by. We picked the one with cushioned seats.

"So, Alan, have you ever been to an Indian flute ceremony?"

"No, this is going to be a first for me," he said. "It's awfully nice of JB to invite us. You know, we may be the only palefaces there. This is all very exciting. We are sharing in on some of their ancient lore. Just think of it, I mean, this is the heart and soul of these people. This is how they pass on their history."

"Alright, Alan, down boy." We had texted JB before we left the motel and invited him to join us for a late lunch. ... "Burningtree will be here any minute," I said. "I wonder what kind of vehicle he drives."

"Well, I take him to be an eco-friendly type. So he probably drives a compact hybrid."

"I don't know," I said. "He may surprise us. I'm going with an old beat-up Chevy pickup."

Colored by our expectations, we keenly spied each vehicle that drove by looking for our friend. We ignored the huge brand-new pitch-black Hummer with dark tinted windows, and sparkled with chrome, that pulled up right in front of us. The door to that tank opened and out stepped a squatty 5' 8" Native American wearing a waist long pea coat, and a silly looking, felt, Nez Perce hat.

"Boy, were we wrong," I said. "This guy is full of mysteries."

"Dear god," said Alan, "he's dressed like a renegade, we better watch out, or we could get scalped."

Once JB had joined us at our table, I couldn't wait to ask, "So, JB, what is it you said you do again?"

"I studied computer engineering in college," he said. "That's a loose term covering a large field, but my degree was enough to open up some important doors for me. I did well."

"Which firm do you work for now?"

JB gave out a snide little laugh and said, "Boy, you guys are sure nosy. What is this? Are you jealous of the Indian who did well?" he said, all the while with a broad smile on his face.

"Come on, out with it," bade Alan.

"Alright, I'll admit that I was luckier than smart. I got in at the right time, and rode the dotcom boom. The small tech company I worked for grew and then went public. I made millions from the stock options. Then I powwowed my money and bought my own company that was very successful. I sold out a couple years ago, and today I own and run a small ad company pretty much as hobby."

"You know, you are full of surprises," I said.

"Yes, but my story is not so odd as an epidemiologist, and a scholar, out chasing UFO's across the Wild West."

"He has us there, Bloome."

The three of us erupted in laughter, and then JB went on to say, "No, I have done very well. Where I can, I make donations to help the cause. Even though my home is now in southern California, and has been for over twenty years, I still feel as though I have a connection to these people. I'm only happy to help them retain their heritage."

Changing the subject, I asked, "Does your black stallion there have a name?"

With a deep laugh, JB said, "Yeah, I call her Guzzler. ... Which reminds me, I've told you two quite a bit about me, but you haven't said much about yourselves?"

I threw up my hands and yelled, "Peace Redskin, no need to torture us, we'll talk."

"Jesus, John, you kill me."

"Oh, I hope it won't come to that," I said.

He then turned and looked down his nose at me, as if he were a hawk about to pounce on prey.

"OK, OK. I'll get you two to talk." With that he stood up, reached to an inside pocket of his heavy coat, and pulled out a small paperback book. Then he threw it down rather hard on the table, sending it sliding towards Alan.

"My god," said Alan. "How did you manage to get a hold of that?" Alan had a pleased yet amazed look on his face.

"What, you didn't think that you could invade our land unobserved, did you? ... You paleface, always thinking you can sneak up on us. Actually, when you told me that you gave a talk at the college in LV, I called my cousin who lives there, and asked her if she had heard about it. She was in the audience that night, and she bought a copy of your new book. I had her get one from the schools bookstore and next day it to me. I read it last night. ... So, is it true?"

As JB was talking, a sudden horror gripped me. I hadn't seen Alan's new book yet—only heard about it. On the cover, the title, *The Devil at 12:01* struck a sour chord in my soul. Suddenly all the memories of that monster, U'buntu, returned to the fore. Chilled, I pulled my arms in and cowered away from any further discussion. I heard Alan talking at me, but I couldn't respond to him.

"John? John!? It's OK buddy. John?"

"Alan, he looks frightened to death."

"Here," JB, "please, hide the book back in your coat pocket."

My head was spinning, and I felt nauseous. I needed fresh air. Getting up, I staggered through the front door and stepped outside. "Alright, get a grip,

John." I told myself. "There is nothing here to threaten you. How long are you going to let this bother you? That's it. Use logic on yourself. No, that doesn't work. Oh god," my gut was twisting and tears of shock poured from my eye ducts. "What is this hold this demon has on me?"

Leaning up against the building's façade support column, my circumspection went on for another few minutes. I did not understand these reactions. To me they were a form of insanity—but I am not insane. In time, I calmed down. Wiping my face dry, and hiding my embarrassment, I went back into the restaurant to eat lunch with my friends.

"Sorry, John," said JB, "I had no idea." Then he stopped short. I guess Alan explained my travails to him while I was gone.

He sat pensive and quiet for a change while we ate. That was a side to his personality I didn't think possible, but what was he thinking about? Then he said, "I understand now. This nexus, you, me, Alan here, it all revolves around Don.

He sensed it beforehand. You see, time flows differently for him. The Nagual is able to see things before they happen, and as a healer, he is able to bring people and spirits together. Yes, it all makes sense now. My dad said that each of our lives revolve as if on some giant circle, and that it is possible for the sides of these different circles to mesh up and turn together—that's the nexus. Your lives are now aligned with the Nagual's. I am sure that you two will meet up with Don again, and soon. I would like you to keep in touch with me, and let me know if he is able to help you in any way."

Alan and I heard JB's astonishing summation, but we sat quiet and did not respond. We didn't want to consider it at that moment. Alan knew of the challenges I had to overcome since Kenya, and he was wise enough to know not to push it—to reopen old wounds—it was time to change the subject.

"Well, if you guys don't mind, I better drive us to the ceremony," said JB, "and it is a long ways away. If we are to get there in time we should leave no later than three."

After finishing with our lunch, Burningtree swung us by the motel so the three of us could freshen and change our clothes. Then we jumped in his black monstrosity, and were off to the flute ceremony.

Driving west of Taos, we left the mountains and entered a high flat dry plain. By my eye, it stretched for over a hundred miles in every direction. What an arid country it turned into; it was much different from the verdure of the high peaks we experienced yesterday east of the city. The mountains here in New Mexico rise like scattered islands strewn across a vast flat ocean of scrub desert. The abrupt change and mix of scenery was breathtaking.

"I was always amazed by how your ancestors were able to eke out an existence in this type of climate," said Bloome. "If it isn't scorching and dry, it's freezing and dry. It would take a very hardy people to survive in that."

"I'm as confused about it as you, Alan. These ancient people managed to occupy just about every little nook and cranny they could find out here, but whether they were my relatives or not is still an open question. I have heard it suggested that there were several different native populations that occupied these lands. We called some of them the Anasazi, which means, *not my people.*"

"This place we are going to," asked Bloome, "what can you tell us about it?"

"Oh, you are going to really enjoy it. Nature has cut the rock formations there into a natural amphitheater. I don't want to spoil it for you, but the acoustic qualities are incredible."

"And this ceremony is part of some sacred Navajo rite?"

"Oh, no, sorry, I hope you weren't misled. No, this flute concert is a recent commercial event. They just bill it as a ceremony, you know, in order to scalp the Whiteman." On hearing that Alan's lips turned down a bit. "But it is usually very good music, and they donate a portion of the proceeds to local aide groups."

While Alan sulked, I had to ask, "Why do you call it the Blue Moon Flute ceremony?"

"It is always held during a blue moon."

We had been driving west on state route 64 for three hours and headed in the direction of the four corners area. A place where the states of Utah, Colorado, Arizona, and New Mexico come together, and all of it sovereign Indian Territory. An hour before sunset JB made an abrupt left turn off the paved surface. We were now traveling south down a dusty dirt road, and at a high rate of speed. As is common in this part of the country; the road ran straight as an arrow.

About twenty miles later, and on toward evening, ahead of us the flat plains that had surrounded us for hundreds of miles suddenly fell away into a wide canyon which lay almost hidden by the dwindling light.

Over the eons infrequent rains, snow melt, and wind had cut had a wide gash into this arid land. Our roadway began to slope away and descend slowly down into the canon. To our right, a wall of rock appeared which grew taller and taller as we descended. It threw a long shadow across the prairie land.

Shortly the terrain changed again. Where the

plains above were sparsely covered with mesquite and sagebrush, the protected lowlands of the canyon grew thick with dark green piñon trees. The change in scenery was welcome one.

JB kept on driving, and my excitement kept building. The narrow dirt road hugged the rock wall as it twisted in, around, and down the natural landfalls. After several miles of twists and turns, we reached the bottom of the canyon, which was now a dry, barren, rocky wash. Tractors had leveled the middle of the arroyo to make a roadway. It appeared that no water had flowed here for as long as a person can remember.

"Almost there," JB called out. Looking behind us, I saw the headlights of more vehicles coming down the hillside. Half a mile ahead, where the canyon bottom spread wide and flat, I noticed a parking lot taking shape. Attendants with flashlights on were directing traffic. Following their lead, we parked and finally got out to stretch our legs.

Once out of the Hummer, I put my hands to my head and rubbed them all about, trying to squeeze the tiredness out of it. I wandered blindly for a moment like zombie. Straightening my spine, I shook and stretched the kinks out of my neck. Alan did the same.

Turing to look west down the long expanse of the canyon, far in the distance, the sun, now nothing more than an orange ball, rested on top of a jagged mountain that sat in silhouette. This would have made a great postcard, but I did not have my camera with me.

It was late autumn, and the evening air was cool and going to get cooler. Overhead cirrocumulus clouds veiled the heavens beyond. In the sun's setting glow, they appeared as fiery angle's wings. Their warm iridescence reflected off the canyon's sandstone walls in surreal splendor painting all the world about us in an orange glow. The reflected light gave us additional time and helped guide our footsteps.

The north edge of the canyon was a miles long wall of rock some fifty feet tall. A narrow chasm cut into it from top to bottom in one area. Widened over the eons, this slit appeared to be perhaps twenty feet wide. I watched as a steady procession of ceremony participants walked into it, and then disappeared, as if swallowed by darkness. "That's where we're headed," said JB, and the three of us walked up to the entrance to this natural hallway.

In the front, high up on its face, the ancients had carved symbols. That excited Alan. Years earlier, he wrote a book on man's symbols, and here were some new ones for him to chronicle. We stood there and studied them for a while. One was a set of parallel wavy lines, and another looked like some extinct creature, but neither JB, nor Alan, could offer clue as to what they meant.

The slot we had to walk through was narrow and deep. Its tall, nearly vertical walls blocked any view of the sky above. It would have been totally dark inside if not for a long line of lights hung alone the wall of this passageway. Workers had leveled the soft sands on the floor for easy walking.

This narrow slit wandered on for several hundred feet, then it ended, and we stepped out into a wide grotto, or side wash, that emptied into the canyon behind us. The wash angled up and rather steeply. It was perhaps one hundred yards wide, mostly flat, but filled with a confusion of paths worn around many large grass covered rocks.

Instinctively we knew that the shortest route to the amphitheater was the one that led up hill. After another quarter mile of huffing and puffing, I thanked JB for the exercise. As the path rose in front of us, we still couldn't see to the end. We kept walking and gaining in altitude; I surmised that we would soon be nearly at the level of the plains up above.

Led onward, we stepped over and around a maze of ever-larger rocks. To our left and right, above the canyon wall, the top of a stone escarpment appeared. It rimmed the sky about twenty feet above us. Soon the terrain underfoot leveled off, and we came to a narrowing in the sidewalls. One huge monolith sat directly in the middle, blocking any view ahead.

A dirt pathway split and led around to either side of it. Taking the left, we squirted through tiny slots between it and the rock wall. Immediately on the other side, the arroyo opened up into JB's natural amphitheater. This was a place where nature, through the process of erosion, had created a large depression into the Earth.

There were already a couple hundred people here, and they were quickly taking seats. This grotto, made of all stone, must reach three hundred feet across. The outside walls rose twenty feet straight up. Nothing here appeared to be manmade, but large sitting rocks had been moved and piled up. They feathered the edges all around, forming a natural grandstand. JB located a great perch for us near the front.

Smack in the middle of this rocky depression at eye height sat a huge table rock. This formed a perfect stage. The three of us chitchatted for thirty minutes as more quests ambled in and took seats.

The sun had now set, but a full moon was already rising in the east. The atmosphere was electrified. I was amazed to see so many people travel so far to sit outside in the cold under a full moon just to listen to music. My skin prickled.

In the dark, I could barely make out the figure of a man taking position at the front of the stage. He sat down cross-legged. Several soft notes from a flute signaled the start of the ceremony, and everyone immediately fell silent.

His solo rendition continued under the umbrage of filtered moonlight. The Flutists haunting notes rang softly forth, and picked up a spooky harmony as they echoed across and around the grotto. Their empty melody matched the nakedness of this vast landscape. The sound was at times lonely, and made me feel sad, and at other times, it was spiritually uplifting.

Just as he began his second piece, a spot light came on. This illumination made him the center of the world. Still sitting, he was wearing a simple buckskin outfit. With a short slender tube in his hands, he again began to play. His notes started out soft and low yet the clarity of each filled my senses. As he increased the timbre, the reverb off the grotto walls produced a tuneful harmonic that shook my soul. With my brain being pleased, I sat in awe, as he completed one solo after another.

For his fourth piece, he switched to a larger Wolf flute. His breath now rang out loud, and his pace was faster, more varied, and upbeat. Additional lights came on and bathed him in bright red and blue colors. I recognized this tune. It is often played in Western movies as a segue to highlight Indian held territory.

The combination of fast and shrill timbre with deep hollow notes had the audience stomping their feet. I sensed they were on the warpath, and my feet jumped and stomped along with them. Suddenly, a second artist ran on stage, and he began to sing. He was singing in a Native American language. Even though I had no idea what his words meant, the strength and beauty of his voice stole me away. In the spirit of the moment, I joined along with the other attendees and sang. The power of music had never moved me in this way before.

Without missing a beat between songs, a third artist, a woman, joined them up on the table rock stage. As she sang, the other two enjoined their flutes in mellow rhythm. I found the silky melody of her voice irresistible. Like a young mother singing softly to her baby, she calmed my kindred spirit. Had we met before?

In a romantic fantasy, I dreamt an eerie connection to her, as though I had known her somewhere in a distant past life. Like the other two, she was wearing a buckskin outfit that accentuated her youthful curves. Her long jet-black hair glistened as it waived in the lights. I fell in love with her. As she played for me, a strange mix of comforting and yet unmet longings overcame me.

The men now changed to large Pan Flutes. I never knew there was such a variety in flute styles, each with a characteristic sound and ability. One was as tall as a man was, and made a hearty deep sound that filled every crevice of the amphitheater. The rocks we sat on vibrated to its heavy resonant breath.

The musicians skillfully blended the hollow empty-bottle sounds it produced into a magical and stimulating rhythm. What these masters of the wind could do amazed me. Their adept combination of various instruments created in me a spectacle of new sounds and emotions. This archetypal music transcended time and space, and transported me to mystical place where the joys of the heart meet with the strength of the soul.

Through its soft lilt, piercing highs, and warbling harmonics I envisioned a forest dressed in morning, or the sights and sounds of a desert canyon on a summer evening, or of an eagle soaring in the sky high above a rocky crag. I sailed to such heights I began to cry. For months prior, all I had focused on were the deaths down in Africa, but now the haunting beauty of this music has restored a balance in me.

Their songs were more than music, they were stories painted in the air, and on the heart, and established a connection in me to this place and its natives. They are called the *People of the Great Spirit*, and a new respect for this ancient race of indigenous peoples grew in me. I have never felt closer to faraway.

For the finale, the lighting technicians projected face of a wolf with bright lights onto the wispy clouds in the sky far above. With the moon showing through behind it, the Flutists built their music to a spiritual crescendo unlike any other. We all sat in silent awe, drinking in the moment. Even without fireworks, the ending left me filled with joy, and hugging that mystical child inside.

12:

Keepers of the Gate

Along the Northern Border of Kenya
I have barely slept. My skin feels like it is crawling with ants. Finding Mike Mills, and gaining his support, have excited me. Now more than ever I am convinced that I will make a discovery to prove Carter and Bloome pretenders and criminals. We may even uncover clues to prove that today.

Last night, Mike and I reasoned out a multi-pronged approach, one that we hoped would gain us access to this questionable Preserve. Part of our plan hinges around the arrival of a missionary at the gate.

No doubt, a considerable degree of luck is involved—unless the guards take a day off. I discussed the plan with Gerald, and he is onboard with it. He is eager to join us, even against his new friend's admonition not to enter the Preserve. He was reticent at first, that is, until I explained to him the absurdity of thinking that Günter's monster would kill an entire city full of people, and yet leave a few scattered farmers, missionaries, and children alone.

Unable to sleep I rose before six. I threw on some clothes, and went out for a long walk to unclog my mind. Something kept nagging at me from deep inside, but whatever it was, I couldn't bring it to mind.

Later I stopped by the restaurant and ate breakfast. By the time I had eaten my fill, the others were already up, and gathering to leave. I found Mike and his news team in the motel's parking lot. They were mulling around at the back of their news van. He and his team had been up here in northern Kenya for two weeks. Their organization put Gerald and me to shame; you could tell these guys meant business.

Several vehicles were at their immediate disposal, one being a giant news van, or more precisely, a customized mini-bus complete with dish antenna attached to a boom lift, and numerous whip antennae. As we gathered to leave for the preserve, I took a gander inside of it. Never had I seen so much high tech electronic equipment.

Today, when we approach the guards of the gate, we want our presence to appear as large and menacing as possible. A news van showing up in their face, recording video, and beaming it live to the world should certainly make for a threatening impression.

Mike was driving a large late model SUV, and invited Gerald and I ride along with him. When we left, Mike took the lead. Two of the technicians drove alone in separate cars. Terry Gelow, the broadcast technician, drove the news van, and took up position at the rear of our cavalcade. And we were off. The plan for today was to arrive at the gate at ten.

It was a beautiful day—no wind, clear, and going to be sunny and warm. We pulled out of the parking lot at nine. With the rough, dusty roads that we have

to travel on, that should get us there with ample time
to harass the guards.

As we drove, I kept silent for the most part, just
chewing the scenery. "What scenery?" I had to ask.
This was Africa, or it was supposed to be. What
happened here? Where had all the animals gone?
What process caused all this devastation? If hordes
of people had caused it, where did they go? Then a
doubt crept in, "Perhaps a fenced preserve isn't such
a bad idea after all, but monsters? Could the rumor
of a monster be just a contrivance by the government
to keep people away?" Looking out across the
terrain, I felt saddened for the devastation to this
onetime Eden, but again wracked with self-doubt my
guts twisted in pained expectancy, "What if I am
wrong about the monster U'buntu?"

We soon turned off the highway and onto the
dirt road leading to the gate. It follows a barren
rocky swale, and the remains of a river for most of
the way there. Not a stick of growth survives along
the river's bank anymore. The entire floodway must
have been heavily forested at one time. Now erosion
has scraped all land along the water's course bare. I
doubt any new growth could take hold, not for years.
For miles around in any direction, all I can see is an
otherworldly landscape devoid of life. The sadness
and despair I feel for this land distresses me. Not
wishing to be trouble with emotions now, I decide to
compartmentalize my feelings. To keep my edge, I
must remain cold and unemotional.

About a mile from the gate, the road curves
around, and rises up out of the river bottom and
meets a broad flat plain. Our approach will be a
complete shock to the guards. They will not notice
our arrival until we are within half a mile. I want to
see the surprise in their eyes when they see our
convoy of vehicles nearing them.

As our cars came up into view of the gate, Mike slowed down. I quickly reconnoitered the gate. There they are—all three of them— and the same guards as yesterday.

We only approached to within one hundred yards, and then made an abrupt left turn. We parked in the staging area where the workers sometimes eat lunch, some two hundred yards from the fence line.

Coming to a dusty halt, Mike jumped out of his SUV, and started directing traffic. In a show of strength, the other drivers parked alongside of us. We were amassing our forces.

Once we were all out of our vehicles, and the dust had settled, we gathered for a last minute strategy meeting. All the while, the guards stood at the entrance to the Preserve, and eyed us with keen interest.

* * * * *

Lieutenant Khan was well aware of who Mike Mills was. He also knew all of the members of his news team. Their manner, presence, and vehicles are totally out of place against the stark backwardness of northern Kenya, and they had been to the gate before. He was surprised to notice Dr. Henderson in his company though. Concerned, he put in an urgent call to his boss in the Kenyan Ministry of Defense in Nairobi.

"Um'fume, it is Khan. The psychiatrist has returned, and he is with the news crew that has been nosing around out up here for the past two weeks."

"So they have banded together. Have they approached the gate yet?"

"No, the six of them are hanging out in a worker rest area. They appear to be setting up their news van to take videos of our operation here."

"They have done that before," said Um'fume. "There is nothing new for them to report, but the presence of Henderson is interesting. That must be it. They must have some new plan in mind, one that involves Henderson. You said that yesterday that he wanted to go into the Preserve. Their only resource for information about what would be going on inside is from someone living in there, and the only person to approach the gate regularly is one of the missionaries. Do you expect him today?"

"No, he rarely makes the journey more than three times a week. I would not expect him until tomorrow morning, but always around eleven."

"If the missionary shows up and decides to talk with them, well, there is nothing we can do about that. However, I expect more from them, I expect them to demand entrance to the Preserve. They may be intent on using the missionary as a wedge to gain access, and with their cameras rolling; it would be difficult and suspicious for us to say no.

This situation could get out of control. I must talk with them. ... Khan, what I want you to do is to warn them off for today. We cannot let them in there. Who knows what might happen?" Taking a long moment to think, Um'fume then said, "Here is what we will do. When they approach you, and demand access, or to talk with the missionary, tell them that he will not show up today. That he will not return to the gate until tomorrow, but do not tell them that I am coming up there. I will be there in the morning. If they show up again tomorrow, I will deal with them."

"Yes, sir. There is something else, sir, the Marks have returned." After a long pause,

"I understand. I will see you tomorrow around ten in the morning."

* * * * *

We had no more than arrived when we noticed Khan move over to his jeep. He jumped in, and held the mic to his mouth.

"He didn't waste any time getting on the phone," said Mike. "Terry, tell me you have your receiver set on automatic? I really would like to know what he is saying."

"Of course it's on. I always leave it on. God knows what juicy gossip we might pick up on?"

"Then why don't you turn the van to face them, and make it look like you are setting up to broadcast. Then go and see what they were just talking about?"

A twinge of discomfort shot through me. I was stunned at how easily and cavalierly they were monitoring every transmission. My concern was for my own privacy. Gerald apparently felt some concern also, and in one of those mysterious moments of universal interconnectivity, we both turned and gave each other a knowing look. Then I turned to Mike and asked, "You can actually monitor and record other people's phone calls?"

With a lack of indignation, he turned to me and said, "Don't be so surprised Bill. The airwaves are free. If you put it out there, and it is not encrypted, we can listen in." I found his response somewhat disconcerting, but at the same time interesting. We were eavesdropping in on, or spying on, the enemy. That excited me, and I threw any concern over invading someone else's privacy out the door.

"Alright, we have plenty of time until the missionary is supposed to arrive. Let's use that time to plan our approach. Barry, I want you on the handheld. And don't be afraid to get that big lens right in their faces."

Just then, Terry Gelow yelled out to us from the

rear of his van, "Hey, you guys should listen to this."

"What is it Terry," asked Mike.

"You were right about Khan. He contacted his boss, Mr. Um'fume. We have his whole conversation on tape. They are on to us. They even suspect that you are waiting for the missionary to show up. However, Khan said he doubts that the missionary will show up today. Here, I'll replay it so all of you can listen in." Terry turned up the volume and we all listened to the conversation Khan had only moments earlier.

"That is very interesting. They have figured out our plan. It is also very odd. Why would Um'fume want to come up here, let alone talk directly with us," said Mike, who took a moment to digest this new information, and then said, "Well, you heard it, Bill. Your plan is going to work. They'll be forced to let us in there if we challenge them in front of the missionary, but that won't happen until tomorrow."

"Huh? What?" I was lost in thought over the last tidbit Khan said to Um'fume, and did not hear what Mike was saying. Something Khan said caught my attention. He mentioned something about a Mark. My thoughts ran to what John Carter had said. He often talked about a mark, one that took the shape of a large moth, but I had never placed any significance in it. Further, there was something about Um'fume's intonation. After hearing of this mark, I sensed fear in his voice.

"Bill, I said your plan is going to work."

"Oh, yes."

"Earth to Bill. ... You alright, buddy?"

"Yes, sorry, Mike. I was just lost in thought."

"OK, if the missioner isn't expected until tomorrow, we might as well pack it in here for now."

"What? Leave now? No. No! That would look too suspicious. ... We had better wait. In fact, we should make a concerted attempt to push by the guards and enter the Preserve today; otherwise it would look as though we are listening to their transmissions."

"Yes. You're right," said Mike. "So let's do this. How about we just sit here and make it look like we are waiting for someone or something. Then, just at eleven thirty, you, Gerald, and I will storm the gate. Terry will stay inside the van, Barry will be on the hand held, and Andrew will pose as back up and bodyguard. We'll have then outnumbered."

"Now that's a plan."

* * * * *

Eleven thirty was well over an hour away. The news crew had several pair of large binoculars with them. To pass the time I grabbed a pair and jumped up on the SUV's rear bumper. It was the perfect height on which to rest my elbows while holding the binocs comfortably to my eyes.

I first used them to leer at the guards. They knew I was watching them, but they didn't flinch a muscle. I then turned my attention to the Preserve. Using the spyglasses, I followed the dirt path, the one supposedly taken several times a week by the missionary. It lead in a straight line south across the wasteland, and then disappeared into a forest. What a strange and unnatural contrast my eyes were bearing witness to. The forest line, about a mile distant, stretched to the mountains way to the east, and filled all of the land southern more. This scene was exactly as Carter portrayed it. At first blush, this shocking and otherworldly visage might cause one to conger up thoughts of monsters on the attack, but I suspected only human forces were at play here.

The air right now was calm, dry, silent—had an almost eerie and unnerving feel to it. Mike joined me up on the cars bumper. Using another pair of binoculars, I watched him scan the waste area. By his intent, I suspected he was searching for something specific; a sign, no doubt, of where his beloved's bones now lay.

I scrutinized his viewing for some time as he scanned right and left inside the preserve. Then he fixed his gaze left of us, about halfway between the fence and the forest. I quickly joined him. In the vast barren waste, one lone dead pole of wood stood crookedly. It had a double nodded cross branch jutting from it about a foot or two down from its top making it appear to be a tall cross. Was it a crude grave marker, or just the remains of a long dead tree? Who knew? This was just one more mystery in this land of mysteries. Inside the Preserve, grasses had sprouted; the tall ones grew in clumps obscuring our close inspection of the ground. Given time, this land would heal itself.

Several times over the next hour, we repeated our viewing. Making it appear obvious that we were searching the open expanse of the Preserve as though expecting to see someone appear. The guards never approached us while we waited, but were quick to eye our every move.

At half past eleven, our gang of five huddled together. We were ready to make our concerted effort to burst through the guards and enter the Preserve. We waited shortly while Terry raised the van's telescopic boom, and then pointed its large satellite dish straight at the gate. This did nothing, but it did look menacing.

Then we made our move. Mike, Gerald, and I walked straight towards the guards. Barry and Andrew followed a few steps behind us. They were carrying a portable high-res television camera, and were filming the whole affair.

Our action immediately caught the attention of Khan and his underlings. Khan, who had been sitting in his jeep, sprang out and forcefully approached us. The other two guards remained at their post blocking the gate's opening. "Stop," he yelled. "You have no business here. You are ordered to leave."

Then Mike put his six foot two, two hundred twenty pound frame, right in Khan's face and said, "Look, Khan, I do have business here." Nearly shouting, Mike said, "The Press have a right to investigate. The people of this country have a right to know what is happening up here. Your building this fence to keep people from moving freely is an international crime." All the while Mike was blathering on; Barry had that TV camera, with its little red light blinking, steady on Khan's face.

Our bold approach proved too much for the poor fellow. We had frightened him. His hands began to shake noticeably. I watched as he fumbled to unholster his sidearm. His hand trembled as he brought it up to threaten us. The muscles of his arm tensed rigid in an attempt to control his onrush of emotion—we had pushed him too far.

His two comrades quickly ran up to join him. Standing at his flanks, they raised their rifles and pointed them at us. Suddenly the fear of a nervous tic jerking at a trigger causing a gun to fire and kill one of us seemed all too possible.

Again Khan raised his voice and nervously said, "Enough, you have no rights here. Now, all of you leave. There is no one coming for you to talk with today. My boss will talk with you tomorrow."

We had pushed it far enough. Further, he had let it slip that we should return the next day. I knew his boss was going to be here tomorrow, but what he wanted to say to us was a mystery. At any rate, we sensed that it was time to back off. Putting our hands slowly up in the air, as if in surrender, we retreated to the rest area, where we gave each other some high fives. Wasting no time, we got into our vehicles and left, spitting a cloud of dust gate-ward.

"Wow, that was intense," said Mike.

"Yes it was," I said. Safely back on the road, I noticed that I was sweating. "Wow, what an experience." Reaching for my wrist, I counted my heartbeats, "Whew. ... Well, we know that tomorrow we have an appointment with his boss, but what could he possibly want to say to us?" My two accomplices just shrugged their shoulders.

About a mile down the dirt road, Mike halted the progress of our caravan. We were now well out of sight of Khan and his guards of the gate. Here, where the road turns west and back toward the main highway, it bottoms out beside the eroded expanse of a river. Frequent traffic has worn a roadway leading out onto the rivers floodway.

Mike turned his SUV off onto this rough passage. There was little water this time of year, and most of what we riding on was hard compacted dry mud. He drove out to the middle of this dry wash and stopped. "I have a surprise for you two," he said. "I think you are really going to enjoy my new toy."

The other vehicles followed suit, and parked alongside. They had secretly planed something. We were far enough away, and below their line of sight of the guards, so they would be unaware of our presence here. He beckoned us to get out, and the three of us walked over to the news van where the engineers were already out and toying around with some object.

"Come on guys," said Mike. "Take a look at this." Terry Gelow and the other two techs were handling something.

"My god," I said in amazement. "It's a miniature airplane. It looks just like one of those predator UAV's."

"Right you are, Bill. This is the latest in non-military aerial surveillance. It's silent, it's programmable, it has GPS guidance built-in, it has two high-def cameras, it has an extended range, and it can soar for hours."

"Wow," said Gerald. I thought his eyes might pop out.

"Now, let's spend the afternoon doing some recon of that Preserve. In particular, I want to search for that supposed site where you said M died. Gerald, do you have those coordinates with you?"

"No, they are on the photos which I left back at the motel, but I do have the proximity of those locations burned into my brain. I can find it. Easy."

"Great, let's scope out the Preserve this afternoon. When we go in there tomorrow, I want the three of us to have a perfect mental picture of the terrain. ... Terry, get that thing in the air."

Along the side of the minibus, the techs hurriedly put together a metal launch rail. It looked to be twenty feet long. The UAV's propeller was located at the aft. Though possible, it would be difficult and dangerous to launch it by hand. We watched as the technicians put the four foot long UAV into a sling, and set it atop of the railing. They started the engine, and then released a pin freeing it. The small plane then shot down the length of the metal rail gaining speed. I watched as it flew off and disappeared into the blue sky and towards the Preserve.

"OK, guys," said Terry, "come on in side."

Though it was cramped inside, we didn't mind. This was exciting stuff. Barry and Andrew were already guiding the UAV with a joystick, and watching its flight on two large monitors. It was sending back high-resolution video of the terrain below. I relished in this voyeur moment as we spied secretly on those below.

"We have programmed it to fly first to the missionaries' village. Once there it will switch to a search program, and fly in an area wide pattern. The video it sends back to us will be processed here in this computer where it will be stitched together to form a detailed stereoscopic map of the surrounding area. Once we have a complete map, we can then order it to focus on a specific spot if you like." The process of flying the search pattern took over two hours. I was so enthralled by the show that I lost track of time.

I was thrilled at how my plan was progressing. It just kept getting better. With this new tool, and with the support of my new friends, I am closer than ever to putting a noose around the neck of Dr. Carter and his tall pudgy buffoon of accomplice, Dr. Bloome. Tomorrow I will have the evidence I need to blow apart his story of monsters used to cover-up a murder. This man not only took advantage of the innocence of the peoples of this country, he also wasted several months of my time while he was lying to me about needing therapy. I will make him pay for it.

13:

Whisper Willow

Town Square, Taos, New Mexico

Being on this escapade with Bloome has been restful and interesting, and there is certainly no stress here; stay out late as you like, sleep in to whenever. Yesterday was no different; our return from the flute ceremony last night was quite late, so we all slept in.

This morning, Alan and I were set to say goodbye to JB. Having grown to enjoy his cheerful and fun loving attitude these past days, we were both sorry to see him go. The three of us met at the town square in Taos; there is a coffee shop there that he likes. It was just after ten.

After eating breakfast, we walked Burningtree out to his tank of a car, or as he calls her, Guzzler. He was returning to his home in Santa Barbara, California, and before he left we shared a few last words together, "Here," he said, "I got these two parting gifts for you two. I think you earned them."

Then opening up, and reaching into the back of his Hummer, he pulled out these two hats. "Now, think of these as official Indian merit badges, of a sort."

He then, as if part of a ceremony, placed the cowboy hats on our heads, took a step back, and with a sly smile, shook his head back and forth several times. Then said, "Now don't you two look ridiculous." Then he let out with one of his characteristic hearty laughs.

He next opened the door to his trusty steed and got in. I did find it comical watching him have to climb up several steps to get into the seat of that black monster. "Now, don't you guys forget, next time you go out in search of ghosts, or UFO's, call me. I want to be there with you." We nodded in agreement, and waved goodbye as we watched him drive away.

"Well, our ranks are swelling Bloome. What do you think of that?"

"I think that it's good, and I really like JB's jovial demeanor."

"Yes, he does add some color to every situation. I'm not sure I like letting him have the last laugh though."

"Yes, I agree, but he is right, you do look ridiculous with that thing on your head."

"Actually, you look quite good in yours, Alan. I think you should wear it for the rest of the day."

"Oh, for once I agree with you John, after all, of the two of us, I am the statelier."

"Statelier? So that is what you call it?"

"Yes, come on, let's walk over to our car and put these amusing gifts inside where they will be safe." We stowed our cowboy hats in the jeep.

Each day a small army of Native Americans come to the square to sell jewelry, art, and other trinkets that they have made. They show up about this time of the morning. You can find them sitting on the sidewalk under the shade of the storefront awnings with their backs to the walls, and their wares spread out on a blanket on the walkway in front of them.

"This investigation went faster than I thought it would," said Alan, "We still have plenty of time to spend here in New Mexico before our scheduled departure, and how do you propose we burn it up?"

"Right now I'm going to check out what the Indians are selling over there, Alan, and see if I can find something for Amy."

"Good idea, I'd better tag along to help you with your choices?"

We walked across the square to where a number of vendors were just setting up. There was quite an assortment of authentic Native American products laid out in front of us. I glanced over the jewelry. "Now just what would my wife like?" I asked. There was also a large assortment of leather purses and bags. The pottery was beautifully painted, but bulky and fragile. I settled on something delicate and ornate. A bracelet and matching earrings made of sterling silver, some orange colored stone, and turquoise.

"I'm sure Amy will love that, John," mentioned Alan.

I finalized my purchase with American made Greenbacks. The morning air was still, and the sun warming. This time of year, it sat lower to the horizon. Looking south, its golden lilt was filtering through the trees in the square. All seemed at peace here, and I was happy again just to be alive.

Just as I was enjoying the warmth of sunlight heating my skin, I suddenly felt a cold chill blow down my back. A flashback to six months earlier in Kenya hit me.

My perfect moment had been shattered. All of a sudden, all of those horrid memories again flooded my consciousness. A bright multi-colored aural flash seemed to rip through my eyeballs. I staggered.

Alan, standing beside me, sensed my unease. With my head pointing down, I covered my eyes with my hands. "This can't be happening again," I said. Fear over the onset of a blinding headache gripped me. I turned to face the square, and asked Alan to walk me over to a bench where I could sit and rest.

As we reached the curb, only feet in front of us, I sensed something, and looked up. The glare of sunlight shimmering through the trees caused me squint. Whatever it was, it drew my eyes to a park bench. There was something sitting there. It seemed to have the appearance of a man, but there was something more, the person's true appearance seemed somehow hidden and unclear.

Was this the bright sun-glare playing tricks on my mind? Although the man was dressed in black, he appeared bathed inside a bright light. As if this person, or this being, were able to control and project, or manipulate the image he put forth.

Unable to stand on my own, I was leaning against Bloome for support. I stopped him from continuing forward.

I analyzed this apparition further. I stared at it. Our eyes locked. We shared an odd sense of recognition. Then I noticed something. The curly, almost blond hair that stuck out from beneath his hat, my man-in-black was actually Oddball Don, or the Nagual. He had returned.

He was clad in all black; deep dark all-consuming black; black shoes, black pants held up by a black belt with a silver and turquoise buckle, black long-sleeved shirt, turquoise bolo necktie clasp with black cord. A black hat even hid his head. I did not know the type of hat he wore, but I had seen them worn before in western movies, and always on the head of some renegade.

"Alan, do you see that?" He looked up and over to where I was staring.

"Dear god, a man-in-black, in real life, and right in front of me. How exciting, I never thought I would ever see one in the person."

"No, Alan, take another look."

Squinting to block out some of the sun's glare, "Oh, yes, now I see that it's Don. That is odd. Could he and a man-in-black be one and the same?"

As I tried to consider the import of what Alan had just asked, Don stood up and waved at us.

My mind at that moment was off in some vaporous world of triple counterpoint. My vision confused by aural color spikes, and my thinking obscured by conflicting thoughts. There was no way I could think to move. The Nagual must have sensed that, and came trotting over to us.

"I told you guys we would meet again," he said, and in an overly happy and hearty tone, speaking as one who has lived alone, and devoid of meaningful company for a prolonged period of time. Then, remarking on my distress, "John, are you alright? You look a bit lost."

My mind was reeling with the onset of an aural migraine, but our King of Gab insisted on making a simplistic understatement. "Don, we need to get him some place where he can sit down."

"No better place than that park bench there. Come on, I'll help you walk him over." Skirting my sides, together they escorted me back to his bench.

"Let's all sit here and rest a while," Don said. "This square has curative power. I come here often to sit and meditate. You will feel better very soon, John."

I heard Don's words. This time he struck me as more caring than oddball, but I still thought of him as different, and I felt his olden times simplicities an affront to my modern sensibilities.

Alan knew all too well the seriousness of my problems, and was understandably concerned for my health. "John, is there something I can get you?"

"Why yes, Alan. What I need is an ice-cold coke, and please, get something for our friend Don here as well."

Alan walked over to a vendor stand located at the southeast corner of the square to get us some drinks. Don stayed with me. My ESP was kicking in again, and I distinctly felt an unusual warmth emanate from the man. I sensed he longed for and enjoyed my referring to him as a 'friend,' as though he had none. Why did this man appear so isolated and alone? Why was his presence so at odds with those around him? Aside from a few quirky beliefs, his aspect was, as far as I could tell, as conversant and as normal as any other persons was. His lonely misery touched my heart, and inside of me, a desire was growing to understand what made him the way he is.

"John, tell me about your encounter with the Skinwalker." Don was a simple person, with a simple and direct manner. He had no need for perfunctory small talk, and dove right for to heart of any problem. Thanks to Bloome's homework assignment several nights ago, my understanding of the term, *Skinwalker* has been refreshed. I took him to be asking about my encounter with U'buntu, but was U'buntu a Skinwalker?

"Don, six months ago I was sent to Africa to investigate a site of mass deaths which appeared to be the result of a virus. There was no virus. The deaths, or murders, were caused by what Alan calls an extra-dimensional creature whose name was U'buntu. That creature made contact with me twice.

Each time it left me scarred, physically and mentally."

"But you weren't killed like the others. For some reason this demon spared your life and it formed an alliance with you. You two, you and it, are still connected, and will be until you sever its control of you, and you of it."

"Me, of it? I have no control over, or need of it?"

"In ways you might not be aware of, you are still using its power."

"But how can that be?"

"Think on it, John. What powers have you gained these last six months?"

"Powers?" I thought on that while I drank down some coke. "Do you mean my new extra sensory powers?"

"Yes, that could be part of it," he said. "Does it also feel to you like a door has been opened for you, enabling you a greater awareness of things?" I didn't have to think long on that question. The answer was obvious. I have had episodes of clairvoyance, and I have also gained a greater sense of truth speak. I can more readily tell when people are lying to me, even though privately I obfuscate this ability.

"You are suggesting that my psychic abilities are an effect shared with that Monster?"

"Our minds can reach out and connect with the minds of other people, other creatures, or demons. I do not understand the science behind this, but experience has shown me that it is true. When we connect-up psychically with other creatures, we can take on and use their powers. I think that religion calls the association with demons possession, but it is a two-way street, with each party taking on some of the abilities of the other. In your case, you seem to have been touched by a powerful demon. If you can't control it, you might consider letting it go."

"Letting "*It*" go!?" I mouthed those words while looking him straight in the face. Was he kidding? I wanted to be as far away from U'buntu as I could get. I was also studying Don's face for tells. There is no doubt that he is convinced about his beliefs. Should I be as certain? ... The caffeine in my soda was helping to alleviate my symptoms. Feeling better, I wanted to know more about our new friend's background. "Tell me a little about yourself Don. I know that Burningtree's father was your friend. JB said that you were from LV. Do you have family there?"

"No, I have no family. They all died many, many, years ago. I was an only child, and no real evidence remains regarding my parents history. The place where we lived is now nothing but a ghost town."

On hearing mention of a ghost town, Alan's ears pricked up. "Ghost town, I wasn't aware that there were any ghost towns nearby? I wrote a book about ghost towns."

"Dear Christ, Alan," I said, "is there anything you haven't written about?"

"No, seriously," he said, "think about it, aside from my historical curiosity, if you want to find ghosts, what better place to go."

Now I was starting to get a headache of another kind. From UFO's to disembodied souls, this man's interests are all over the board. Well, he might be quirky, but he is a friend, and there is nothing wrong with a little harmless curiosity.

"Alright, Alan, let's let Don continue to tell us about his own life."

"Those many years ago, our little town came down with a plague. Everyone got sick, and then they started to die. After my parents died, I was left all alone, that is when my mentor found me and adopted me. He was Navajo, but not of pure blood. He had some Apache in him. Though his mixed blood kept the Navajo of that time from accepting him as a member of their tribe, they still feared him for his power, and allowed him access to their lands and sacred grounds. He knew the Navajo Way well, and taught me the healing ceremonies. He also gave me my own Skinwalker, and I use it unto this day."

Bloome was excited to hear of this supposed Indian lore, and eagerly jotted down all of Don's non-sequitous drivel on a notepad, no doubt, for later use in another one of his many books on the unreal. I was content to be amused, so I just sat back and listened as they talked.

"Could you tell us how you came into contact with this creature?" asked Alan.

"You mean my Skinwalker? ... It was in the summer following my parents death, and the death of the little town of Whisper Willow. When we left that place, we traveled west for many miles. We were living then in the Canyon Lands. We built a Hogan there. These were very tough times, and with little to eat, my mentor said that I needed the help of a Skinwalker to survive. He took me to the top of a tall Mesa. There, at the edge of a cliff, I sat out on a flat rock. We were high up, and I could see forever. He told me to sit still in the center of this circle he made.

For safety, I had a rope tied around my waist. Then, while he chanted, he made these sand paintings inside of the circle. Hours passed and nothing happened. I became weary and struggled not to nod off, but it was too much. My head would fall down in dream sleep, and I would have a thought of some animal. Afraid, I would jerk awake.

Several times, I would see these creatures in my mind, and snap out of my sleep. Finally, I nodded off into a deeper sleep. That is when I had a dream of an eagle. I saw it soar over me. In tight circles, it flew above me, and I could hear its loud scree, scree.

Then in my dream, I saw it dive down and hit me.

Frightened, I immediately woke from my dream. Curios over my vision, I turned to look at my mentor. He put his finger first to his lips, telling me to be silent, and then he carefully pointed straight up into the sky. I looked up. There, above me, was what appeared to be an eagle circling above us.

My Nagual cautioned my not to move. The creature circled several times. It kept screaming out its loud call again and again. Then, in a moment of terror for me, it dove down. I was looking right at it as it hit me. I felt it dissolve into my body, and we became one."

"My mentor went wild with joy. He said I had received the most powerful of Skinwalker—the eagle."

Don continued to relate the story of his early life for us. Alan was ecstatic. All week he had wanted to hear some real Indian lore. Our times spent with Burningtree, though fun and interesting, provided him with nothing new regarding the heart and soul of the aboriginal people of the southwest. However, here was a man who possessed a wealth of arcane knowledge.

As the morning wore on, Alan and Don continued to yak it away. The Nagual did not seem to mind having his personal life probed by Bloome's inquisitions. While they talked, the fierceness of my infliction waned, but so did the warm sunlight. A cold front was moving in. The sky above first hazed up, and drew ever darker. As the cloud layer lowered, the air cooled, and chilled my spirits as well. I suggested to Alan that we invite our friend to a warm spot where we could sit, talk, and eat lunch.

Over lunch, Don talked more about his parents, and this old town of Whisper Willow, now turned a ghost town. I did not know that Alan considered himself the penultimate ghost hunter, but he was really into that stuff, and practically begged Don to lead us to his old and forgotten home. Apparently, the lost town of Whisper Willow was only a few hours away to the east. We had the time, and with nothing else to do this afternoon...

Drive to Whisper Willow

I was warming up to Oddball Don, but that doesn't mean that I still don't think of him as quite off. He doesn't fit in with today's world; that much is obvious. It was as though he had been ripped out of time, say, from somewhere back in the eighteen hundreds, and he would not be a person well socialized for that era either. Yet again, there are those who think he possesses extraordinary knowledge, including Alan.

We left the artsy village of Taos for the ghost town of Whisper Willow. Don said that it lies some twenty miles east of LV. With him as our guide, he directed us to a road north of town that ran by a ski resort, which then led to a state route that skirted the eastern side of the Rocky Mountains.

This shortcut would take hours off our drive time. While I drove, I listened as Bloome burned his tongue off pumping Don for his secrets of Indian ceremonies. Though I liked Don, I must admit he does project a creepy aura about him. He was dressed in all black. Alan initially thought him one of his Men in Black. This brought back memory flashes of my own encounter with a real Man in Black earlier this year in that infamous bar in Kisumu, Kenya.

That man was there in the bar, I know he was, but he wasn't. He sat at a table behind me, yet none of my friends saw him sitting there; then he seemed just to disappear. Interesting, and now I have somewhat of an apparition sitting in my back seat.

This was in some wise spooky, and as we drove, I eyed him in the rearview mirror many times. With my imagination twirling, I wondered if he could be a man in black. Moreover, could he be the very same man in black that I saw in that bar?

When we first met Don, he was sitting in a window, alone, and staring blankly out into the vast emptiness of the plains east of LV. What was he thinking of, or viewing in his mind at the time?

Perhaps he is practiced in the art of remote viewing. Able to sit, and in his mind, actually see distant places, as though her were really there. As Burningtree suggested, the three of us are caught up in some strange nexus, one where the flow of time and the problems of distance matter not. If so, then Don could've been my man in black in that bar six months ago.

His appearance there, sitting, studying me, could've been from some place here in far off New Mexico. He could have been witnessing the events that played around me in Africa. Then he waited, somehow knowing that I would show up here in the future. But why? What could he want?

Of a more stable note, I was still searching for clues to what made him the way he was. It is more than his odd belief in demonic possession, or that paintings, made of sand, can have the power to heal. No, and it was more than his backwards, yesteryear style of speech. His personality showed a detached humbleness to it, yet he wasn't a timid person. I suppose that kind of social awkwardness comes with being out of place, or out of time.

Just as my mind was thinking on what life's events could have moulded this guy, in a weird case of synchronicity, I heard him say, "You know, I had a very harsh time growing up. Life on the plains was very hard. Then my parents dying ended my childhood." It was almost as though he knew somehow in his mind that I was trying to figure him out, and he answered me.

Then Alan continued, "I am sorry to hear that Don. How old were you when they died?"

"Only twelve."

"That must have been very sad time for you."

"Sad? Was it sad?" he said. "Contrasted with what? People today have no idea. Life back then was so demanding we had no time to be sad. Even as a child, I was forced to get up at dawn, and the chores usually lasted into the evening. When your every day is a struggle, sad takes on a different meaning. Kids today have no idea how easy they have it. There were not any other kids out here to play with anyway. I do know I loved my mom and dad, and I missed them so."

We had already passed the small town of Las Vegas, and had turned east on the interstate, and were now swallowed up by the Great Plains. As I listened to Don's saga of his early life, I gazed out and across the plains trying to imagine what it might be like to live here even today. There isn't much out here, just miles and miles of empty grasslands. It's not bad if you are a prairie dog, sky hawk, or even a cow, but for people, the boring desolation must have been mind crippling. It is a beautiful place to drive through, but to spend day after day with nothing other than a lizard for company—that's not for me.

Fencing lined both sides of the highway we were driving on—hundreds of miles of it. Roughly forty miles east of LV, Don directed us to turn south, and off the interstate. Well, so much for his accuracy in judging distances.

There was no intersection where we turned, just an opening broken into the barbed wire fence.

A rusted steel fence enclosing an ancient, yet barren wasteland, I found the contrast prescient. Man, battling against nature, with all his myriad contrivances at hand to divide and control her, yet with time on her side, in the end, she always wins.

We had turned onto a dirt road, one that received rare use. The land here is fragile, and scars, such as those made by a car tire, or wagon wheel, can last for centuries.

As wide and open as these lands are, one would expect to be able to see where the road turned or · ended, but this one just kept on going, and seemed to vanish into infinity.

"Almost there guys, just another twenty miles, or so, you will see it. There will be a large stand of trees surrounding a natural spring, the only one for miles," chimed Don.

Don's directions were as bleak as his syntax. The place we were looking for was not located on any map, and there are not any visible landmarks within eyesight to guide with. How frontier man navigated out here is a mystery.

"Don, you say there is a natural well there," I asked. "This land is flat and dry, how could that be?"

"It is a spring actually. You will see. It is all part of an ancient aquifer underlying this entire area. In a few places, it comes rushing to the surface. The Indians knew of all of them, but when the white man came, he built towns around them, and pushed the Indians away."

Roads conditions forced me to slow to thirty and below. After driving for half an hour, we approached a small rocky rise. The road made a long lazy sweep to the right and circled around it. After we came around the corner of the rise the terrain gently fell away to reveal a wide shallow valley that was previously completely hidden from sight.

There, not more than half a mile in front of us, was a large stand of trees. "That's it," yelled Don. "That's Whisper Willow."

The stand of cottonwood trees stretched laterally in front of us, east to west. The west end of it looked up and far off into the nothingness of the prairie. At the east end, a pond, overgrown with reeds, and circled with willow trees, spilled a gentle flow of water down into a swale. The swale wandered off to the east, and then turned south and disappeared.

"So this is Whisper Willow?" I asked.

"Yes, this is where my parents died. Come on and park, and we will have a look," he said excitedly.

"So, where are all of the buildings?" asked Alan.

"Oh, no buildings are left. Time has turned them back into the dust they came from. The last time I was here was some forty years ago. At that time, you could still see the basic outline of where the structures stood, and there were still quite a few artifacts left strewn all about. I suppose that pickers have been here since, and have scavenged most of what remained. The main street was there on the north left side of the pond. The graves were over there at the far end of the grove of trees. Come on and let's have a walk around."

We parked, I was careful to wait for Don to open his door and get out, and then I turned to Bloome and gave him a quizzical look. The non-appearance, or ghost of a ghost town may have mystified me, but Alan looked crestfallen. He wanted haunted buildings to creep around in. Yeah, as though ghosts are tied only to structures. To cheer him up, I said, "Come on big fella. Let's get out and stretch our legs. Remember, ghosts don't need houses."

The stand of trees was huge and growing wild. At about two acres in size, it stood in stark contrast to the barrenness of the surrounding prairie. If this place had ever been occupied, no obvious evidence remains. Nature had won out again.

"It is not what I expected as a ghost town," mentioned Bloome. "I was looking forward to seeing old rundown buildings from yesteryear."

"It was here," said Don. "Our house sat there. Our barn and stable were just over there. At the time of its death, the town consisted of only four main buildings. A dry goods store, a place to eat and drink, a multi-purpose building for meetings, and my dad's blacksmith shop."

"So, what happened here, Don?" asked Bloome. "How did your parents die, and where did the buildings of this the town go?"

"It was all part of the changing times in the old west. If you look hard enough, you might still find a few ruts over there along the path of the creek. Wagon trains used to follow it. It used to have more water in it. This town was once considered as a possible route of the famous Santa Fe Trail, but that never happened. My parents and the other families who moved here had gambled and lost. The main trail ultimately formed north of here."

"That spelled doom for our little town. Fewer and fewer travelers found their way to it. Then the building of the train lines forced development elsewhere. We found ourselves nearly cut off from civilization. Then the sickness came."

"What I remember is that it was late fall. On a cold and overcast day, like today, a caravan of only a few wagons wandered in. My ma said they had the sickness, and the town's folk sent them on their way, but it was too late. About five days later, people in this town began to come down sick. I mean really sick. Then my parents caught it. They all died you know. Everyone in town got ill and died."

"My dad went first. Then other residents caught ill, and in a few days, they were dead. My mom was the last to go. I was at her side when she passed on. She knew the Great Spirit would take her that morning, and that then there would be no one to care for me. I recall her last words; shaking with a terrible fever, she turned to me and said, "Sorry, Donny." Then she gave out a big gasp, and went away. Frightened, I ran out of the house. With tears in my eyes, I ran to the middle of town, looking, hoping, to find someone to call out to, but there was no one."

"It was right over there." He pointed to a patch of barren ground a few hundred feet away. "I remember standing there and crying. I was all alone in a town full of dead people. As tears fell, I stood trembling, and I tried to think about what I should do. That is when something caught my attention and I turned around. I saw the figure of a man approaching the town from the east. He was on foot, and dressed in all black."

"I stood in front of him in the middle of the road as he walked up to me. He seemed to have a knowledge of what had happened here, but he wasn't afraid of the sickness. As I thought on my parent's death, a tear fell down my cheek. Stretching out his hand, he wiped away my tear, and then said in broken English, do not worry little Nagual, I will take you with me. That was the first time I ever heard that term, and did not know what it meant. But I sensed a gentle kindness in him, and accepted him as my mentor."

"He said we should put the bodies in a place where they would be safe. The town was only a decade old, and had no cemetery yet. We found a restful place at the edge of the stand of trees. That is where we lined up the bodies."

"We covered them up with dirt as best we could, and placed pieces of wood shaped into a cross on top of each. Then he told me we had to set fire to the buildings. I ran into my house to grab a sack and put some of my things in it. He ran in after me and stopped me."

"He said, 'No, take nothing; it will only hurt you later on in your life.' At that time, I had no idea what he meant. I dropped the sack, but one thing I could not part with was a picture of my mom and dad. I quickly bent it and stuck it into my back pocket, and have had it with me ever since."

"After taking the horses to safety, we set fire to the buildings. Without wanting to stay and watch the fire, he told me to get on a horse, and we rode off to the west."

Alan was in near tears from listening to Don's story. Don was misting up too, and needing time to recompose. He wandered off to the far west side of the stand of trees to be alone.

I was still questioning whether a town could have ever been here or not. If his story was true, time and the elements had erased every sign that civilization ever visited this remote oasis.

Looking down at the ground, I noticed a change in the color of the dirt. The sandy brown clay had an orange-red rusty spot in it. I kicked at it with the tip of my shoe, and hit something hard. Using the heel of my shoe as a pickaxe, I rammed it into the dry soil and unearthed an old iron object. Reaching down, I grabbed it, and gave it a good jar to remove the encrusted dirt. "Hah, look here Bloome, I just found a horseshoe."

"Yes you did, they're supposed to be good luck," he said.

"That was one of the most tragic stories I have ever heard, Alan. That is if it's true."

"You have doubts?"

"Well, let's snoop around a little and see if we can find more evidence that a town full of tall buildings once sat here."

While Don was off having a moment of solace in the woods, Alan and I scuffed around in the dirt trying to see if we could kick up another relic from the past. If a town did stand here once, nature had done a very good job of erasing any trace of it. If scavengers have been here to loot artifacts and antiques, they must have brought vacuum cleaners along with them.

It had been over a century since Whisper Willow supposedly burnt, and I know that primitive settlements thrown up quickly were probably built without cement foundations. Therefore, I asked myself the question, "If they were built out of all wood, and then torched, wouldn't some ashes remain, or had enough time elapsed for them also to have blown away?"

Not having a map of the town, or specific directions as where to poke around, the two of us just walked side by side, up and down the spot where Don said was the center of the town. The scene of two guys scuffing in the dirt, and walking stick legged like penguins must have looked hilarious.

"I'm not seeing anything, Alan."

"No, neither am I."

"Do you suppose that they could have erected buildings here without scoring the dirt? I mean, I don't see any depressions, or unusual lines, or anything that would hint that modern humans had built a town here."

"It is perplexing," said Alan. I was having a hard time getting him to engage in conversation. He was still in a bit of a funk. Things old have never enthralled me, so the absence of rotting structures didn't bother me, but Alan had built up some high expectations, and was saddened not to have rickety structures to snoop around in. Thinking on ways to cheer him up, I then said, "Come on Alan. Cheer up. I am excited just to be here. This is a beautiful place. If someone were to build a town out here, this would be the best place to do it."

"Yes, I guess so."

Still getting only four word answers, I decided to try another tactic. "So, Alan, are you picking up on any ghost vibes?" All he gave me in return was a throaty, "No."

We had scoured the town site several times, and were now standing down toward the bank of the creek. Very little water was seeping from the spring—barely enough to keep the dirt muddy. Scarce patches of green grass followed the track of this ancient drainage ditch. Rainwater was so rare here on this side of the Rockies, that most of the ground was barren of grass or shrub. A few scattered clumps of low growing sage cluttered the view, but not much else.

"John, how did you know where to kick the dirt when you found that horseshoe?"

"There was an orange discoloration in the dirt."

"You mean like this one here?"

"Why, yes." Alan scrapped away a few small stones and a shallow layer of dirt, and managed to kick up a small object. Bending forward he reached down and picked it up.

"What have you found big buddy?"

"Oh, look. I believe that this is an old style nail. See how it is square, not round. That is the way they used to make them."

"Huh. Well, you would need nails to build a house." We looked at each other, and then shrugged our shoulders. Just then, Don rejoined us.

"Did you two find anything of interest?" Bloome held up his nail, and I showed him my horseshoe.

"Yes, those were some very common items in this town when I was a kid. There isn't much else that remains here."

"Are you alright, Don?" asked Alan.

"Yes, I was just thinking the future," he replied.

I thought that an odd thing to say, and asked, "What do you mean, 'thinking the future?'"

"Oh, that is just my term for when one reflects on what is to come. ... Here, before we leave, walk with me, and I will show you where we buried the bodies of my parents and the rest of the townsfolk."

Don led us back and into the far west side of the stand of trees.

"This is it here. Time has washed away what they were. They have grown into trees now. The little grave sticks we put down to mark their bodies have long since passed to dust. Just like everything else we brought to this desolate place." He sounded a little peeved over what had happened here long ago. And, if his story were true, he certainly had reason enough to be angry, but at what, or whom?

Don then took off his Indian hat and bowed his head, apparently in silent prayer. Out of respect, Bloome and I did the same. A stiffening breeze carried the cold air of the afternoon. With his head still bowed, and his eyes closed, Don said, "If you listen really closely, you can hear whispers coming from willows?"

The quiet solitude of this place was powerful. Even though we were standing amid a forest of tall cottonwood trees, for miles around us in every direction, all was flat, barren, and dead quiet. The only noise to break the aloneness was the whining of the wind. If you used your imagination and listened closely, the sound it made as it blew through the branches of the willow trees over by the pond did resemble shrill haunting whispers.

Could they be the long forgotten voices of the town's dead? Perhaps, they were calling out to us from their ancient burial ground. Their sad empty whine a requiescat whose eerie lyrics will forever haunt this place—a song from the ghosts Alan had so hoped to meet.

We all stood quiet for a moment—just listening, wondering. Then Don said, "Goodbye, Mom. Goodbye, Dad."

There was emotion pouring from Don's face as we got back in the jeep to leave this place. I thought it interesting that his feelings could be so strong. If his story was correct, and I was beginning to think so, then this Nagual was well over one hundred and forty years old. His parents have been dead and buried for nearly seven generations. Apparently, memories do not fade with time.

Before Alan got in, he took the nail he found earlier, and tossed it in the direction of the ground from which he had plucked it. Its worth was more as a memorial to this place than a memento to him.

I was still holding my horseshoe, now eroded beyond recognition. Like Bloome, I tossed it to the ground, knowing that time wasn't done with it yet. Nature does not respect memorials.

Reversing our tracks, we headed back to LV. Sitting in the back seat, Don sat quiet as he gazed out across the flatness of the plains. He still wore a sadness on his face. I know what it is like to lose someone close to you. Tragic lessons from life we will never be able to forget.

When we hit the interstate, his somber trance

broke. He turned and looked over the back of the rear seat of the jeep and noticed our cowboy hats. Reaching for one, he picked it up and looked it over. Then he said, "These are some really nice hats you have here."

"Those were gifts given to us by JB," I said.

"Yes," said Alan. "He said they were our merit badges, and that we had earned them by our trip into the sacred mountains the other day."

"Oh, don't tell me he used that old honorary Indian routine on you two?" Then he broke out in riotous laughter, just like Burningtree. We both knew at the time that we had been had by JB. Made the butt of one of his silly jokes, but that realization didn't make us feel any better.

Alan pursed his lips and turned to look at me, then shook his head. I knew what he was thinking, and said, "Don't worry, Alan. We are going to see JB again. I'm sure if we put our heads together we can come up with a swell form of initiation for him."

Alan didn't answer me he just nodded his head.

Wondering if he was going to be in a foul mood for the rest of the day, I glanced up at Don in the rear view mirror. He was smiling and talking again. I found it strange that his mood had switched so dramatically. For him, it was as though emotions were nothing more than a dance. He had tired of the blue one, and now decided on one with a more upbeat and livelier step. I only wish I could trade moods as easily.

The trip back to LV passed quickly. It was well on to dark when we arrived there, and the three of us were starved. We immediately hit the same eatery we were in when we first met Don.

With food now on the near horizon, Alan's mood improved. As we sat and waited to order I said, but in a rather stern tone, "Well, this is nice, Don. It is kind 'a like a reunion of sorts. It has only been five days, but I feel like we have come full circle. Only now we accept each other as friends."

"You're doing what my Ma used to call beating around the bush, John," he said. "If there is something on you mind, why not just come out and say it."

"My, aren't you the clever one," I said. Alan winced and gave me a throat clearing sound. He didn't want me asking Don any targeted questions. I didn't care. I was going for it. "Alright, here it is. If you were only twelve when you lived at Whisper Willow, then you would have to be around one hundred and forty years old today. You don't look a day over fifty. I think it is time you explained yourself."

Alan winced and looked away.

"That's funny," Don said. "I have been explaining myself to you constantly each time we have been together, John. Is it possible that you haven't been listening?"

Hearing that, Alan bust out in laughter. "Right on, Don, let him have it. It is time he had his eyes opened up."

"Two against one," I said. "That's alright. I can handle it."

In truth, I wasn't prepared for an all-out assault on my sensibilities; not by either, or both, of them. I sat with my fingers meshed, and resting on my empty belly, while I bobbed my head trying to gather a thought. "OK, let's assume that you are very old, and that you are a Nagual. Remember, you said that you survived a disease that killed everyone else in that town, but that happened before you became this Nagual, and gained you your powers. How do you explain that?"

"John, I don't have any scientific answers for

you. All I have to go on are my life's experiences. I know that you have a hard time believing in the mysteries that surround us, even though you suffer from the effects of one. That is a quite common reaction among modern man. But trust me, John, the machines and medicines of science won't be able to help you. You are going to have to have faith in a different kind of power if you want to rid yourself of this monster, U'buntu."

"What is that you said?" I had thought to correct him. "Don, listen to what you are asking me to believe. You want me to believe that some magical power exists in sand paintings on the ground, or that some potion brewed from plant leaves and animal guts can open some door to the unseen world that allows ghosts and demons to come and go. ... So far, all you have shown me is a town that seems to have never been, and the many people who supposedly lived there have all disappeared. Even their bones have vanished. Their personal histories erased, and any proof that they ever existed now lost to the winds of time."

He didn't answer me. He did not seem upset or perturbed by my doubting rant. He simply sat across the table from me, and stared blankly, silently, right at me. This cold reproach lasted for only a minute. Then, before we changed the subject, and went on to enjoy a repast, he said,

"When I am gone, John, much will be lost. I am the last Nagual, and, unlike my mentor, I have no apprentice. If nothing else, you should show respect for an old man. Humor me, and participate in the healing ceremony. You two are my friends. I only want to help you."

We spent the rest of the evening involved in lighter conversation. Alan again pumped Don for more

Navajo lore for a new book he is going to write. Before we parted for the night, I did acquiesce to attending Don's healing ceremony the next day. He said it would have to be performed on a power spot, and that the best one was inside his Hogan located in the Canyon Lands up by Four Corners. It is a long drive from LV to Four corners. We will have to leave early the next morning.

14:

Perdition's Gate

In the small African town of Kilali, Kenya, it is 3 AM. Those dark early hours, a time in which monsters of all kinds and sizes roam our dreamscapes. In mere hours, Dr. Henderson will at last gain entry to the Preserve, an area, and an idea, which have haunted him since hearing about it months earlier from his patient Dr. John Carter.

Dr. Henderson is an imperfect man, one riddled with self-doubts. He also harbors an intense suspicion of others. This is jealousy bordering on paranoia, but it is not his personality quirks, or personal demons, that trouble his sleep tonight.

* * *

"NO! No, don't. Please no.
"John," yelled Gerald.
"Oh, god! NO! No. Don't."
"John, wake up buddy. ... Come on, snap out of it."

"What?" ... "Oh, god." ... "Fuck!" ... "What the hell was that?"

"You were yelling in your sleep. Geez, just look at you. You're soaking wet."

"Oh, Christ. What a fucking nightmare." ... "Thank you for waking me, Gerald. Boy that was a first."

Still shaking, my body wet with sweat, I rise from bed and walk into the bathroom to take a hot shower. "Dear, god. I have never had such a horrifying dream, and where did all of this come from? I am anxious about the coming events later today, but what on earth is there about that, that would give me the cold sweats? The Preserve, is that it?"

"Carter's monster; that face I saw. What a vision from hell. ... Why am I letting his stupid tale affect me? Now, I am the one talking with monsters, good one, Bill. ... Visions of monsters, warning me not to enter the Preserve, this is just nervous apprehension. Imagine me talking to monsters, monsters talking to me. Christ, Bill, get a grip."

I have never experienced that kind of fright in a nightmare. Yet it all seemed so real.

In a confused state of mind, I turn my shower into a long, hot soak in the tub, and try to forget the torment that just went through my mind. Afterward I returned to bed and was fortunate enough to fall asleep and grab a few more hours rest.

When I awoke again, it was already eight. The sun was already up over the horizon, and shining brightly through the motel room's window. Our plan for the day was to arrive at the gate at ten thirty. The trip there is only an hour, so I still had plenty of time to shake the sleep out of my head, and eat something.

After a freshening shower, I took off for

breakfast alone. After eating, I noticed Mike Mills and his crew gather around the back of the news van. Gerald was with them. Time to leave was nearing, so I walked over and joined my comrades.

A brief tailgater strategy session erupted, and some last minute doubts crept into my accomplice's heads forcing me to deal with them.

"We know from listening in on Khan's transmission yesterday that Mr. Um'fume will be at the gate today, and that he wants to talk to us. I don't get it," said Mike. "Why, after all our attempts to get into the Preserve, if we force the issue today, are they going to let us walk in there now? There is something fishy about this whole situation."

Mike was having second thoughts about entering the Preserve. With one word, he could ruin all of my plans. I can't let that happen. This opportunity will never come again. We must go ahead. We must. What can I say to keep him on track? I had to think quick.

"Yes," I said. "Something more is on Um'fume's mind, but remember, he is a government official, and probably just wants to get some camera time. There is nothing mysterious about that."

Then unfortunately, Gerald chimed in to share his doubts, "Mike is correct, Bill. Something isn't right about this. I'm getting a bad feeling about entering a forbidden zone. You know about the warning Günter gave us."

"Gerald, come on. Are you still worried about spectral monsters running amuck and killing humans? Gerald, the deaths that occurred there happened six months ago. Have you heard of any deaths since then? No, you haven't, and furthermore, no self-respecting extra-dimensional monster would hang around for months hoping to catch a few trespassers and kill them. That idea is just crazy." I wanted to hear nothing more about U'buntu, and I didn't mind rubbing Gerald's face in his stupid worries.

"Well, never the less," said Gerald, "if we are to go in there, I would feel much better about it if we were accompanied by someone who had permission to live in there."

"I think Gerald may have a good idea, Bill. It might be wise to wait and see if the missionary shows up."

"OK, I agree, he supposedly arrives at eleven. Let's play it by ear. We will meet with this Mr. Um'fume, see what is on his mind, and then, with luck, the missionary will show up. Now, if there isn't any more silliness to deal with, can we go?"

As we did on the previous day, all of us jumped into vehicles, and our caravan was off and heading for a destiny unknown. I had forced aside any memory of my nightmare from last night, and the dreadful warning inside it. All I felt was a mounting excitement. At last, I was on the way to find evidence to prove Carter a fraud, and put this murderer in prison. Nothing else mattered.

We had a twist planned for today. On the way to the gate the news van, followed by cars driven by Barry and Andrew, veered off the dirt road, and entered the wash where we gathered yesterday. This wide, flat, dry, wasteland was over a mile from, and out of sight of the Preserve gate. Once out in the middle they would prepare and launch the UAV. The three of them would spend their day maneuvering the aircraft to circle overhead; in essence spying on the spies. It was comforting to know that we had eyes in the sky. They would be recording everything. The UAV also doubled as a cell phone link; we would be able to call out for help if needed.

Mike, Gerald, and I continued in Mike's SUV without stopping. As we approached the gate, I noticed that the same guards were there. I began to admire their dedication—albeit misguided. There was another person with them today. He was a tall, slender, well-dressed individual.

"That must be Mr. Um'fume, Khan's boss," I said.

Mike drove to the rest area and parked. The three of us sat inside his SUV for a moment.

Experiencing a rush of adrenaline, we were trying to feel a way forward, and to calm our nerves. We had no grand scheme cooked up. As events unfolded, I would attempt to control and manipulate them to achieve my ultimate purpose. The appearance of Mr. Um'fume added a layer of confusion. Who was he really, and why did he want to talk with us?

It was just before eleven and there was no sight of the missionary. We exited our vehicle. The three of us gathered in front of it, and in plain view of the guards. Mike shot several quick gazes in the direction of the keepers of the gate. They stared back, but didn't budge. They just stood and stared at us. I supposed they were waiting for us to make the first move. Mike then said, "OK, let's do it."

Casually we started walking the two hundred yards to the gate opening. We did not want to be taken as threatening today, so it was a slow, casual, and easy gait. We were all friends. We talked and smiled with each other as we closed the gap. On seeing our approach, Khan and Um'fume came forth to meet us.

With fifty feet to go, Um'fume stretched his right hand out to his side, and Khan stopped. Um'fume, still walking, then put his hand in the air to gesture for us to stop where we were, and we did. He came up to us, and after a momentary face-off, introduced himself. To maintain the appearance that we had no idea who he was, we introduced ourselves and told him how nice it was to meet him.

Then we asked him if he was in charge of the gate today, to which he replied, "Please Mr. Mills, we know who you are, and we know that you have been monitoring our transmissions. Please don't treat us as though we are just a clueless bunch of third world idiots." They were on to us all along. That realization stung. Were all of our efforts now in vain?

Mr. Um'fume continued, "I want the three of you to listen to me, and I want you to know that I am committing treason by telling you this. You do not want to go into the Preserve. You, more than any of the others should know that, Gerald. I was the one who sent you the copy of Dr. Walter's last report. I could go to prison for that. I am putting my life in your hands by taking you into my confidence."

Then he turned to me, "And Dr. Henderson, I am surprised by your actions most of all. You know Dr. Carter well. You should listen to what he told you. He didn't lie when he told you how those many people died."

Then he turned to look at Mike, "Mr. Mills, no good can come from exposing the secrets within the Preserve. We already have the situation under control. Any light you bring to this story will only cause more pain to a nation, and a people, who have been traumatized enough." His admonition only seemed to anger Mike.

"Oh, yeah," said Mike, "and what about the death of M. Apurna. You didn't investigate her death, and you quite probably have let her killer go free. Why you didn't even try to bury her body."

"Bury her body?" argued Um'fume. "My god man, have you any idea what has been going on in there? Mr. Mills, there were thousands of innocent people in Kenbe. Everyone there died. Everyone! They were all left unburied. ... The truth is that we did secretly send in a SAR team the next day. Eight men! We almost immediately lost contact with those eight men, and they were never been seen or heard from again. Even our UAV's began to fall from the sky. We couldn't risk sending in more people to bury those already dead."

I sensed Um'fume's speech was having an impact of Mike and Gerald, and I had to act quickly to counter his heartfelt appeal,

"For Christ's sake, Um'fume, listen to what you are saying. You have bought into this whole monster story. Ghosts do not murder people. Kenbe was a tragic accident. A wind whipped conflagration that tragically destroyed a city, nothing more."

"No, you are wrong about that Dr. Henderson."

"Then, let me ask you, how many people have died in there in the past six months?"

"Thanks to our efforts, no one, and we would like to keep it that way."

My exchange with Um'fume continued. I found him to be an interesting and well-educated man, and his un-argumentative discourse showed uncommon professionalism. His tall and slender stature, and skin as ebon as the night sky, were characteristics shared with many Kenyan people. His speech was accented with lovely foreign tones that I could not specifically place. Was this Afrikaans, a blend of many languages; I couldn't say? I thought I heard a tinge of English coming through and possibly also a touch of Indian, and of course, Swahili.

While we argued back and forth, none of us had notice that a man leading a burro, and accompanied by a medium sized dog, had crossed the wasteland of the Preserve, and had arrived at the gate. He became involved in a forceful discussion with the guards about something. His loud pleas caught our attention, and we broke off our discussion with Um'fume.

It sounded to me as though he was arguing in French. Mike craned his neck to listen in on what the old man was saying. "I speak French," he said. "The man seems to be saying that they need a doctor. One of the old missionaries has come down ill. He is suffering from some kind of mental trauma."

The guards then yelled out to Um'fume. Apparently, the problem needed his attention to resolve.

"Well, there is your missionary, Dr. Henderson," he said in a pained yet concerned tone, and then he hurried over to inquire as to what the problem was. The three of us with guarded curiosity followed him.

I was impressed to see that Um'fume spoke French fluently, as though it were his native language. He and the aged missioner spoke at some length while Mike translated for me.

The priest was pleading for help. Apparently, an old man at the mission had come down ill. He was extremely agitated and ranting out of his mind. The missionary was asking the guards to send in a doctor to treat him. Well, three cheers for fortune.

Um'fume refused to acquiesce saying, "Sorry Father Kitunzi, you know that no one from the outside is allowed to enter the Preserve. It is just too dangerous."

Not deterred, the old priest said, "After a lifetime of service, surely god would not punish us for accessing modern medicine, so why should your government. It is not for you to interfere, Um'fume. Listen to your heart, and do not fear destiny."

A look of scorned indifference overcame Um'fume's face. He turned to me and said, "Alright,

Dr. Henderson, obviously you know what the priest is asking for. You are the only doctor here. I have informed you of the dangers that await anyone on the other side of this fence line, so I will ask you not to go in there, but if you choose to do so, I will let the three of you accompany Father Kitunzi back to his village. However, remember that I have warned you, and I am washing my hands of this. Whatever happens to you and your friends inside of the Preserve falls on your shoulders."

It is mysterious how the universe works. Just when I thought Um'fume had persuaded my friends to give up their pursuit, heaven steps in and forces our obstacles aside. Of course I said, "Yes, we will go with him, and I will treat his ailing colleague."

After I blurted out those words, a shiver of doubt coursed through my body, "What, now I am responsible for the lives of my friends? What if something does happen? What if everything Um'fume and Carter told me were true?"

My guts twisted. I fought off the urge to cower over in fear—people were watching— they were scrutinizing me closely. I must stand tall and show resolve. But these doubts. Where did they come from? I'm afraid. That's it. It is only fear of leadership. Fear of being in put charge. There are no monsters. These feelings tearing away at my innards are nothing more than an adverse reaction to a new and unfamiliar situation. We will all be just fine.

Shrugging aside my fears, I was relieved to have finally gained entrance into this fanciful Preserve.

Mike, speaking in French, explained to the missionary who we were. He said that I was a psychiatrist, and that we had permission to accompany him to his village to treat his friend.

The priest then thanked Um'fume and the guards, turned his burro around, and started walking back to his home.

Still a bit stunned by our apparent good fortune, and self-absorbed in my own doubts, I lost track of what was happening around me. However, I did manage to hear Um'fume bark something in Swahili to the guards, and they moved out of the way.

The priest was leading his burrow with a makeshift rein tied around its neck. With the dog at his side, he took the lead on the narrow trail. Mike fell in behind the man of God, and Gerald followed closely behind him.

I stepped back for a moment to survey the sight, and watched as my friends passed through the giant steel poles that made up the gate's frame.

Workers had not yet installed the gateway's door, and its enormous empty hole silhouetted my friend's bodies against the stark nothingness that lay immediately in front of them. This surreal vista had me in awe. I was standing at a gate, the only gate, built into a hugely tall fence—a fence that stretched to the horizon on my right and on my left. Nearly finished, it now enclosed a vast area. Only the first half a mile or so of the terrain before me was a desolate wasteland, what lay beyond were miles and miles of verdant jungle. Was I now peering into the Garden of Eden, or was I viewing something sinister? Did this gate lead to a heaven here on Earth, or does perdition wait for me just on the other side? That jumble of commixed possibilities had me feeling confused and fearful, and yet at the same time, I was eager to press forward into the unknown.

I ignored the guards, emboldened myself, and started walking. My friends were already well on their way. Just as I reached the entry to this paradise, something on the gatepost to my left caught my eye. There, facing out, and about ten feet up, was a Mark. Clearly visible against the shiny new galvanized steel, this large black tarnish had the appearance of a flattened "V." It somewhat resembled the wings of a giant moth, and looked to have been burned right into the metal post.

Remembering Dr. Carter's description of the Marks left by his monster, U'buntu, a brief twinge of queasiness hit me in the stomach and parts below, but I was on a mission now. Nothing will dissuade me. The guards put that Mark there to scare us I told myself, and marched on.

About one hundred feet inside the gate, I stopped and turned around. Um'fume and his gang were still standing outside of the Preserve in front of the gate. They simply watched us walk away. Um'fume had an aura of calm disquiet about him. His concern for our wellbeing touched me. As I looked at him, my eyes noticed a small black object hanging from the right front side of his belt. I had notice it when we first met, but at that time I gave it no thought. It looked to be a cell phone type device, but there are cell towers up here. "He must be just wearing it out of habit," I told myself. Then, as I turned back around, I half way put my right arm up in the air, and gave them a casual wave goodbye.

"Um'fume, why did you allow them to enter the Preserve?" asked Khan. "You know that death awaits them in there."

"Well, my friend, one of my religious beliefs is that every man should be allowed to find his destiny. And who knows, nothing is set in stone. Remember, Dr. Carter survived two run-ins with U'buntu. Who is to say that some good won't come out of this?"

"And what if they do survive? What do we do then?"

"Don't worry. I already have a contingency plan in place."

The missionary's pace matched the slow clop, clop, clop of his pack animal. Shaking off my feelings of unease, I quickly caught up with the others. It was now mid-day, and the sun although bright and looming high overhead imparted only a gentle warmth to the air about us. All was still here, and other than the sound of our footfalls, all was quiet as well. With my friends close-by, this easy stroll gladdened me. My senses whelmed with joy. Finally, I am free. I am accomplishing a greater good. My journey today will uncover clues, hidden truths that will shine a fresh light on a crime too long ignored, and with my assistance, Mike will avenge his lost loved one. At last, I will expose Alan Bloome, as a fraud, and I will see his coconspirator, Dr. Carter, jailed for murder, what could be more perfect?

* * * * *

As we strode along Mike involved the Missioner in casual talk. I don't understand a word of French, and couldn't follow their conversation. We were already three quarters of the way to the entry of the forest. Its verdure and dark inner recesses showed in mysterious juxtaposition to the stripped bare patch of land we were crossing. Looking to the trail front, I noticed the priest's dog walked with a slight limp; there was also a silver dollar sized scar on his game left hindquarter. Curious, I asked Mike to inquire of the Missionary as to what befell his poor pooch.

"Bill, he says that it is not his dog. That he belongs to this place. He said the dog just wandered in to the mission compound about six months ago. That he was injured, but that someone had already treated his wounds." I heard the missioner continue to babble something to Mike … "But, he says, 'we do not know who it was. The dog was starved, so we fed him, and he has stayed with us ever since. He loves to walk with me.'" My stomach fell. Sweat began to bead up on my forehead. This couldn't be the dog that Carter treated. It couldn't be the one he said saved his life.

A preponderance of strange happenings had my mind reeling. Many arrows were piercing my theories, and now odd coincidences were lending support to Carter's story. How could this be? Stunned, I fell into a mental fog, but I could not let the others sense my doubts. I pretended to be oblivious to the uncertainties ahead, and walked on.

We soon entered the tropical forest. Its thick green vegetation appeared healthy and vibrant, and much of it so overgrown and dense that if not for the well-worn path you could easily become lost. Our estimations, derived from viewing the UAV data from yesterday, put the village not more than a mile farther, or at this pace, another thirty minutes, but right now, I couldn't think, or more correctly, didn't know what to think. Had my analysis of Carter been wrong?

No, I will not accept that. My hands were shaking. A slight pain grew behind my eyeballs. My stomach felt empty, as though I hadn't eaten in days, but I wasn't hungry. Fearing an anxiety attack, I put my head down, and tried to concentrate on path in front of my feet. A jumble of roots and ruts crisscrossed the trail—plenty to hold my tortured focus. I remained mute, while my friends gabbed away. I let them get a little ahead of me while I pretended to be touching and examining the surroundings.

Falling back, I did not want anyone to notice my confused suffering. Tortured by conflict, and fearing the unknown, the passage of time became unpleasant. It seemed to stop. How much longer must my torment last? The village now seemed a hundred miles off.

My stomach hurt, and I felt like vomiting. But I ambled on dizzy, disoriented, and with nothing more than the chatter of my friends to cue me to which direction to fall. Then, from just up ahead, I hear the playful laughter of children.

Almost immediately, the trail opened up and we broke out into a large clearing. The priest said that we had arrived. I spied around to gain a perspective on this village, but it was not what I had expected. What met my eyes were only a few quite dated and simply constructed buildings. Several were not much more than huts.

They were open and airy, and banded all around with screened windows. Shutters, hinged above each opening, and raised open by wood sticks, doubled as awnings. None of these makeshift windows contained glass. I found out later that these summer-camp style cabins were the bunkhouses.

A group of young children ran up and surrounded us. Father Kitunzi handed the burro's reins to them, and shooed them away. I watched as they playfully led the beast elsewhere.

A familiar looking building stood apart from the others. It looked like a small chapel. Set on the northern edge of the mission compound it appeared half eaten by forest. A man was standing in front of it. He waived to us, and Father Kitunzi led us over to him.

Mike introduced himself to the man, and they had a short conversation in French. He then turned to me and said that his name was Father Hamidi, the mission's superior.

As I moved forward to introduce myself, he reached forward and grabbed my right hand with his. Then he put his left hand on my right arm just past the wrist. With a broad smile on his face, he uttered, "Very nice to meet you, Doctor."

We shook, and not being an expert in introductions, I simply nodded in agreement and said, "Yes, nice to meet you also."

Our trip to the mission had not taken as long as I had thought. It was just under an hour, and it was now half past noon. My stomach was growling and my head still in a state of confused purpose. Before I saw the old man, I needed time to relax and eat. I spied some picnic benches in what looked to be the communal eating area. Pointing a finger in their direction I said, "Mike, would you ask the missioners if it would be allowed to sit over there and eat?"

My request was met in the affirmative. Father Hamidi motioned in that direction with his left hand, then put his right hand on Mike's shoulder, and led us over to the eating area.

Without waiting for the others, I rudely dragged some grub from out of my backpack and dug in. A teenaged girl brought out some pitchers of water with lemon slices in them, and put them on the rickety picnic table.

These people did not have much. From what I have seen so far, they lived a very Spartan lifestyle. The question as to why they decided to locate their mission in such a remote area did cross my mind, but I thought it might be rude to inquire.

Mike and Gerald joined me and had some lunch. The two priests sat with us, but remained oddly silent while we ate.

The act of eating calmed my stomach, and the atmosphere here was very relaxed. Children were playing unsupervised all throughout the compound, and by the sound of it, they were quite happy. No one was hiding, or cowering in fear from some murderous monster. No, everyone seemed quite at peace. That helped to further ease my tensions, and I reminded myself that all of Carter's story could be true. All of it, that is, except his insertion of a demon into the mix, but that was good.

I was on a hunt for clues, and so far, I had managed to track his travels of six months ago perfectly. All of the pieces were falling into place. Secrets to finding M Apurna's body must lie with the school's proctor. He, or one of the other priests, must be the one Carter met and talked with that day.

I should ask him, but not yet, no, Mike's ardor for M, if he hears about where M went, I know he will bolt after her, no, it is better to wait, wait until I am ready, I will wait until I have treated the stricken old man, then, and only then, can I inquire if they knew of Carter, and if so, what direction he took that day.

15:

Journey to Don's Hogan

Northwestern New Mexico
We were traveling west on State Route 64, and had
passed the tiny town of Farmington hours ago. I
enjoyed the old west vistas, but these daylong drives
are wearing on my patients. I cannot even be sure we
are still in New Mexico. Four states come together
and share a corner here, and we are traveling off
map. I trust in Oddball Don not to get us lost. He
asked us to drive him to his home he says is located
deep in the Canyon Lands. It is something he calls a
Hogan. Supposedly it is a safe place in which to hold
a scared Navajo healing ceremony. About that, I am
skeptical. However, with the abrupt onset and
severity of these aural migraines I am willing to try
anything.

* * *

"OK, we need to turn right up here, a little ways,"
blurted Don. "At the next junction, there, turn right."

Following Don's instructions, I approached the intersection and stopped. It looked like a place I had seen on a TV commercial. Here there are, two roads, four corners, and four stop signs—all stuck out in the middle of Nofuckingwhereville. Each leg emanating from this nexus of nowhere stretched as far as I could see across a flat barrenness, and from my perspective, at the end of each road lay nothing more than lost. I gave myself a hearty, "You have to be kidding. People can't possibly live out here."

I turned right, and I am going to guess north. There are no markers to reference by, or fences, or trees, or shrubs, or grasses, just a thousand square miles of two-dimensional boredom. We drove for another hour or so, and then even the sky darkened to hide the sun and obscure our passageway.

A thick blanket of clouds, colored perse to dark gray, were pressing down and looked menacing. It might snow soon. In front of us, off in the distance, I can see a long line of low-lying mesas, but their similar corporealness made them indistinguishable one from the other.

The bland nakedness of our surroundings was hypnotic, and I lost track of time. We were driving through a land void of human presence. Suddenly a terrible thought ran through my mind, and I shot a glance down at the gas gauge. Whew! Good thing we filled up back in the small town of Shiprock. There was no emergency yet, but if we do not get to somewhere soon the gas in our tank is going to lower beyond that point of safe return.

"Almost there," shouted out Don. He and Bloome have been lost, in a sense, in a world of their own. Alan keeps pumping him for his lore and knowledge of Native Americans. I hope the Nagual gets more than a footnote in his new book.

Several miles ahead, we branched off on a new

and smaller road, still paved, but remote enough that it received little maintenance. The surface was cracked, and grasses had begun to grow in the roadway. We were totally alone out here. The last vehicle we passed was a hundred miles ago. Such a sad and lonely place this is—who would want to live here? Then Don shouted, "There, that dirt road there. Turn right, and take it."

I turned off onto the dirt road; it cut an oblique angle toward the mesas, which still lingered far off in the distance. As we slowly approached them, the terrain changed—visible signs of life have returned—some scrub brush and a few piñon trees lay scattered here and there.

After many miles of driving at an angle to the hills, the mesa's cliffs slowly approached on our right side. Interesting how hills in this part of the country have that tabletop look. Their ancient rocky faces eroded to expose beautiful bands of earth colors. Even in the storm-gray afternoon light, they painted an iconic western scene in varied hues of orangey-pink to dusky vermillion, and oatmeal beige to a faded puce.

The road had turned once again, and now skirted the base of the mesa. We continued driving on it for another thirty minutes. I soon realized that the many mesas I thought I saw earlier were in reality only one. Wind, rain, and time had breached her crown, and cut many narrow canyons deep into her skeleton. They extended back, bending like the joints of fingers, creating hidden and unexplored realms that appeared lost to time. Their mystery excited the explorer in me, and I began to thirst for a chance to trek into one of them.

"It is the next canyon, John. There. You see how it is wide and flat here in the front? If you turn off to the right side of the road. There. In front of the arroyo. There. Do you see those two tall piñon trees? Why don't you park it there?"

Following Don's hand gestures and modest directions, I maneuvered the jeep off the dirt road, and parked aside two evergreen trees. Finally, after half a day's travel, we had stopped, and could get out and stretch our legs.

"No roads lead into the canyon," said Don, "We will have to walk the rest of the way."

Always eager for a hike, Alan perked up. I was excited, too. The three of us jumped out to survey the sights.

First, I did a big stretch of my limbs, and yelled "Aaah," and then took a deep breath of fresh air. My nose was instantly treated to a sharp, wet-cold, smell, one people who live in snowy climates recognize well. The weather was closing in, and it could begin to snow at any time.

This place was remote and private. I do not think you can get any farther away from anywhere than here. The gray clouds had descended down below the mountaintops, and now their chilling storm-mist filled the canyon before us, partially obscuring our view.

I took a gander down the canyon entrance. Its rocky sides had weathered and fallen to form a wide flat "V." The floor was sparsely populated with scrubby piñon trees, but I saw taller pines growing farther back. This walk should be fun and easy. After freshening up, the three of us zipped up our jackets, donned our packs, and started our walk to Don's Hogan.

A quarter of a mile in a shiver ran down my neck. It wasn't storming yet, but my body told me it was getting colder. I loved the change of seasons, and today the air possessed a musty sent and an eerie stillness, which bespoke to the coming of winter. My senses told me that soon snowflakes would fall and silently weave a white blanket to cover all. Neither of us was dressed for prolonged exposure to wet and freezing temperatures. I hope Don's place has a heater.

From our vantage point, I could see the top of the Mesa. It appeared to be barren of vegetation of any sort—just a dry, windblown, sandy tabletop. The scenery below the top and inside the confines of the canyon was a dramatic and wanted change.

Following Don, we walked slowly along the canyon bottom, winding around scattered piñon and large boulder alike. There was no trail worn into the dirt, in fact, I saw no signs of previous human presence anywhere. This was pristine wilderness untainted by human foot or garbage—I found it beautiful—you couldn't help but imagine that deer, elk, or mountain goat must roam wild here.

The sides of this long valley were broken up into several terraced layers, each a wide life-supporting shelf. Rising spires of orange-brown hued sandstone, or hoodoos, framed the edges of each terrace, and numerous scrub evergreens lent their wistful dark green shapes as contrast amid the exfoliating tiers of rusty rock. The canyon floor was flat and wide as a two-lane highway. What trees there were grew scattered and alone in the cinnamon colored soil. Our view ahead was for the most part unobstructed, making for an easy traverse.

We hiked for perhaps thirty minutes filling our senses with the primitive beauty that encircled us. Perhaps a mile in we came to a natural stair step cut into the rock of the lower left side terrace. Our leader, noticeably spry for his supposed age, trotted up them with ease. It was amazing how his appearance and abilities changed with different situations. Yesterday, as we left Whisper Willow, his wan aura of sadness had him looking much older. Today his attitude was a one eighty, and he looked and acted now like a man my age. There was mystery that surrounded this man.

The rubble staircase took us up to the middle tier giving us a fresh perspective. We were now some forty feet above the canyon floor.

Shortly we came to a point where the canyon branched. One leg of it curved around and to the north, the other opened toward the southeast.

"This is it here," said Don. He could not have picked a more picturesque place to build a house. The wide-open vista from this ledge afforded a perfect view of the valley below, and of the morning sunrise. However, after turning around twice I didn't see a house, or any other kind of structure.

"It is well disguised," said Don. "If you didn't know where to look, or what to look for, you wouldn't notice it."

So, I thought like an Indian for a moment. So did Alan. Then, in unison, we both turned to face the canyon wall. There it was. Seemingly built right into an outcropping, and partly hidden by boulders and an old tree, sat an earthen structure. The canyon wall made up two of its sides. The rest of it was sculpted out of adobe mud supported by dried tree branches. This roughhewn structure, slightly domed on top, stood barely taller than a man, and was not much more than ten feet to a side, and nearly indistinguishable from its surroundings.

"This is it?" I asked. "This is your home?" I was aghast. It was nothing more than a mud hut.

"Yes, this is my old home, well, one of them anyway. My mentor and I built many Hogans across this land, but this was my favorite. There is everything you need to survive right here in this canyon. I lived here for many years."

"Yeah, there is everything here alright, everything except human contact," I thought to myself. No wonder this guy is a bit off.

"It looks unoccupied. How long has it been since you have been here?" asked Alan.

"The last time I came here was well before Burningtree senior died. After he passed, I traveled down into Mexico, and lived on tribal lands there. So, it has been over twenty years."

"I'm astonished. … I am surprised that it hasn't fallen in over the years you were away," I said.

"Nah, this type of house is time tested. The walls are a thick adobe, and it doesn't rain here much."

Then this ancient urchin of the Wild West asked us to help him make his earthen hut habitable. First, we had to clear the front door.

Made of just a simple grate weaved from twigs, it had been sealed over with reddish mud. We also had to clear a small vent located on top of the hut. It had been covered up with an old and tattered horse blanket, which was in turn covered with a thick layer of mud.

Once we had cleared away the obstructions, I stole a look inside, and was shocked to see nothing but a barren dirt floor. Don went inside and had a quick look around. He seemed excited to be back here. Even with its stark nothingness, obviously this place meant a lot to him.

Then he zipped outside, ran over to a lone piñon tree that was standing some forty feet away. There he ripped off a long bough, stripped it of a few pine needle bunches at the fat end, and then ran back inside his hut.

Taking his pine branch, he swished it all around in the air hitting the sides and ceiling sweeping them clean of cobwebs. Then he used the bristly end as a broom slash rake to sweep, level, and clear the floor. Giving the air a chance to settle, he dipped his head to miss hitting the low doorjamb, and came back outside.

"Now, I think we should build a nice hot fire," he said.

I snuck a quizzical look at Bloome. I was stunned by the prospect of spending the night in a mud hut, but the brisk walk while heavily clothed had me hot and a bit sweaty, and now that we had stopped, the cold was getting to me. I felt a shiver coming on. A fire right now was a great idea—I will explain to Bloome later how I hate camping out.

Alan seemed happy. He loves Indian lore, and this place was a page ripped right out of the old west. Don instructed us to round up some firewood. We set about foraging for anything that would burn. There wasn't much dead and dry wood lying around, but we did manage to find enough to fill our arms. We walked firewood back to the hut where I dropped my load just outside, and next to the front opening.

"No, not there, John," Don said mockingly and with a little laugh. "Here bring the wood inside. We will fill the fire pit, and place the rest over there. I like to have a nice stack against the far wall and within easy reach."

"Well excuse me," I didn't say that, and wasn't angry over his pointing out the obviousness of my being out of place in the woods. So what if I grew up in a city, I'm proud of it. I never was a boy scout, and I have never built a fire in the wilderness. Now I am getting scorn from a country bumpkin. "Ah, alright, just get your fire going," I thought.

A dozen or so stones, perhaps ten inches in diameter, lay in a ring out in the middle of the floor. We carefully placed our foraged sticks and short logs in a pile inside of this rock circle.

Backwards Don arranged them in some order inside of the fire pit. Then I halfway expected him to start rubbing two sticks together, but instead he took a modern day lighter from his pants pocket, and lit a fire. Bloome and I stood in front of it for several minutes warming our hands against the flames. It soon got cozy inside.

Don said, "At night, and on cold days, the thick adobe walls pickup and retains the fires heat and makes everything inside warm and cozy. The ceremony can be quite long. We will need several more arm loads of wood."

Once warmed by the fire, we went back outside and gathered more firewood. All the while Alan remained mute. Neither from his silence, nor from his attitude, could I tell what he was going on inside his head. Personally, I was wondering if we were expected to sit on the dirt floor. Our friend had no chairs, or other furnishings of any kind. Wasn't room for them anyway. I assumed that Alan wanted to partake of this ceremony, so I didn't raise a stink. The things I do for friendship.

After two more forays into the cold, we had amassed a healthy stack of wood, which we neatly placed in a pile along the sidewall.

While the two of us did the work, Don cozied himself by the fire and supervised. "That looks good, boys. Now, if you two would help me. We need to grab some things out of storage."

Storage? We both looked at him questioningly. "Follow me."

North of the Hogan, the canyon branches around to the left. We followed Don around this corner for about two hundred feet where he stopped.

"OK, it's still here. This pile of stones heaped up here against the rock face covers a storage locker. Help me pull them down." We did as he asked.

Behind the stones was what looked like another adobe and wood grate. Don worked on loosening an edge. With his fingers, he grabbed a hold of one of the wood sticks, shook it several times, and then gave it a hard tug. It came loose, and he set it aside.

To our surprise, behind it was a cave perhaps ten feet deep and five feet across. Our Nagual had a hidden cache. In it, we saw many crates, or wooden boxes, of varying sizes. They were covered with dusty old horse blankets.

Stooping, Don entered the cave and began to riffle through things. I was surprised to see how well his belongings survived considering they had been stowed in this manner for over twenty years.

From one crate, he handed Bloome an arm full of old blankets and said they were to cover the floor with. I received a load of colorful woven blankets. He said these were for sitting, sleeping, or wearing. One box had bedrolls in it. Another contained an assortment of cooking utensils.

He also pulled out a couple of buckskin leather bags and secreted them back to the hut. We made a couple roundtrips each before replacing the cover grate over the cave entrance, and hurried back to the warmth of Don's Hogan.

Once inside we closed the door. Don fitted an old blanket over it and adjusted it so that only a sliver of light shown through. It was toasty warm inside, yet not overly smoky. A draft from the door help funnel fumes up and out of the top hole. It did not take long to spread out the floor coverings, and now with something other than dirt to sit on I crossed my legs and parked it. Alan sat to my left. Don was sitting across from us and facing the doorway.

Inside of the Hogan it was dark. The fire's flames put out dull yellow light that reflected poorly off the darkened interior walls. This place wasn't much, but it was a warm welcome from the worsening conditions outside.

Don clanked together some pots, and then pulled a small sack from out of his leather bags. Filling his pot with water, he put a pinch of something in it, and then held the pot over the hot coals saying, "This is one of my own blends of tea."

Once the tea brewed, he handed us each a cup, and poured us some to sip on. It had a nice aroma, and drinking something warm helped sooth my hungry stomach. We socialized around the fire for a while—just enjoying each other's company.

16:

The Old Man

Missionary's village, Inside the Preserve
Finished with our lunch, we sat quietly and rested.
The sound of young children running, laughing,
playing, so familiar, slowly blended into a
commonality of experiences and then faded from my
immediate awareness. The ideal of this place crept
in. I heard a loud caw, caw, caw, of an unfamiliar
bird as it flew overhead. I became aware of an
underlying din from insects hiding just inside the
wall of verdure that surrounded us. The mission
village was located inside a circular clearing, one
imposed by man upon nature, nestled inside a sea of
lush greenness. Briefly, I reveled in my newfound
adventurism. Never before had I thought myself an
explorer. That field of pursuit seemed so distant
from my capabilities, so far flung from my education,
and so ancient from my personal mythos, that it
never entered my mind, even as a dream. Now I was
awash in deepest darkest jungle. I convinced myself
that I was living the life of adventure and
exploration, and I loved it.

Relieved and emboldened, I was ready to press on. It was best to treat the old man before continuing with our quest. For that, I needed a translator, and I wanted to keep Mike close to control him. Looking at the Proctor, I said to Mike, "Mike, I will need you to accompany me and translate when I visit the old man. You can tell the Proctor we can go whenever he is ready."

They spoke a few words in French, then with a pleased smile on his face, the priest motioned for us to follow him. He led us over to one of the camp style buildings we had passed earlier.

The buildings simple construction used no foundation. The floor and framing rested on short wood stilts that raised it above the ground by two feet, and you could see all the way underneath it. Nothing more than a rectangle, it was perhaps twenty feet wide and fifty feet long. It had only one entry that was located on a short end that faced south.

We walked over to a set of steps. They led us up to a landing. Opening a screen door, Father Hamidi let us pass by him, and we entered into a screened-in porch that made up the length of the end of this structure. The porch was furnished with several wooden park benches and low tables all of which appeared to be handmade.

They protected the interior of the building from bugs, chiefly mosquitoes, by a second screen door. Once we were all inside of the porch, the priest closed the outer door, then walked over to the inner door, pushed it open, and bade us to follow him.

The interior appeared bright and airy, and no walls partitioned it off. You could not only see from one end to the other inside, through the band of open screened windows, you could also see everything that was going on outside.

A row of sleeping cots lined either side of the long walls creating a long empty pathway that ran down the entire length of the middle of the room. The lower portions of the outer walls were covered with wood paneling that had darkened with age. They had painted the upper walls and ceiling in an off-white hue more akin to beige. The floor was covered in large brown tiles. It squeaked clean, but did little to liven up the room. Fortunately light pouring in from the plentiful windows helped to brighten the white canvas of the cot fabric. They were daytime, and being daytime, they fought back against the obscure nighttime palate of the floor, walls, and ceiling.

The bare minimum of distance existed between them—perhaps three feet, and each rested neat, clean, and perfectly square to the wall. At the moment, the room appeared empty. All of the children were outside playing. Atop the outside end of each empty cot laid a neatly folded blanket, and on top of it, square in the middle, rested a small pillow. This military uniformity spoke to lessons being taught of discipline, respect, and gratefulness.

Father Hamidi led us down the middle of the row of cots. At the far end of the room, I saw that five cots separated from the others by white sheets hung over a simple frame to make a moveable partition; they offered little more that the idea of privacy.

As we drew near the far end, I began to hear some confused mumbling. It got louder as we approached, as if to tell us, "The person you are nearing knows you are there."

The Proctor pulled aside one of the white partitions. What greeted me was the sight of an aged man; he looked to be well into his nineties. He lay reposed and vulnerable. His venerable skin was as black as the African night, and deeply wrinkled. His

Tynan 218

hair had turned not gray, but an unnatural snow white color.

His cataract eyes opened wide to gather more light. On seeing us before him, he turned his head and fixed his stare on me. Our eyes met. His arms moved with a pronounced shudder, and he began mumbling incoherently.

"There, there," I said, "it's alright, just relax; we are going to get you some comfort."

I sensed he took his current debilities to be a weakness that troubled him. His inability to reach out, to move, to talk cogently, touched me, and I took pity on him.

He was quite agitated, but at what? Further, we were out in the middle of a jungle. There was no pharmacy on the next street corner, and I did not have any medications with me.

"Mike, if you would, ask the Proctor if they have any medicines available."

To my shock the Proctor responded himself in a slow and cautious use of English.

"Yes," he said, "we have limited drugs Dr. Henderson. As you might expect, with so many children about, we need to have a supply of medicines."

I slowly turned and eyed the man. My expression was shouting out at him in disbelief. Then he said, "Sorry doctor, I am not fluent in English, and my use of it is rare, and as a result imperfect. Your friend spoke in French; I thought you understood what he was saying. If you feel mislead, I apologize." I found it difficult being angry with a man dressed in a black robe.

Thinking for a moment about what I might need, then I said, "I will need to look through your medical supplies."

"There isn't much, doctor. What medicines we

have are all in one small box kept in a storage locker in our one-room infirmary. I will send Father Kitunzi to bring it over here."

That was a good idea. The priest went for the box of drugs. Gerald and Mike went along with him. That left me alone to talk with the Proctor. I needed some history on the old man, so I asked,

"So, who is this old man, and what is his name?"

"This is Father Mahbub. He is one of the founders of this school. He has worked tirelessly for over forty years to aid the orphans of this country."

"If he is one of your priests, then why isn't he resting in a bed in his own house?"

"This is his home. His hands helped build this structure those many years ago, and this is where he has lived ever since."

"What? He has no other possessions?"

"Father Mahbub chose to live a very humble life. He has few possessions. God was his love, and devotion his life. Dedication filled his daily needs, he needed nothing else to make his life meaningful, and believe it or not, he considered himself a very happy and lucky person. Yet, sadly, time wears on all of us, even men of God. I pray you can ease his torments?"

The thought that this man's lifetime's accumulation of things lay within three feet of his cot was humbling. A modern man who took no thought for his own comfort, and had spent his whole life in service to his fellow man. I didn't think that anyone alive today could be so selfless. Touched by his story I decided to focus my attention on alleviating the suffering of this old priest.

"I promise you Father Hamidi, I will do the best I can with what we have. Can you give me some insight as to how he came to be in this condition?"

"Up until a few days ago he seemed in prefect health. He was happy, he often played out in the compound with the children, he walked with us on our daily hikes into the jungle, or up into the hills. Then, one day last week, he seemed very anxious, and said he wanted to go off to meditate. When he did not return for dinner that night, we became worried, and the next day went out looking for him.

We found him that afternoon at the niche; it is a secluded outcrop farther up on the mountain. There, many years ago, we constructed a sort of religious a place for quiet prayer and meditation. He was lying there on the niche's floor unconscious.

We could not wake him. So we carried him back here and laid him on his cot. We treated the reddish marks on his arm where he was burned from exposure to the sun, and we gave him comfort by washing his skin with cool wet towels.

The following morning he woke up, but could not talk, sit up, or walk. He just kept babbling the nonsense you are hearing now. That is when Father Kitunzi offered to walk to the gate to ask for a doctor, and by God's providence you showed up."

My examination of Father Mahbub was so far confusing. He displayed signs of dementia; however, that is a progressive disease; one that does not come on instantly. I ruled out heart attack, and a diagnosis of stroke didn't fit well either. A person his age could have passed out for a myriad of reasons. The twitching of his arms looked to be more a reaction to extreme fright, but the confused babbling could only be a result of brain trauma, not something that I was able of diagnose, or treat here in the jungle. The red mark that ran down the length of his arm was already fading. Fading, not healing. That was odd. Severe sunburn always leads to skin damage and pealing. Always. It never just fades away.

Before I had finished with my thought process,

Father Kitunzi returned with the box of medicines.
Gerald and Mike remained outside, and were
standing in the shade of the building just below the
open window.

I took the box and riffled through it in search of
anything I could use. As Father Hamidi said, they
didn't have much. Mostly antiseptic liquids and
creams, some outdated antibacterial, over-the-
counter painkillers, etc. the only medication of any
use was valium. Something I could give the old man
hopefully to calm him down.

Father Kitunzi asked me, "Dr. Henderson, is
there anything you can do for Father Mahbub?"

"Yes," I answered, and told him that we were
going to give his friend some valium. At that point,
the two priests looked at each other, and then Father
Kitunzi begged his leave, and left the building. I
noticed him walking just outside of the window
where he met up with Gerald and Mike. It sounded
as though he was furthering a conversation.

Even though they were standing just below the
window that fronts Father Mahbub's cot, I could not
make out the details of what they were talking about,
but I didn't need their distractions right now
anyway. What I did need were a few more private
moments alone with the old man; just let them talk
while I finish tending to him.

* * * * *

Mike Mills had a photo of M Apurna in his back
pocket. He has kept it with him ever since she
disappeared six months ago. He also had a
newspaper clipping showing a picture of Dr. Carter.
He and Gerald had been talking to the priest about
the activities there in Kenya six months prior. The
priest, being from such an isolated village could

reveal little to them. Then Mike took the photos out of his back pocket and showed them to Father Kitunzi.

"Yes, I remember now, they were here," said Father Kitunzi. "I was the one they talked with. I was the one who reported the deaths at the settlers' site to the authorities. They told me they would be sending someone to investigate. That man was your Dr. Carter there, and I remember there was a young woman with him.

I gave them the directions to the death site, and then they left. I did not see them return that day, but Father Mahbub said he saw someone running through the compound that evening at dusk. It must have been him, and I thought nothing more of it.

Then, as you know, a day later there was the conflagration at Kenbe. We were all in shock, and sat in quiet prayer for them for several days. Our supply line from the south stopped, and things remained hectic here for a couple weeks until we managed to start up a supply line with towns to the north.

I did not return to the settler's death site for many weeks, but the thought of those bodies lying unburied tormented at me, and I wanted to go there and put up a cross.

Some months had passed before I did return. Such a horrible sight, there were skeletons everywhere. The vultures had already done their gruesome work—they had picked each body bare of flesh. I needed to make a cross to sanctify the area, and ease the pain of the departed.

I noticed a woman's faded and weathered white top lying under one of the bodies. I carefully pulled it away from under her bones, and used it to tie a stick to a long pole making a cross. Then I stuck it deep down into an animal burrow for a grave marker.

I said a few words of prayer over the site, and

then left. With all of the deaths here in Kenya, those got lost in the furor surrounding Kenbe. Even I forgot about them until you showed me that photo today."

Mike turned away. He couldn't listen to any more. Tears welled up in his eyes. Silently he mourned. Previously, in his mind, he peered through the narrow slit of a door of hope slightly ajar—the brilliant lights shining forth from behind it blinded him to reality. "Surely some glimmer exists that she might be alive somewhere, somehow," he had thought. Now that door had slammed shut, and the harsh realization that M was truly dead hit him hard—he sobbed. Then, turning back, he said, "Tell me, Father Kitunzi, how do I find her grave?"

"Just there, to the left of the chapel, there is a trail that leads straight to it. If you follow it, you will first come to the cleared area. Then, perhaps only half a mile ahead, you will see the cross I put in the ground. The bodies are there."

Mike looked up, and in the direction the priest had pointed to. Then, with no more discussion, he took off at a fast pace, and disappeared into the lush growth of the jungle.

"Mike, wait, I will go along with you," yelled Gerald. But he was gone.

"Bill!" yelled Gerald, from below the window, "Mike has taken off. We learned of the location of the young woman's corpse, and he took off after it. What should I do?"

"Damn! ... Gerald, you best run off after him. I will be along shortly, after I have had a chance to calm down the old man here."

Damn it, I knew this would happen. Now they will get there first. Well, why not. Let them go and search for clues. Those bones have been rotting there for six months. It is not likely they will jump up and run off. Just let me have a few more minutes' time to comfort Father Mahbub. Then I will go.

With Father Hamidi standing behind me, I poured some cool water into a cup. Pressing it to Father Mahbub's lips, I gave it a little tilt. Some water spilt and trickled down his face. "Father, try to drink some water. I want to give you something to ease your suffering."

Awake and aware, he knew well what was happening around him. Mustering some strength, he raised his head slightly. "There, that's it, slowly, take a little more." With his eyes staring at me, I managed to give the nonagenarian a couple valium. Then he exhaled and fell tiredly back onto his cot relaxing— all the while his eyes wide open and staring at me—a bond was forming between us.

Some unspoken form of communication had passed between us through our locked eyes. He was straining, I sensed it, but he couldn't talk. "There, there, Father, try to relax, the drug will help to calm your nerves, just give it a minute to work."

He still appeared agitated. Standing, I moved closer to him to put a caring hand on his shoulder. Suddenly he reached up and grabbed my left wrist.

As his bony fingers wrapped around my wrist, I felt his intense fearful trembling's shoot up my arm. Immediately, we shared a thought; a sense of extreme terror flashed upon my consciousness. As a reflex action, I jerked my arm away from his grasp. His eyes opened wider and glared at me, and then he cried out, again, and again, "U'buntu, U'buntu, U'buntu."

Those words sent shivers down my spine. My gut muscles clenched, and painfully so. Scared realization burst upon my mind. Finally I got it—the Priests sunburn that disappeared, the unusual white hair, the Marks on the gate, the injured dog, the old man's mind numbing fear, the fenced Preserve, the *unknown* cause of deaths. It was all true. The monster U'buntu was real.

Then I thought of, "Mike, Gerald. ... What? No!"

I yelled out, "Gerald, Wait! Stop! Wait!" But it was too late. They had left minutes earlier.

"Oh my god! What have I done?" Now cognizant of the danger, fearful, and concerned for my friends safety I ran off after them.

17:

Prayers of Intercession

The Healing Ceremony
Don's Hogan, Four Corners, New Mexico

We were quite relaxed and sitting in a circle before the comforting fire inside Don's Hogan. He began to speak about how the ceremony would proceed. Amused, but interested, I listened on. "Now," he said, "it is important that the three of us enter into the spirit world together. Once there, I will call to my spirit guide. You'll see him. The spirit guide is very powerful. You must let him direct any interaction. Just let him do his work. Do not try interfering with what he is doing. Remember, you are only spectators in his world."

"John, you were touched by a powerful spirit, your U'buntu. It left a piece of itself inside of you. It attached itself to your soul. That is how it communicates with you, but its power is too much for you to handle. To be free of its influence, we must remove this scar from your soul. I will call upon my Skinwalker, the Eagle. It is he who will do battle with the demon that possesses you."

"Alan, you can aide your friend here by joining us in the spirit world. Three is more powerful than one, or two. All that is required is your willingness to participate. I will direct the ceremony; you two should do nothing other than watch. But be warned, we are entering a dangerous realm. Do not take it lightly. Stay focused, or you could get lost and never make it back.

There is no set time, and it could take many hours to complete. The two of you will see things. Do not be alarmed by them, I will be right at your side to protect you. Whatever you do, do not break the circle by getting up. We will continue with the ceremony until John's soul is healed."

Without us saying another word, the Nagual dug into one of his deerskin sacks, pulled out a small pouch, and put a pinch of a powder into the teapot with some water. "This is a special tea. It'll help your body to relax, and it will allow your mind to expand. Your goal is to enter a trance state. I will guide your entry into the otherworld with some chanting, and my willpower."

Though not comfortable with the idea of ingesting god knows what, neither of us asked what was in the powder. I suspected some sort of hallucinogenic mushroom, perhaps even snake venom, or even peyote button   something I read about once.

The tea brewed, we each drank a cup full. Don kept the fire stoked. I sat quiet for a moment staring at the glowing embers. I watched as the smoke and sparks gathered and twisted up and out of the hole in the top of the Hogan.

Suddenly I felt queasy, like lying on a bouncing waterbed. The world around me began to twist and turn, like the fires flames. I knew the Nagual's potion was taking effect, but I was not prepared for its immediacy or consequence.

At one point, I felt as though my body were falling. Slightly sick to my stomach, I closed my eyes, and lowered my head. Then I had a more intense sensation that I were falling. I was falling and falling, then spinning dizzily around and around.

Then I heard a sharp loud crack. My eyes opened, and my head snapped upright. An eruption of sparks spewing from the fire grabbed my attention. Staring at the flame, its spires rose out of proportion, they licked ever higher, biting at the air.

The fires glow became all-encompassing. It was the only thing lit. The walls of the hut became a blackness unseen, the faces of my friends, now only flickering shadows. Time dissolved, awareness of my body—gone—now only an endless stream of hypnotic visions played across my consciousness.

Mesmerized, too enrapt to disobey, I ceded control of my consciousness over to the whims of the universe unfolding before me.

Freely associating, vaguely aware of my surroundings, or myself, I hear a man's voice. He is chanting in some native tongue, but I do not hear his words in my ear. It is as though a tiny bug had flown deep, deep, inside my head, and was vibrating his words directly to my brain.

Then I see in my vision the man, he is dancing. He is dressed in colorfully adorned buckskin clothing and Indian headdress. He is dancing around an enormous fire, its flames reaching far up into an orange-yellow tinted sky full of white clouds. The surreal vista which lay beyond him was aglow; the rocks of the mountains and valleys appeared as if painted in brilliant reddish-orange to purplish-brown, and contrasted little from the fiery flames.

His words, his voice, echoed across this landscape. Then my vision changed. I witness scenes of a fantastic realm, but I sensed that my mind had wandered off track. Then I hear the man's voice again. It snares my attention, and draws me back to the scene at the fire pit.

Chanting, as he circles the fire, his arms moved up and down in counter rhythm to his dancing feet. His head bobbing low, then high, all synchronized to his powerful native song. Around he danced, and around, and around. My gaze now locked on him.

I noticed he now had a small drum in one hand, and some other instrument in the other, and making noise with either of them. Around and around he went, all the while looking straight ahead, or at the ground. I cannot look away, my focus locked on his visage, and the ever-growing flames he circled.

Without a sense of time—hours could have passed—I did not know. Locked in a trance, one controlled and directed by my spirit guide from some nether in-between world, I found his chanting song beautiful, and I listened intently and unawarely.

Then the man straightened up, and stood still. Raising his gaze upward, he stretched his arms out wide and high, as if beckoning to the sky. His song grew louder, almost ear shattering. Suddenly an eagle emerged from the clouds. I hear its piercing cry, "Scree! Scree!" Over and over again, it cries, "scree, scree," as it circles high above...

* * * * *

The Bones of M Apurna
Inside the Preserve, Kenya, Africa

I immediately left the ailing priests side, and ran out of the bunkhouse. Father Kitunzi was standing in front of the chapel. Grabbing him by the shoulders, "Quick, tell me which way they went." He pointed to a trail alongside the chapel building.

Running in that direction, I rounded the side where I found the trail. Slowing, I knew I couldn't keep up this pace, I hit a fast walk. Catching my breath after a moment, I sped up again and jogged along. Slowing and then speeding up, I ran then walked in this manner until I had reached the clearing. There I broke out into the open.

The path vanished, but spying ahead, my friends were easy to locate. Not much more than half a mile farther to the north and east, they were standing at the spot where Mike and I had notice a pole in the shape of a cross the day before.

"Thank God. They are still alive."

They were still too far off to yell at. Walking as fast as I could, I crossed this forbidden land. I now knew it was all forbidden. Everything inside of the fence line was Marked, and the penalty of trespass was death. Forgetting the dangers to myself, I ran, I had to warn them.

My adrenaline was in overdrive. By the time I had reached them, I was totally out of breath, and couldn't speak. Bending forward, I put my hands on my knees, and tried to catch my breath. I tried to call out their names, "Mike ... Gerald," but further words would not come—I was too exhausted.

A stench hung over this small plot of land. Several intact and unburied human skeletons were still visible. A remaining testimony to the hardships of a life made cruel by an uncaring and unthinking human presence. Here, bones laid bare, rest as silent yet shocking witness to the futility of life—did it have to end this way? Must man always spoil, ruin, and desecrate. When will he learn to live in harmonic balance? When will he learn that it is as easy to share the natural beauty of life, as it is to destroy it?

And what leads to a more fulfilling life, playing

the role of killer and user, or living as giver and healer? The old man at the village had lived as a giver. He had little, yet his life was as full and happy as anyone with plenty—perhaps even happier. He will pass on a legacy of goodwill, built over a lifetime of sharing and living peacefully within the bounds of nature. According to John Carter, that is what the spirit monster U'buntu was attempting to force on us?

Carter had mentioned that many of the dead were left to rot out in the open where the sun and natural decay would return them to the dust from which they were made. Still panting, with my hands on my knees, and my lock-jointed arms supporting my torso, I turned my head to the right. There was the grave marker Father Kitunzi had fashioned, and there was M's faded white crop top, the very one John Carter mentioned she wore back on that fateful day. It hung now, as a thread, and used to tie two pieces of wood together to form a cross. How pitiful.

Mike was standing twenty feet in front of me to my left. He was haunting over a woman's body—now just a sun-bleached set of rotting bones. He was in mourning, ostensibly, he had found the remains of M. Factual identification would be difficult, but whoever it was, she wore a friendship ring on her little finger—it was still there. Lying face down, her left arm crumpled beneath her breast, her right arm extended slightly, as though hugging a lover in an eternal embrace.

Gerald was behind me and to my right. A sense of death permeated this spot. He must have found it difficult to withstand, and had backed off from it. Finally, my breath caught up, I stood to warn them.

Before I could utter a word, a bloodcurdling scream shook my soul, the hair on my neck and head straightened. Frightened, and fearing the worst, I turned.....

* * * * *

The Fight

As the eagle screamed above, my spirit guide, with outstretched arms, beckoningly sang to this apparition. His song was loud and pointed. Its timbre projected a force uncommon, as though each word carried the utmost intent. Harkening to his song the huge raptor broke left on its wing, then dove down from the sky, and began circling over the tips of the ceremonial fire.

Next I saw the vision of a giant hand, ghostly in appearance, reach out from inside of the supernal flames. Its fingers splayed open as it stretched out toward me. With astonishment, I watched as it dug deep into what was my essence. There, it grasped ahold of the piece of that beast that was inside of me, that scar it had left upon my soul by U'buntu, and pulled it out and away from my body.

The visage of what it pulled out, dark and massless at first, morphed into an image of the monster U'buntu. Clutched inside of the giant hand, he was drawn back and into the flames where the eagle waited.

Was this a dream, or was I witnessing actual events taking place, only in a subaltern universe? The symbolism before me was obvious, but how could my scientific mind accept this fantasy as substantive and real? How could a drug-induced trance open a door to another world, another dimension? These were things my mind could not determine, could probably never understand. I am left with the prospect of taking it all on faith. That is something I cannot rest easy with.

The two specters, the eagle and the demon

U'buntu, fought as foes inside the flames. What were they fighting for? What was the prize? How could I know? I was only a spectator to this bout of otherworld phantoms. U'buntu moved about as if to avoid the eagle. The eagle, with talons stretched out long in front of it, kept swooping in and tearing at the spectral monster.

I saw wounds open up on U'buntu's shoulder area. As they widened and stretched white light began to pour forth. The demon, injured, now fearing for its life, turned to make eye contact with me. I sensed an angry sadness inside of it, as though it felt betrayed by me.

Had I betrayed it? What was it anyway? Was it a friend? Someone I could get to know better? Something I could spend time with? Was it a force, an ally, a Skinwalker I could control the way the Nagual did his eagle?

For hurting it, a feeling of sadness cast my eyes downward. I was participating in an action to rend its presence from me, and from our phenomenal realm as well. The sorrow I felt for causing it harm personalized my feelings, and changed my perspective of the demon from an it to a him. He was now something corporeal, an anthropomorphic inter-dimensional extension of me. And I, in a strange twist, had become my friends betrayer, a disloyal former accomplice turned witness for the prosecution, an ex-possessor, a traitor, and a deserter.

As U'buntu struggled, I rethought my relationship to it. Images of past acquaintances flashed before me. I saw my old friend Sam. U'buntu had taken his life, and now possessed his soul. Briefly, I saw the smiling face of M. Apurna, it was from the day we hit the trail for the missioner's village. U'buntu had taken her from me as well.

Many more faces shown before me as he struggled for his existence. Images of people that I did not know, victims all of this spirits infernal desire to teach us a lesson. "No," I reasoned, "the human cost of contact with this inter-dimensional being was too severe. It must be vanquished from our perceptual world," and I steeled my resolve against it once again....

* * * * *

Judgment

Frightened by a loud scream, I turned around. It was Gerald who had screamed. He was attempting to run away from something, but then, oddly, he stopped in mid tack. I turned farther to my right to see what had him so fearful.

A vaporous apparition was taking form. Even against the bright daylight, its unfathomable black emptiness shimmered with an intensely wicked glow. Huge eyes rayed forth amid its dreadful head. Gleaming white gems, piercing, and full of menace, stared right at me. Instantly I knew it was the U'buntu monster Carter had warned me about, and now its hideous outstretched wings for arms threatened to enshroud me in its dark and evil pall.

Fear has struck me hard. Like an animal when frightened, my bowels wanted to empty. I thought to turn and run, yet my legs would not respond. Frozen with terror I cannot move. Neither can I avoid its malevolent gaze. It is irresistible, and I'm forced to look deeper, and deeper, into those ghostly orbs.

Some mute force has robbed control of my mind. Like falling into a deep pit, I lose awareness of the sensory world. An empty darkness now surrounds me—it was like darkness falling into darkness.

In the throes of impending death, a deep sorrow

swelled up in my heart. I began to reflect on my past life. Scenes from my past, moments when I gave harm to another, the time I yelled at my mother, times when I sat and raged at drivers on the road, an incident of cheating on my former wife, began to flash across my consciousness. I was bearing sad witness to all of the hurtful incidents where I physically or emotionally harmed another.

Then the visions playing forth on my consciousness switched to scenes of life here in Africa. I was shown the entirety of what happened across this vast plain of northeast Kenya, and I witnessed what had happened here at the settler's death site.

In pained condolence, I watched the senseless slaughter of the farmer's family. My eyes bore witness to the grief he felt that led him to take his own life.

I saw the faces of the two criminals who had savagely murdered Umb'we'bwe's family, and then I watched their terrifying judgment before U'buntu. I saw him burn through their bodies, killing them, and searing a Mark on their chests where the heart is supposed to beat.

In pitiful acknowledgement, my psyche endured the deaths of all those people in the small town with whom the murderers shared their savage plunder. Then, I stood in grief-stricken horror, as I paid mournful observation to the nightmarish visage of the Kenbe conflagration.

In inconsolable fear I watched as every soul in that city was judged by U'buntu, and then fell dead at their feet. Cowering in self-loathing, I watched as the flames from the helicopter crash, whipped by a hellish wind, spread and reduced every building and everybody in that town to nothing more than ashes. That was their judgment, which was to be my judgment; in context, we all share in the sins of others. For not caring, for not respecting laws of nature, the laws of man, or the laws of universe, they, we, I—will now pay the ultimate price—nonexistence.

I pitied myself for my past misdeeds. Sullenly I hung my head down. A feeling of utter unworthiness to live further has crushed my spirit, and in gloomy indifference, I waited to die.

In my mind, I then saw a whirlwind of smoke and fire, bright red-orange flames intermixed with dull gray-black smoke twisted and seethed, sparks spewed, and rose up inside this cloud of smoke. Peering through the veil of flames, I saw the vision of a man's face. In startled recognition, I yelled out his name, "Carter!"

* * * * *

Circling high overhead like a vulture was Terry Gelow's UAV. He and his crew had been sitting inside of the news van staring at their computer screen all day. They have had the trio under surveillance, and have followed their tracks ever since they entered the Preserve. Right now, the UAV is flying in tight circles directly overhead of the settler's site.

* * *

"Looks like they have found something. Can we zero in on that area there where Mike is standing?"

"Yes, the UAV is in a stabile hover. With the joy stick here, I can zoom in tight."

"Oh, look there. Those are human skeletons. Mike seems to be standing over that one there. Oh,

Poor guy, I wonder if he's found M's body. ... Looks like Carter's story checks out."

"Yeah, there's Carter now. I wonder why he was last to get there?"

"Pull back again. I want to get an overview of the entire area. ... There, that's good. How much more air time do we have?"

"About thirty minutes. Then we have to fly it back."

Just then, the computer screen flashed and went fuzzy.

"Oops, there, what's that? ... What just happened?"

"I don't know, Terry. There was a bright flash, and then the screen pixelated."

"What's happening there? Look. The three of them, they have stopped moving, they appear to be looking straight ahead, and are standing still like zombies."

Then the computer screen went completely black.

"What caused that? Did we crash?"

"No, it wasn't a crash. We were in level flight when we lost video."

"Get it back."

"I can't Terry. There is no video signal coming in from the plane."

"Shit! Now what do we do? ... We have to get over there to the fence. Isn't that thing supposed to return home when there is a problem?"

"Yes, I can send it a signal to return. Its homing program should bring it right back here without our help."

"Then do it and we won't wait for it to return. ... We need to get to Mike, and right now. Let's go."

* * * * *

Inside the Ceremonial Hut

U'buntu was mortally wounded. I watched as his ghostly vision waned. His grip on me was fading as well, and I felt some degree of clarity return to my consciousness, or was it Don's tea wearing off?

I knew well what Mothman wanted to accomplish half a world away in Kenya. Through our mind meld, it had shared with me the horrid slaughter of a farmer's family that led it to our world to begin with. Through U'buntu I had further witnessed the devastation wrought by non-thinking humans upon humans, and upon our environment—crimes all deserving punishment—but U'buntu's way of thinking held no shades of gray, no degrees of culpability, and it alone played judge, jury, and executioner. Sure, we are all, and too often, cruel to each other and many of us are perfused with a quality named evil. However, to condemn an entire civilization for the misdeeds of a few is an unattainable ideal when dealing with imperfect creatures as us. Fallible man was not ready for its form of absolute judgment, absolute punishment.

As U'buntu's presence ebbed, soon to be severed entirely from the inter-realm, he briefly shared with me a scene from his last moments. His specter hung as a menacing shadow over the settler's death site—the place where M had died. I saw three men standing in front of him. They were in the process of being judged. I felt the strange rage in its psyche—it hated the men—and I knew full well they would in a short moment all fall dead at their feet.

I recognized one of the men. Still in a quasi-trance state, in my mind, I tried to yell out his name, "Henderson." But, how could that be? How could he possibly be in Africa?

Then U'buntu's eyes glared. In one final fit of

raging fury, I watched as he swooped through one of the men, killing him. Then the other man felt his murderous wrath, and his body fell dead to its feet. Then I noticed him switch his attention to Henderson.

In my mind's eye, I see an enraged red flash zero in on, and then rapidly move toward his chest ... but then U'buntu, and our shared vision, vanished. In that last fraction of a second I saw Henderson slump to the ground.

* * * * *

Returning from working on the fence-line three miles to the east and farther up the mountain, Günter was driving in his construction truck, passing along the outer rim of the Preserve. By happenstance, he turned his head to scan out and across the barren expanse. To his surprise, only two hundred yards away, he spied his new friend Gerald.

Giving him a short honk of the horn, he then put his arm out of the window and waved. Gerald and his two comrades did not respond. The three of them just stood frozen, as if at attention; not moving, not looking, not talking, not pointing, just motionless caricatures of human form.

He honked and waved again. Then, frightfully, his friend, and the other two men with him, fell to the ground, lifeless.

"Gerald! No!"

Knowing of the tales of U'buntu, knowing of the stories of the deaths from inside of the Preserve, he feared the worst, and he knew the worst.

Immediately he wheeled his truck around and drove it straight for one of the metal fence posts. Grabbing a length of chain from behind his seat, he hurried tied the chain around the post and his trucks front bumper. Climbing back in, he sped backwards in reverse, yanking the post out of the ground, and laying down a section of fencing. He shoved the trucks gearshift into neutral, and without bothering to set the brake or turn the engine off, and without regard for his own safety, he got out of the truck's cab, and ran the short distance to his friend's side.

* * *

After a short respite, Um'fume returned to the northern gate. The guards and Khan dutifully had remained at their post all day. They were, as yet, unaware of the tragedy playing out only half a mile away. Suddenly Khan notices something and yells out:

"Um'fume! Look! The Marks! The Demon's Marks, they are fading away."

The others turned and fixed their stare ten feet up on the huge gateposts. The Marks, taken as a territorial warning, would mysteriously appear, but never before had disappeared. The four of them looked on in astonishment. ... Then, half a mile to the east, Um'fume's attention was drawn to some unusual commotion. One of the contractors had pulled down a section of fence with his truck.

"You three," yelling at Khan and the two guards, "go, go. Find out what he is up to, and stop him. I will be there shortly."

Um'fume then pulled a black cellphone device from the right side of his belt, and placed a call.

"Alright Lieutenant, bring your troops on in. We will be about half a mile to the east of the gate." He then took off running to catch up with the others.

* * *

Dead silence. It's like being enveloped in dead silence. My head, the pressure inside of it, this blinding pain is pushing outward on my temples. I have awoken, and I am lying on the ground. First, my eyes opened. It was still daytime. How much time had elapsed—I could not say? My head—god the pain. My head—still spinning. My god, am I alive? Had I actually survived the attack? Or, am I, is this, death?

The muscles in the back of my neck feel stiff as bricks, and it hurts to move. Slowly I raise my head, and turn to my left. There is Mike, he is lying on the ground, and not moving. Only a few feet away, I see that his right arm is stretched out and reaching across the bones of M's corpse.

Sitting up, I try to ease the ringing in my ears—stop the spinning. I can see, but my other out-world senses are still locked up. I haven't noticed Gerald yet. Closing my eyes, I put the palms of my hands over them to block out the light; oddly, the daylight causes me intense pain. Gently rubbing them seems to ease the suffering and the spinning.

Suddenly, like pulling the cork out of a bottle, my hearing returned, and my ears are barraged by the sound of a man sobbing nearby.

"No, no, no. Gerald, oh no. Gerald, it's over buddy, come on wake up."

I knew that voice; it was Günter sobbing. My head was killing me, but I made the effort to turn in his direction. He was kneeling on the ground and cradling Gerald's body. Sobbingly, he kept calling out to him, "Gerald, come on buddy. Come on. Please, please wake up. Oh, dear God, no,"

Laying there, his head resting in Günter's lap, Gerald's sweet innocence looked so peaceful. I tried calling out to Günter, but he did not respond to me. I turned back to where Mike was lying. Rising on all fours, I crawled over to him and touched him on the shoulder. He felt cold and still. Softly, gently, I called out his name, so as not to rudely awaken him from his slumber, but he didn't stir.

Putting my right hand to his shoulder, I shook his body gently—several times—but he was gone. At last, he had found his lost love, and now once again held her in a tender embrace.

As yet, standing up was not an option. Then I hear an onrush of people. ... It was Um'fume and the guards. Respecting my space, and remaining silent for the moment, the four of them took up positions around me. Sitting on the ground, the trauma of what had just occurred still had me in a fog. My current lack of emotion was curious. I should be happy to be alive, but I feel no brightness radiating from my face. My friends were dead, yet I have shed no tears to fall to wet and sanctify the ground they rest on. My training as a psychiatrist tells me that I am in shock, but I do not feel that diagnosis accurate. Amazed stupefaction best describes what I'm thinking—but—I do not express it.

Noticing movement coming from the direction of the fence, I turned to see that Terry Gelow and his technicians were now running towards us. As the only member of my group sitting up, still aware, still alive, I became the focus of their immediate and confused ire.

"Henderson, what the hell happened? What have you done?"

Terry's noisy bark broke Günter from his spell, he rose, turned to find me, and with venom spit some choice words at me, "Henderson, you bastard. You killed Gerald. I told you this would happen."

He then made a rush for me; intense anger bulged from his eyes. He was a big man, and could have easily harmed me. Fortunately, the guards managed to catch him by the arms and held him back.

"You bastard," he yelled. "You should die for this." In gawking dismay, I just sat on the ground and listened as Günter kept yelling at me. His vicious foaming at the mouth would not abate, and the guards had to drag him away and out of the Preserve.

They escorted Günter to his truck and stood by while he got in and sped away. I would learn later that he left his job and northern Kenya that afternoon. Left Africa and its sorrowful hell as well.

Still sitting on the ground, I watched in silent amazement as Günter sped away in his truck.

No sooner had he left than a cavalcade of military jeeps came to a dust spewing halt. The soldiers in them jumped out and took up positions around the news van, which was parked outside the Preserve, and next to the torn down fence section. Then several of them entered the vehicle.

Terry yelled, "Hey, you guys stop. What are you doing there?"

Um'fume quickly moved in front of Terry, and put his right hand up to stop him from interfering with the soldiers work.

"Mr. Gelow, let me introduce myself. I am Mr. Um'fume."

Terry looked him in the eye, but at first didn't say anything. He didn't try to play the part of the, "I'm surprised to meet you," and "I don't know who you are," role. Which was just as well, their gig was up, and he knew it.

"That is a news van," he said, "and we are registered members of the Press. You can't search us, our van, or take our property."

"Please don't interfere, Mr. Gelow, or I will be forced to arrest the three of you."

"But you can't do this. That is our property. We have rights."

"Seriously, Mr. Gelow, is that your contention? This is not your country, and how do you justify your spying on us? Yes, we know about your little airplane flying all about. We have given you and your friend's unprecedented leeway during your stay here, and you repay our lenience by spying on us, by listening to and taping our private conversations. ... Now, I could have the three of you put in prison for life for spying on us, or I could let you peacefully leave Kenya. Let it be your choice."

"But what about Mike's body?"

"I will have his body released and sent to his next of kin. There is a process we must go through first in order to do that. It will take a few days."

The soldiers who were searching the van exited and one of them raised something up in the air. I assume signifying that they had gotten what they were looking for. Terry saw this gesture, then turned to me and said, "Damn it Henderson. This is all your fault. You fuck. You have killed Mike. You and your maleficent blood hunt. You knew this could happen. I hope you rot in hell."

With that said, he, Andrew, and Barry kicked up some dirt at me with their shoes, shrugged their shoulders, and left. Too busy reflecting on what he had just said, I didn't follow their exit of the Preserve. Never had I felt such scorn from people I took for friends. Did I deserve this bitter derision? Did I deserve to be equated with evil? ... They didn't know the hell I had just gone through.

How could they know the depth of my shock? That I had been face to face with true evil only minutes earlier. ... If only I could have shown some emotion, shown some concern for the deaths, said something meaningful to assuage their fears and mitigate my distant and uncaring mien. However, there I sat, untalking, unemoting, unengaged, all the while with a stupid little smile on my face.

The soldiers approached our little gathering. They placed Mike's body on a stretcher, and were about ready to take it away. Then I remember something and yelled out, "Wait, wait."

Crawling over to his body, I then knelt down beside him. Lying there, Mike's final expression was not one of abject fear, or even of hatred. His death mask to me appeared to be one of resolved contentment, as though his final slumber would be one of restful peace. "Forgive me friend, there is something I need to see."

Reaching across his chest, I loosened the top buttons of his light-blue pinstriped shirt. "One last clue remains, sorry my friend, but I have to see it."

Call it morbid, but my curiosity could not be denied. Pulling open his shirt to expose the area of his chest right above his heart, "My god. There it is. There's the Mark, just as Carter described."

"Are you satisfied now, Doctor?" said Um'fume. I shot a glance at Um'fume, but did not answer him. I had not said a word to him, or anyone, since waking. My silent existence bore testimony of the strangeness I was feeling within, and the strangeness I was seeing without.

Um'fume knew. Of course, he knew. He had foreknowledge of the events that played out here. Not a psychic foreknowledge. His was a pre-understanding gained through experience. He had tried to warn me this would happen. I didn't listen. Bloome had tried to warn me, I didn't listen to him either. Now the consequences of my unwillingness to heed advice have resulted in the death of two friends and the embitterment of everyone else.

I sat back down on the spot where Mike last rested. His body was now being strapped to the rear of a jeep. Then I thought of Gerald. I snapped my head around to the right. He was left lying on the ground, and was balled up in a fetal position some thirty feet away.

"Gerald," I mouthed. "Gerald, my fuzzy haired friend. … What have I done to you?"

Some cognizance returning, and deeply saddened, at last tears welled up in the corners of my eyes. Feeling wetness track down my face, a tear dropped to my lower lip, its slight saltiness melted into my mouth. My eyes opened wide and peered out and across the expanse of this wasteland. With my friend lying dead beside me, the cruel reality of what we had done sunk in, and I remembered what U'buntu had shown me. In the aftershock of this horrid trauma I cried, "What have we done to this place and to ourselves? We have destroyed this land. We have devastated our Mother, our environment. Nothing lives here now. All that is left is this scarified earth, which now lays barren and desolate. … How could man ever hope for atonement when our wounds of hate have pieced so deep?"

Gerald's body was last to be carted off. The guards brought another stretcher over, lifted his delicate-framed body onto it, and slowly carried him away from me. With teary eyes, I slowly turned and looked at Um'fume.

He and his guards were now the only people left out here with me. Still sitting on the ground, I felt so all alone.

"Well, Dr. Henderson, what shall we do with you?" asked Um'fume. I deserved reproach from him as well. With contemned and calumnious intent, I had disrespected the guard's authority and person, but Um'fume proffered no hatred toward me. Perhaps he sensed I had learned my lesson, or perhaps he knew the hurt I felt inside would continue to grow and haunt me the rest of my life.

I could not divine his rationale, but with mysterious insight and perplexing calmness he simply said,

"Come along, Doctor. We can't be having you left alone out here, can we?"

Helping me up, he led me out of the Preserve, a place I was never so happy to be away from. A helicopter flew in. Without him saying a word to me, or I to him, we boarded it. I was flown back to the Nairobi airport. There I was put onboard a plane for my home in Chicago.

18:

An Abstruse and Cloudy Future

The Nagual

"John, wake up. ... Come on buddy, wake up. It's time to wake up." I heard some commotion, and felt the warming glow of a rekindled fire on my face. Was the ceremony over?

Alan was tapping me on the shoulder. Slowly I came out of the trance. Upon waking, the first thing I become aware of is my head hanging down against my chest. From being locked in that position for a length of time, my neck was stiff and I felt a terrible headache building. I needed to get up and move around. Apparently, I was the last one to come out of it. Don was already in the process of making a fresh pot of tea.

"Wow that was pretty wild. How long were we out?"

"It's already morning, buddy."

"What?"

"Yes, it's already morning. Go ahead, take a look outside." I didn't need to look outside. Peering up, I could see filtered daylight coming in through the vent hole in the ceiling, but the necessity for fresh air and to pee had me moving to the makeshift door.

Putting it aside, my eyes were treated to a wonderful sight, "My goodness, it snowed. There is a half foot thick blanket of snow on the ground."

I left the warmth and comfort of the Hogan to answer nature's call. It wasn't snowing at the moment, but the day was still a cloudy gray. The air, thick and foggy, hung low and enwrapped all in a suffused winter slumber. Walking over to the ledge for the view, I sucked in several deep lungfuls.

Although the air was cold, it was country clear, lightly scented with the smell of pine, and held an under-scent of that crisp, clean, smell of fresh fallen snow—it felt great to be standing and alive. Braving the cold, I stood for a long while just admiring the untainted winter vista, and let it fill my senses.

I could not believe that so much time had elapsed. No doubt, I was asleep for much of it, all thanks to Don's magic tea, but hunger was setting in, and we hadn't brought food. Alan poked his head out of the Hogan and asked me to come back in. The tea was ready, and they wanted to discuss their experiences of last night.

"This tea is my morning blend, it will soothe your hunger pains," said Don, "and it will also take the edge off of your headaches."

"Oh, what is in it?"

"Birch bark, pine needles, and a few of the things your mother told you to stay away from." Don's morning brew was strong and not something I would want to acquire a taste for, but it did fill and warm my empty gut, and the hunger pangs subsided.

"John, the healing ceremony was a success. Your Mothman spirit has been completely removed from you, he should no longer cause you harm. Your bouts of blinding headaches and frequent nightmares should be over as well. Don't worry about them anymore."

"Well, that is good news," chimed Alan, almost mockingly. Then he asked me, "What do you remember seeing?"

"Yes, John, tell us how your experience went." This felt uncomfortable. The two of them sounded like childish pothead hippies who wanted a blow-by-blow account of my drug induced hallucination for their entertainment. If they were expecting a recount of my LSD trip, they are going to be disappointed. I wasn't sold that what I witnessed in a dream trance was real, and recounting it wouldn't bolster that impression for me. Further, I am a private individual, and do not really like divulging what I consider quite personal, and I was not about to embarrass myself by resorting to using empty, unsubstantiated, and juvenile jargon. I did offer up what I thought to be the most interesting and salient points.

"What I will say is that I remember seeing an image of Mothman. I did see him in a struggle with what appeared to be an eagle. The eagle injured him, and I remember his appearance fading away as he lost the battle. Right before he disappeared completely and I lost awareness of the vision, I thought I saw Henderson, but he was in Africa."

"Africa, Henderson was in Africa?" asked Alan. "Huh, now that is interesting."

Yes, that was interesting, and I also found it interesting that Alan and I apparently had different visions. "So, Alan, you and I didn't share the same visions? You didn't see the Mothman, or Henderson?"

"I would say not. After I fell into the trance, I went back to a time I spent with my long dead wife. I relived several of the wonderful times we spent together. We touched, we talked, and it felt and seemed so real. But no, I didn't see any scenes of Africa, or of your monster, U'buntu."

I was sitting on the ground in front of the fire, twiddling my fingers over my stomach, wondering.

The coziness of the Hogan was becoming claustrophobic, and the smokiness of the air inside was stinging my eyes and causing me to choke. My hunger had returned. It was time to go.

"Well, it is obvious that our experiences from last night are going to take some time to personally digest. I suggest that we head back to some town and grab some breakfast."

"Yes, John, you are right about that," said Alan. "Come on, Don. Let me buy you something good to eat."

"I know that you two are hungry and need to eat," said Don, "and that you are probably a little bored with my accommodations. Sorry that my house isn't larger and more modern. I'll walk the both of you back to your car, but I am going to stay here. This is my home, and I intend to stay here through the winter, and then we will see."

"Stay here?" asked Alan, "but there is nothing here, Don, what will you eat?"

"Oh, there is small game. I might come across a deer or goat. In the past, in hard times, we caught and ate lizards and crows. We crossed the trail of a number of squirrels on the hike in. Once I had nothing more to eat than squirrel and tree bark for a couple weeks, but don't worry about me. I will get along. This is the life I have come to know and love."

"Don, my friend, please, it hurts me to hear you say that. How can we leave you here all alone, and with nothing good to eat?"

"Thank you, Alan, I appreciate your concern, but

this is where I belong. This is the world that I know. I have grown tired of your world. I just want to be alone for a while."

"Alright, as you wish." Without wasting any more time the three of us headed back to our jeep.

I led the way. I thought it unusual that Don took up the rear. He wasn't as spry as he was yesterday. He looked older. His face had now weathered with the marks of time. Wrinkles and pockmarks had darkened his skin, and darkened his aura. Was his true self now showing through? How can this man's outward appearance change so radically? His step was slow and uncertain. Several times I worried he might fall on the slippery snow covered rocks.

The winter cold grew harsher as we trekked along. The darkening gray sky drew ominously low, and a wind had kicked up. Sensing it would storm again soon, I turned up my jacket's collar, and hugged myself to warm a shiver. Glancing at the Nagual, his now aged and frail appearance seemed ill prepared to handle these conditions.

Why he would choose to live alone out here was beyond me. A week earlier, when we first met, his almost youthful appearance was vibrant and lively. Today it was as though a century of years had sapped his vitality. Was this a result of the ceremony? Had his Skinwalker been injured in the battle with U'buntu, and abandoned him? Its clasp on his essence gone, would he be returning to the natural progression of time? And does the spiritual realm really wield that much power over the physical world?

He is a man who told a story, his story might be true, but my belief in the supernatural, colored over by my scientific education, prevents me from viewing the spiritual realm with much credence. Moreover, if his story is true, and now that that story is ending, is his existence wrapping up along with it.

He body showed he was surrendering now. Surrendering to the inevitable tic, tic, tic, of the universe, a clock to which all things in the corporeal realm succumb.

It wasn't a long hike out of the canyon, but the cold had already gripped me, and my ears were about to freeze off. At the jeep my legs danced up and down, I couldn't wait to get inside.

"Don, please come with us," begged Alan, one last time.

"No, thanks for asking, but I'm home now. This is a special time of the year here in the canyon, and I want to enjoy it to the fullest. ... Now, before I go, John, turn around, I want to put this pouch in your backpack. It contains some of the tea we shared this morning. Use it anytime you have pain in the head or hunger in your tummy."

"Why thank you, Don." I said with a shiver in my tone.

"Alright, I better let you go. Remember me to Burningtree, if you will."

We said our goodbyes, and then the Nagual turned his back on us and retraced his steps back to his Hogan. Braving the cold, I watched for a moment as the path he walked took him past and around scantily boughed piñon trees, then slowly up a low rocky rise, all the while his visage grew smaller and smaller.

Soon my observance of his image faded into the dark obscurity of the storm-fog—and he was gone. In a way, it hurt me to think of him living way out here so totally alone, with no human companion with which to share a warm touch, or a knowing smile. This place has a beauty to it, but at what point does solitude end, and the bitter cold of loneliness begin?

He was odd, he was kooky, but he was my friend, and I wondered if we would ever see or hear from him again.

"You did remember to bring the keys, didn't you?" asked Bloome.

"Alan, before you start in on me ... let me just say that this has been one of the oddest, yet finest, vacations I have ever had. In addition, I thank you for inviting me to come along. That being said..." I didn't finish my sentence. I have found that he hates silence and elided thoughts much more than reproaching disputes.

"But you don't believe what you witnesses last night, do you?"

"I don't know what I believe, Alan. Let's just get the hell out of this remote desert, and get something to eat."

Alan took the keys, said he wanted to drive for a bit. God save me, but I didn't object. The cold infinite white landscape, cave-hidden by storm and clouds, produced a surreal dreamscape. I just wanted to let my eyes scan out and across its blankness and think of nothing for a while. Alan and I were headed back to civilization, back to the warmth of friends and family, the Nagual, back to his dark and empty Hogan with only lizards and scorpions for company—how strange.

* * * * *

Requiem for a Psychiatrist
Sitting in my seat, and flying high above the Earth's surface, I was now thousands of miles away from the tragedy that played out a day ago in northern Kenya. I am headed home. I am safe. I am alive.

A days long cry has tortured my face. Tears continue

to ooze into the corners of my blood red eyes. I no longer try to wipe them dry, there is no point; I just let the tears fall, the towel on my lap is now an ocean of wetness. I thought of Gerald a moment ago. His sweet innocence was taken so soon, and for what, my pride, my arrogance, my unwillingness to open my eyes and acknowledge the truth. I caused his death, and the thought of that will torment me for the rest of my life. Oh, better that I had died than to suffer this eternal living hell.

As I reflect back on my previous life in Chicago, I see now that I was nothing more than a scared soul hiding inside a deeply shadowed life-scape. My life then was like looking into a mirror in a dark room, all I knew, all I could see, were the obscured layers of my own ignorance. Hiding in that mirror, shadowed by obliviousness, understanding never touched me. Obdurate, callous, pitiless, I was a man trained to listen to what people say, to listen to how they say it, yet the years of listening to nonsensical problems hardened me, and prevented me from seeing the simpler truths. That lifestyle had blinded me into thinking that I was better and smarter than the rest of my peers. It was not renown my arrogance had won me. My false beliefs had only brought me shame. Nevermore! The sleeper's eyes have been opened now. Nevermore! shall I hide behind these profligate lies. Nevermore!

Suddenly cast out. Freed, freed I am, freed from those endless, self-imposed repetitions we call our lives; freed from the repletion that drones us into a lifelong slumber of stupidity. What lies ahead? Will the weather be sunnied and warm, or cold and filled with harsh realities? I did not know. What I did understand was that Carter was being truthful with me all along. I also knew the truth behind the horrors that unfolded there in Kenya. I understood now how the powers of the universe are our ultimate judge and jury. How I escaped with my life remains a mystery. What happened to that Mothman monster, U'buntu, remains a mystery. The two people who understand that mystery are Carter and his friend Dr. Alan Bloome. When I get home, I am going to contact them. I am going to tell them they have a new friend now, a new ally. I am going to work together with them in search of life's mysteries.

19:

Endings

Their vacation to the Land of Enchantment now over, the duo is on a jet plane and heading back to Chicago. John is fiddling with his carryon bag, digging around inside looking for something, drawing the ire of Alan, and then he happens upon something unexpected.

"John, what on earth are you looking for now," shot Bloome.

"Chapstick. I know that there is some in here."

"Dude, you're frantic searching is making me nervous."

"Don't call me dude, Bloome."

"Look, there is a logical way to search for items inside a purse, you know." I turned and gave Alan quite a stare for that one, Oh, but pointless.

"Here, Alan, be useful and hold these things for me?" I started taking items out of my backpack, and handed them to him to hold for me while I searched. My lips were dry and cracked from the cold.

I needed Chapstick, but then we found something more interesting.

"Well, look at this. This is the tea pouch that Don put in my backpack, isn't it something?"

"Yes, that is something; let me have a look at it.

My, that is some beadwork on the cover flap. It is just beautiful. ... Amazing how the Navajo perfected their art work."

"Yes, well, they had a lot of spare time." As Bloome examined the little pouch, he untied the cover flap and opened it up. Inside, at the bottom, was an ample amount of Don's special blend of tea, but something else caught his attention.

"Well, that is odd. Just look at this."

"What is it Alan?"

"Looks like one of those old-time photos."

The picture was folded over. Alan unfolded it, and then fell oddly silent. Curious, I turned to see a look of astonishment fill his face.

"Huh," he said, "it's an old pictograph. The kind they took towards the end of the civil war."

"An old photo? No kidding. What does it show?"

"It is of a couple standing together, and they have a young boy at their side. Behind them, there looks to be a barn, or livery stable."

"My god let me see that." I took the photo back, and scanned it carefully.

"Is there any writing on it?" asked Alan.

"Yes, there is something here on the back. Alan, hand me your wallet magnifying glass, if you would?"

"Eyes giving out on you, buddy?"

"No, it is just that the writing is faded a lot, and some of the letters have rubbed down."

With Alan's wallet magnifying glass in hand, I closely examined the lettering on the backside of the photo, "There are a couple of names written on here, Alan. I can make out an Ida and Rudolph Hornbakker, son Donald, Whisper Willow, August 1880. ... Oh, you don't think?"

"Oh, no," sighed Alan." I watched as his facial expression went sallow, and a sadness grew in his eyes.

"Alan, are you going to be alright?"

"Don't worry for me; it's Don we should be concerned about."

"Christ sakes, what is it now?"

"John, don't you see? He gave you the one last thing holding him to this Earth."

It always amazed me how quickly Alan's mind made jumps of logic. I got what he meant, and its truth caused me to sigh along with him. We had only known Don, or the Nagual, for a short time, yet in that time we came to know him as a dear friend, someone we had hoped to see and talk to again. He was a man who gave everything, and asked for nothing in return. My intuition led me to suspect that all he ever wanted from life was for someone to call him a friend. For several minutes, our shared silence, as we sat, became Don's unspoken epitaph.

Later, as judged by Alan's constant inquiries, it seemed he was intent on getting me to talk about my experiences this past week, but I still needed quiet time to sort and file them away. I did not want to be bothered now with meaningless drivel, but we were still hours from home. I am sitting next to a world-class blabbermouth, all the while locked inside a small cabin, and flying at thirty-five thousand feet—I feel a headache coming on.

"John, what did you mean when you said that you saw Henderson in your vision?"

"Alan, I was just trying to make interesting conversation."

"Oh, stop being thick."

"Thick! ... You see, Bloome, my Vassar trained mind took only two nanoseconds to consider and dismiss your characterization."

Alan then exhaled loudly, his lips releasing a noticeable flapping noise, and then he said, "Oh, that is just another obfuscatorialism."

"What? What's that? What did you just say? ... Don't talk to me that way, Alan. Not while we are flying."

"You know John; you have a unique way of compartmentalizing your experiences. I know that it is a protective mechanism used by your brain, and is probably what kept you from going crazy when U'buntu attacked you. However, it is also something that is keeping you from advancing spiritually. You have personally experienced many exceptional and unexplained phenomena, yet you still insist on denying the possibility of paranormal events. The truth is out there, buddy. Just open up to it, and it will be yours."

"Well, maybe you are right. Just give me some more time." I enjoy Alan's kooky musings because they are usually just wrong, but I hate them when he is right.

"So, John, since you brought it up, I forgot to tell you that I met Dr. Henderson."

"Oh, dear god, Alan?" Rubbing my head with my fingers.

"Yes, I did. It was right before I left for Chicago; he met me in front of my house in Amsterdam."

"In Amsterdam. And you just happened to think that you could defer any mention of that meeting right through our trip?"

"Sorry, his visit was a confusing conjunction of fates, and I didn't know how to handle it. Perhaps I should have told you right away. Are you angry?"

"No, honestly, I knew he never believed what I told him. He always had such a suspicious look when I related the events of Africa to him. The nerd. I am surprised at the lengths he was willing to go to though, wonder what was driving him?"

"What do you suppose happened to him down in

Africa anyway?"

"My guess is that he came face to face with the truth. If he lived through it, he is going to be a changed man."

"By the way, I am seriously considering moving back to Chicago."

The End.

www.ingramcontent.com/pod-product-compliance
Lightning Source LLC
Chambersburg PA
CBHW070814180626
46818CB00001B/253